Early Praise fo

"What a grand story for a first-time writer. E. Reed dives deep to create a new fantasy world full of interesting personalities, unique ideas, and big moments. So much thought was put into worldbuilding, ethics, and characters you will care about. Look for surprise twists and grand battle sequences. An enjoyable romp!"

~ Brian Fargo, CEO InXile Entertainment

"A very well told and exciting journey from beginning to end. E. Reed has a great way of filling out his fantasy world's details in a telling and descriptive way. The relationships in the story were multidimensional and had an excellent way of being both emotional and very real at the same time. If you're a fan of fantasy novels, I highly recommend this engaging story from an author we will no doubt hear more about in the future."

Chris Keenan, CFO InXile Entertainment

"Dawn Crusade is a wildly entertaining novel that appeals to adults from all backgrounds. Host to a dynamic range of characters, the island of Somerset immerses readers from the very first few pages. If you are interested in an expertly crafted fantastical realm conveyed through careful storytelling, intense emotion, and masterful wit, look no further."

Ryan Wilson, Harvard Undergraduate Senior

"Reed combines coming of age, the call of destiny, and fanciful adventure into a jam-packed, poetic novel. Through connective characters and delicate diction, Reed creates a movie in your mind that will keep you turning to the next page."

Dylan Field, USC Undergraduate Senior

"E. Reed's storytelling is much more advanced than it should be at his age. His capability to weave between stories and convey his characters' inner workings is captivating. Dawn Crusade is an enchanting story of heroes, magic, and prophecy, with characters that enhance the world they are set in. Reed's alluring, magical world isn't plagued with the immature elements of similar works but cuts deeper. Dawn Crusade is mature and at times raw, making it an attractive story for older audiences, while still maintaining a whimsical feel that makes the reader want to read more."

Cameron Platt, Marketing Freelancer

DAWN CRUSADE

A Tale from Somerset

by E. Reed

ISBN: 978-1-7371850-0-0

Contents

Dedication

For Nova

Prologue

A shooting star tore through the midnight clouds in a flurry of red flame. The world of Dawn was still that night. Deer swung their heads up to the sky in anticipation. Bats darted into the open air from pits hidden beneath the earth. From atop a crumbling stone watchtower on the island of Somerset, Absal followed the falling star with a hollow gaze.

Long ago, generations before Absal's birth, the *Great Spirit* made the woods of Somerset her home and rose the island out of the merciless tide cast by the Aged Sea. Now the isle clung to the air, a jagged mass of earth resting high above crashing waves.

Timber and gathered stones lined the empty dirt streets. The many burnt homes and shops had recently been torn down with hopes of rebuilding. Absal could still imagine the town as it once was, teeming with merchants and welcoming faces.

"Absalom, are you hiding from me?" Beth asked as she rounded the narrow steps of the tower. Her eyes were tired, as were Absal's. Beth's brown hair was freshly washed and rolled down her shoulders. Absal rubbed the sleep from his eyes and felt crevices and creases etched in his aging skin.

"No, I was waiting for you," Absal told Beth while wrapping his arm around her. Bright gray eyes flashed up to him like thunder clouds. Underneath her chin hung a chain holding a silver pendant. It was in the shape of the numeral X. Absal sported a similar pendant, except it resembled the numeral II.

"Have you made a wish?" Beth inquired with a finger pointed at the line of smoke trailing behind the ball of fire in the sky.

Absal grunted in amusement.

Beth settled her head against Absal's chest and spoke in a hushed voice. "Don't go."

"I'm the Spirit's champion, and she demands this war for the good of our people. My soldiers are ready," Absal responded with hands sliding down to Beth's hips. "Come with me."

"We have a family here," Beth said, pushing herself from Absal with a heave of her arms.

"One day, our children will fight too," Absal told Beth, and he grabbed her waist once more to yank her close. "It's their destiny and ours."

"You'd gamble the lives of our children, and for what?" Beth's eyes narrowed and widened like she was searching for light in utter darkness.

"Vengeance," Absal responded. "Vengeance and justice."

"I don't recognize you," Beth whispered with pools of tears beginning to spill from her eyes like traces of rain before a storm. She slipped away from Absal's arms. "You're lying to yourself."

Absal became defensive in the face of her agony. His voice grew cold with rage as he spoke. "Perhaps you've forgotten, but our home was burned, pillaged and raped. Maybe you can bury that memory, but I won't. I've kept this anger inside me for four years. At night, the only image I see is of the empress who tried to take my island lying dead with her throat slit. You won't stop me from leaving."

Beth became pale and still. Absal saw her as a shadow, a ghost of what he once wanted. She tightened her jaw and said, "Then go." A red glow cast by the falling star mingled with the moonlight. Taking a step forward, Absal gently pinched Beth's chin and pulled her lips into his. He felt her sink against him, not out of love but sorrow.

The star pierced the island of Somerset miles away. A plume of dust and ash burst into the air. Absal mistook the trembling of the earth for his beating heart. Then a chill shuddered down his spine and caused him to force his wife away.

Beth's face was drained of color. Absal knew that she recognized the terror in his eyes. With a bitter voice, he told her, "The Spirit is calling me." He peered out to the rising pillar of smoke forming deep in the woods.

Hurriedly, Absal gathered his sword, shield, and black cloak. Beth stood on the old oak porch of their home, lantern clutched in hand, and watched him lumber away on the back of their mule. As he journeyed down the town's single dirt road, Absal envisioned the light from his wife's lantern dimming and shrinking to a faint shimmer. She would be staring at the symbol stitched into the back of his cloak, a white diamond separated into fourths by an X.

The forest was still and quiet. No creature wandered across Absal's path. No sound or sight shook Absal's gaze from the way ahead. Out of the trees, he came, a broad clearing beckoning him forward. Moonlight basked the rolling green pasture and kissed the tongues of fire that lapped out of a mighty crater. He dismounted from the mule and walked to the crater's edge. What otherworldly treasure had he been sent to claim? Had a human ever laid eyes upon a star?

Absal strained his gaze against the harsh light of the fire. Between the rising and falling of flames, he caught a glimpse of the star. It was a small child, no older than six years, sprawled out at the bottom of the fracture in the earth. She was sun-kissed in complexion with eyes shut tight. The most remarkable feature, Absal surmised, was her thick, winding hair. It spun down to her waist in heavy cords of gold, auburn, and ginger.

Taking several steps back, Absal drew in a deep breath. He spread his legs in a firm stance and focused on the growing wall of flames. Exhaling hard, Absal shoved his hands down toward the ground and called upon the powers taught to him by the Great Spirit. In an instant, the fire surrendered into the earth. The child now sat on her knees. Luminous blue eyes with flecks of green were fixed on Absal in curiosity. Hesitating for only a moment, Absal slid down the crater's slope and wrapped his cloak around the naked child.

He carried her to the mule, and they rode back toward his home. The forest had turned against him now. Wolves stalked Absal from the cover of trees, and a cougar perched itself on thick branches above him. Absal pulled out an unlit torch from a bag on the mule's hip. He snapped his fingers against the torch's head, creating a yellow spark of light. The torch ignited, and Absal waved it about himself in warning. Held against his chest, the child reached out for the light playfully. Absal swatted her hand away. Low growling rumbled from the foliage, and the feline predator leaned onto its front paws to claim the first strike.

The child stretched out her hand once more. A light surged from the torch, bright and pure. Growls erupted to frightened yelps, and the large cat scurried into darkness along the branches. Absal could not stand to stare into the torchlight, yet he held it tightly ahead of them. He had begun to understand his purpose. Slowly the Spirit's intentions were becoming illuminated.

Before the sun could rise, Absal brought the young girl into his home. Beth had not gone to sleep. She was sitting in a wicker chair near the dwindling fire wearing a somber fret. Her worry melted to awe and bewilderment upon seeing her husband and the bundle in his arms.

"Who are you?" Beth asked as she rushed over to inspect the child.

"A little star," Absal told her, and he stroked the girl's long hair free from underneath the cloak.

Two tiny heads poked around the hallway. Absal caught the eyes that came with them, causing his son and daughter to dart away.

"Ike, Bridget," Absal called toward the pattering footsteps. "It's all right. Come here."

A boy came around the corner rubbing his eyes. He was four years old, had rigid brown eyes like his father, and was topped with a mop of chestnut hair. He and Beth had expected it to stay blond, but it had darkened over the last year.

Bridget rushed past Ike, knocking him over. She was two years older than Ike, had thin blond hair like her father, and a toothless grin. "What's that?" the little girl asked curiously. Ike popped up to his feet and approached Absal warily. As

Ike and Bridget closed in, the girl who fell from the stars clutched Absal's shirt and looked at the children intently.

"Say hello," Absal instructed them. Bridget waved hesitantly, and Ike's lips parted, yet no words left them. Absal recognized the gleam in his son's eyes. He was looking upon something more beautiful than he ever thought possible.

Part 1

Somerset

☼☼ I ☼☼

Deep in the forest of Somerset, hidden within a labyrinth of winding vegetation, dots of light floated on the summer breeze. They moved toward what appeared to be a massive tree formed by hundreds of trunks twisting together. An arching doorway gave passage to the tree's hollow center. The wind carried the specs of multicolored light into the cavern formed by spiraling branches. The morning sun cut through the roof of leaves but left a shadow at the grotto's center.

From the cover of thin darkness, a heavenly voice spoke to the droplets of light dancing in the warm air, saying, "My children…Listen closely…My sight will soon fade forever…The *Starchild* will return home by the next sunrise. And her arrival will bring the resurrection of the *Deathrid*…It is time for the one we have watched to journey here and receive my sacred quest…If he fails to reach me, all will be lost. Lotis."

A ball of green light sparked a shade brighter.

"Go to him…"

The glowing sphere raced out from the cavern of trees and soared through the forest of Somerset. It zipped up in the air and rose above the towering foliage. All of Somerset was spread before the dot of emerald light. Far from the dense woods, the village rested. Cottages fashioned from the forest's timber spotted the cliffside and overlooked the Aged Sea below. Shops, eateries, and the Temple to El lined the newly paved roads. Pausing in the air, the speck of light searched for the one she was to seek and found him near the forest's edge.

He dwelled within a hut of white wood that clung to the top of a great oak tree. Below the humble treehouse was a flock of grazing sheep in a fenced pasture. Spiraling down in the sky, the spirit's messenger made her way to the tiny, rounded window.

☼☼ *II* ☼☼

Ike was dreaming. He walked across floating stones in a world of endless sky. The footholds were growing farther and farther apart. His strides grew longer and longer to accommodate. Eventually, he had to muster a leap to reach the next stepping-stone. There was something ahead. A doorway of bright, warm light poured open. Exhaling hard, he made another leap and then another. Without warning, night began to swallow the infinite sky around him. A bitter cold nipped at Ike's back. The door was closing, but he could still reach it. With a grunt, Ike jumped and caught the next stone with his outstretched arms. Struggling with the weight of his body, Ike yanked himself onto his feet with great effort. Just a few more stones. He could make it.

Suddenly, a shiver rushed down Ike's spine. There was something behind him. Like vapor, a shrill voice permeated his skin.

"Careful, Ike. The closer we are to the light, the greater our shadow becomes."

Slowly, Ike turned his heels on the narrow stone. A silhouette of himself stood on the previous foothold like a reflection of total darkness. It raised a black mask over its face, one with huge, bulging, round eyes. The long path of stepping-stones dropped from its place in the air. Ike fell from where he stood, but his shadow remained. From a lone stone, it peered down behind two gaping eyes.

Ike awoke, his heart shivering in his chest. Perspiration melded his back to the sheets, and for a moment, it was difficult to recall where he was. Within a few breaths, he recognized the decrepit ceiling of his treehouse. Dread was still gnawing at his chest. Every flutter of his eyelids left him with the image of those massive eyes. However, Ike had grown very accustomed to dread. Yawning, he rolled out of bed and stretched his sore muscles. Already the details of the dream were fading. Something about the sky and rocks.

He walked to a small mirror that hung over the water basin. Unremitting training had begun to leave hints of muscle. He had grown large in the last year. The traces of infantile fat that his father once scorned had evaporated from his body like burnt fuel. Now he was on the cusp of manhood.

Eyeing his bedhead, Ike lamented the streaks of gray that had sprouted in his chestnut hair. He felt his stomach burn at the sight of them. Not even eighteen years old, and he was losing his hair's natural color. To make matters worse, thanks to his heavy sweating in the summer heat, acne had sprung up in the night.

A tapping against the window caught Ike's attention. Taking a stride toward the sound, Ike could only see the harsh morning sun spilling through the glass pane. Perplexed, he approached the window and pushed it open. A ball of green light shot inside the hut and darted about the single room. It knocked over cups and plates stacked on the kitchen table and banged against the cooking pot in the corner.

Ducking and dodging the erratic light, Ike shouted out, "Hey! Hey!"

The ball froze in the air. In an instant, the emerald light expanded and bloomed to the shape of a young woman floating overhead. She was green-skinned, shimmering, and had a long braid of brunette hair filled with white flowers. Her body was shapely and sparsely covered with grass and vines. It seemed that she had dizzied herseßlf because her shoulders swayed clumsily above him.

Ike's cheeks became flushed, and he stumbled in place. Suddenly his arms felt awkward, so he tried crossing them. That felt wrong, so he took a half step forward and placed a hand on the table. "*Hey,*" Ike murmured.

"Ike Ryder," the woman of light proclaimed in a light, airy voice, "son of Absalom Ryder and Bethany Tempest."

It was then Ike became cognizant that he was half-naked. Slowly he reached for a wool shirt on his dresser as if the gradual movement would be invisible to the beautiful, glowing woman in his bedroom.

"I'm a child of the Great Spirit, a nymph of the forest," the floating woman proclaimed. "You've been summoned to stand before her and fight as a champion against terror. It has been foretold." Her body sparkled and became transparent. "Be warned. This journey is a treacherous one." In a flash, the shimmering nymph retreated to a speck of emerald light and darted through the window into the open air.

Left alone, Ike felt more blood rushing to his face. He tossed off his shirt and collapsed back into bed.

✪✪ *III* ✪✪

Miles across the tumultuous Aged Sea on the rugged cliffs known as the Serpent's Edge, Knights of Tenshi loyal to Absalom Ryder clashed with seafaring bandits. The three ships carrying the Knights were set ablaze long before dawn in an ambush. Now smoke clouded the banks of the rock-infested island and enveloped the dwindling bloodshed that had endured from the depths of night to sunrise. The northern tip of the island was where the Knights had retreated. There the young commander of the fleet, Markus Julian, drew in a ragged breath. His meticulously crafted black jacket marked him as one of Dawn's legendary protectors, a Templar of Tenshi. Sweat spilled down Julian's body, and his dirty blond hair was matted with soot, mud, and blood. Today was his twenty-third birthday.

Julian stumbled over the fallen soldiers. His face was sunburned and ached in the sunlight. It was difficult to distinguish which corpses belonged to his regiment. Their mouths were gaped open in similar mannerisms, and crimson blanketed the bodies in shallow streams. Hundreds were piled dead along the Serpent's Edge. The Aged Sea stretched before Julian. The smell of iron mixed with the sea breeze. He managed to focus his gaze enough to see the enemy ships sailing in from the west. An empty awareness washed over Julian. They had lost the battle.

Gulls descended and began to pick at a corpse, squealing at each other in exasperated gluttony. Julian recognized the body as Tiff, one of his Squires. She was no older than sixteen and had bronzed skin from reading in the courtyard. As the birds dug their beaks into the open wound on her cheek, Julian spotted a single enemy. The Marauder was large, yet his frame was stooped by exhaustion. Like many of the pillagers, he wore makeshift iron armor over patched wool clothing. Julian clenched his hand, expecting to feel his bow, but he gripped only air.

They ran for each other, hobbling over the piles of dead. A sharp pain gnawed at Julian's leg. It was an arrow lodged in the side of his thigh. Injured and without a weapon, Julian searched for an advantage. A sword rested on the belly of a dead Marauder just a few feet away between Julian and the enemy. The huge man barreled toward him, revitalized by bloodlust. Julian limped hurriedly and reached down for the blade. His finger grazed the hilt as the man tackled him onto jagged rock.

The Marauder's massive palms throttled Julian's neck. From below him, Julian stared intensely into the man's black eyes and observed his features. His dark skin was dry and cracked from months at sea. He had many lines on his face, like suffering had gifted him a permanent fret. Even with failing breath, Julian found it odd that the man's bloodshot gaze was full of tears. Drool spilled from Julian's mouth, and he could feel the blood flow thinning to his head. As he reached his hand around the arrow stuck in his leg, Julian realized it had been a long time since he had truly seen the face of a man he was going to kill.

Agony tore through Julian's entire body as he attempted to rip the arrow free from his leg. He fell in and out of consciousness, adrenaline igniting his will to survive. Julian yanked the arrow from his flesh with all his strength and jammed it into the Marauder's neck. Blood splattered from the wound as the enemy fell on his side, dead.

Murmuring from across the battlefield barely registered in Julian's mind as he gasped for air and spat the Marauder's blood onto the dirt. He had to escape now before the adrenaline faded and left him crippled. In a moment, Julian pushed off his fallen comrade and began to sprint for the cliff's edge. Marauders pursued him, their shouts battling against the sounds of crashing waves below. "The Templar is alive! He's alive! Alive!"

Three enemies leaped and clawed over a mound of corpses. Julian felt only a shadow of where his leg should be. He turned his head to see a Marauder twenty feet away drawing back a bow. Another was sprinting toward him yet caught his foot under a corpse's limb and slammed into the earth. The edge was close, the blue sea stretching out for miles. As Julian readied himself to jump, a sharp pain pierced through his shoulder. A steel arrowhead poked out of his skin and black jacket. Suddenly he became very tired and felt himself slip forward. Hissing wind awoke him, and he spotted a Marauder watching him fall to the ocean from atop the cliff.

Julian smashed into the water and sunk deep. Death was reaching into his chest, but it was all right. He had escaped, and that was enough. Now he could rest with the soldiers he had failed. Illumination cut through the sea in thin lines. Julian began to release the air in his chest with a forceful huff.

An arm wrapped around him. He was being pulled up toward the surface. Kicking his one good leg, Julian tried to help the mysterious savior. They broke through the waves and sucked in air. "Help him!" the rescuer holding Julian called out. It was a girl with a sharp and ornate voice. She was guiding him to the side of a tiny sailboat, one of the scouting vessels used by the Marauders. Julian surmised the craft must have been stolen, as there was another woman at the mast clad in the lightweight leather armor given to Julian's Knights of Tenshi. Feathers and beads were braided into her silvery hair, and her sky-blue eyes scoured the cliffside above like a bird of prey.

Reaching down, the silver-haired girl pulled Julian aboard as his rescuer hoisted him by the hips. When the savior climbed on board the ship, Julian was astounded by her beauty even in his barely conscious state. The girl's wet hair spun down to her waist in thick cords of auburn, ginger, and gold. Her skin was the color of polished copper and shimmered in the sunlight with drops of seawater. She leaned in close to him, and two eyes speckled with blue and green stared intently as she said, "Can you hear me?"

Julian managed to nod.

Suddenly, the copper-skinned girl turned to face the cliffside. High above, a row of about a dozen archers had gathered. A trill sounded in the air as arrows cut through the sky in unison toward the little boat below. Spreading her legs into a fighting stance, Julian's savior thrust her open palms up toward the raining archers. A barrier of thin, translucent light formed. It sparked and flared with the color of fire. When the barrage of arrows met the barricade of light, it burst into puffs of ash.

"Hanali!" the copper-skinned savior called to the silver-haired girl. Planting herself securely on the deck, the girl called Hanali threw her fists toward the sail of the boat. A gust of furious wind slammed against the back of their vessel. The sail inflated with the pressure of the gale, and the ship hurtled forward with enough force to nearly topple everyone on board.

Blood spilled heavily from Julian's shoulder. He pressed a hand against the wound. It was difficult to tell where the sea ended and the clear sky began. It was a massive, racing blur fading and fading away…

An unfamiliar voice shouted while Julian shut his eyes, "Alina! He's dying!"

☼☼ *IV* ☼☼

Bridget,

It's Ike. I didn't know who else to confide in. Last month I stole all of Lieutenant Asim's left boots. All the Squires ran sprints until Flynn Quan puked, but it was worth it. That's not why I'm writing. I just wanted to brag a bit.

The Spirit Festival is today, and so is my day of initiation. By dusk, all of us remaining Squires will become Knights of Tenshi. Soon we'll be joining you on the battlefield.

Oh, I've also been chosen to see the Spirit. No one ever told me how beautiful the forest nymphs are. You probably didn't want to hear that from your brother. If I had more ink, I'd cross it out. But I don't.

The Spirit made our father her champion and sent him to war. You and Alina are gone now too. I have no interest in whatever sacred mission she has to offer.

My family has suffered enough. Whatever the consequences are for disobeying her, I'll embrace them even if it means exile. Or death.

It's been so long since I heard from you. Write me —

"Ike!" someone called from outside. Ike rolled up the letter and stuffed it in his pocket. Poking his head out the window, Ike spotted Flynn Quan standing amid the flock of noisy sheep. "Hurry! We'll be late for training!" Small in stature, Flynn had narrow black eyes as well as stubby, dark hair. He was nine months younger than Ike and perhaps his oldest friend. Still, Ike used the word "friend" loosely. Flynn was a person he had to actively tolerate.

Behind Flynn stood Nathan Abara. He had caramel skin and wavy black hair extending past his ears. Like always, a red strip of fabric covered Nathan's eyes. The Squire was born blind, but Absalom Ryder's war demanded every youth be made into a Knight of Tenshi. Nonetheless, blindness did not hinder Nathan's athletic abilities. Even now, his stance appeared solid and unwavering. Nathan's chin flinched up to Ike's window as if he sensed his presence. Ike smirked at the blind Squire, his closest companion in the world.

"Coming!" Ike yelled down. By now, Ike had donned his traditional white gi, blue belt, and fitted brown pants. This outfit was reserved for special occasions only. To conceal the gray in his hair, Ike sported a knitted wool cap. He would have to hide the hat before seeing his mother. Before opening the trap door, Ike slipped the sheath housing his father's broadsword onto his back.

When he reached the ground, a sheep was gnawing at Flynn's ankle, causing him to flail his leg around and mutter obscenities.

"Peeko!" Ike called to the sheep with an insistent finger outstretched. "Drop it." Peeko released Flynn, who tumbled onto the grass and cried out, "I'm okay!" As Flynn got to his feet, Ike shot a thumbs-up toward Peeko and mouthed, "Good job."

"Listen, man," Flynn began while the three of them walked through the flock toward the stone road, "I had the night of my life yesterday! The Spirit Festival makes everyone crazy. And today is going to be even better — we're becoming full-on Knights of Tenshi!"

"Uh-huh," Ike responded absentmindedly. His thoughts were focused on the gorgeous green nymph who had visited him and her message. The Great Spirit wanted to meet him? Ike's gaze drifted to the island's edge. If he threw himself off it, the whole mess could be forgotten.

"Last night, Juniper was crying about how she was sure the Spirit would choose her to speak with this year," Flynn recalled just as they began trekking down the road. "I mean, the Spirit hasn't spoken with anyone since she told your old man to start this war. But Juniper's afraid of ghosts, you know?"

"Yeah, I remember," Ike sighed.

"Anyway, I was comforting her and drinking that moonshine Freddie's cousin made last winter."

"Freddie still lives here?"

"No, but his cousin does. Anyway, anyway." Flynn grabbed Ike by the shoulders and said, "I finally told her how I feel. I said she was the most amazing person I have ever met."

"Wow," Ike responded, feeling trapped by Flynn's tight grip. Nathan remained quiet beside them. He probably felt content being left out of Flynn's ramblings.

"I know," Flynn said with eyes wide as saucers. "I almost threw up, but then we kissed, and honestly, I don't remember much after that." Flynn looked past Ike as if he was forcing a recollection. "Freddie's cousin makes strong moonshine."

"I'm happy for you," Ike said genuinely and stepped out of Flynn's clutches to continue down the road. Nathan began walking as soon as Ike's step hit the ground.

"Now we just got to find out if the Spirit actually picked someone this year," Flynn said as he hustled to catch up. "I mean, the guy she spoke to before your father went insane and cut both his feet off. Before that, Quentin's grandmother blinded herself with a brooch. People say the person before her never even came back! I'd hate to be the sorry bastard who—"

"Yeah, Flynn," Ike began to say before halting in place. Flynn nearly skidded on the road from stopping so abruptly.

His hollow expression told Ike that he already knew what he was about to reveal. "It's me. I'm going to see the Spirit."

Ike turned his attention to the sea to avoid staring at Flynn's gaping mouth. Far below Somerset, waves tumbled over each other. Breathing in the sea air, Ike hardly noticed Nathan mutter, "Shit."

Not much else was said on the walk towards Somerset's keep. Soon all the Squires training to become Knights of Tenshi were seen working relentlessly in the training courtyard. The stone keep had been built just behind the old watchtower generations ago. Now twenty-six teenagers ruthlessly trained their bodies beneath the dim light of early morning. All of them wore padded training pants and boots. Ike recognized the lightweight materials from his parents' Templar clothing. Blue, white, and black gis were the only colors allowed. Ike mostly wore blue as white stained too easily and black absorbed far too much heat. He had changed out of his formal attire and into a smelly, blood-stained gi he kept in his trunk under the keep.

Every few days, Ike would wonder how he ended up here. His father had never asked if becoming a Knight was what he wanted. Then again, the rest of Dawn was never given a choice. War was all Ike's generation knew. They'd been raised as weapons, blades to pierce the Great Sands' horde of savages.

Sweat drowned Ike's vision and caused his fingers to sink into the dirt. He crawled on all fours with a sled attached to his waist by a rope. Lieutenant Asim dropped another weight onto his load. "If you stop, I will assume you are dead," he declared over the boy. "And I'll have you dig your own grave."

That's a bit much, Ike thought. Asim had a gaunt face, long black hair, and rough white skin. Of all the people Ike had encountered in his life, Asim was among the most hated.

His entire body trembling, Ike mustered the strength to push himself forward. After one's pain tolerance is surpassed, time dilutes into an indistinguishable fog. Every day, Ike searched for this point of breaking, of release. It came to him then. His body worked monotonously. Soon he collapsed near the edge of the courtyard.

"Mr. Quan, this is not a vacation," Asim barked at Flynn, who held a handstand against the wall.

"Sorry, sir," Flynn said and continued performing pushups with his feet in the air. "I didn't know you had returned from the Templar Trials, sir."

"I have," he responded smugly, "and rather successfully." Asim revealed a silver chain. At the end of it was a pendant in the shape of the numeral V. It was then Ike realized that Asim was wearing the black jacket signifying a Templar of Tenshi. The design Asim chose was more of a coat draping down to his ankles.

"Oh shit," Flynn chirped before falling over. "You won? You're a Templar of Tenshi? One of the twelve strongest people in all of Dawn? You are?"

"Indeed, Mr. Quan," Asim said with a slight roll of the eyes. "It seems I am no longer your lieutenant. I've joined Mr. Ryder's parents among the—" he paused and let a smirk slide across his face, "—supposed legends."

"Congratulations, sir," Ike said politely through exhausted pants of breath.

Lieutenant Asim kicked Ike's limp frame against the wall. "Join meditation," he commanded.

Ike spotted Nathan only a few feet from him. He sat doubled over in the dirt, breathing heavily. The familiar red fabric covered his eyes. "Hey, buddy," Ike huffed.

"Hi, Ike," Nathan managed to murmur.

"Want to steal all his underwear later?" Ike pointed toward Asim.

Nathan nodded.

Summoning the strength to stand, Ike joined meditation. Twelve Squires were lined up in two rows before Captain Katya in the center of the training courtyard. Dense, black hair had been tied up above her brown skin and piercing eyes. Katya was disciplined; her thin lips were always held in a firm line. Despite her rigid demeanor, she moved her hips like a dancer. Ike and the other boys had always fought to look away from her curves and tight figure. On this day, she wore special armor crafted by artisans for high-ranking Knights. Metal-looking shoulder plates blended with a navy fabric that seemed to be padded. A white sash on her shoulder had a design stitched on its center: a diamond separated into fourths by an X. This symbol represented the League of Tenshi, the four allied kingdoms of Dawn. A yellow tree stood just behind her. Its golden leaves were beginning to fall.

"Ra-Chi-Ro!" the Squires all yelled in unison while following the meditative motions. For years, Ike had followed the rhythms. "Ra" — cross hands at the waist, pulling negative energy to each side. "Chi" — twist the hands to the right side and let the energy converge in a tight ball. "Ro" — release the energy forward with a tight thrust of both hands. A tinge of pain in his shoulder made Ike shudder. Every muscle in his body was sore due to their ridiculous training schedule. Still, he didn't feel that his physique looked appealing or mature. If anything, Ike felt more awkward than ever.

"I heard in the last recruits, Brantley Adams blasted through the keep's wall doing this," Ike muttered to Adrianna under her breath. She had tanned skin and a crew cut. Her eyes were like charcoal and carried a pronounced warmth.

She wasn't listening to Ike. Most girls preferred not to.

"Yesterday, I swear, there were sparks on my fingers," Flynn whispered on the other side of them. He was smaller than the rest of the Squires but had the biggest mouth. "Sparks, man!"

"Ryder!" Captain Katya called. Ike shuffled his feet together and held a half bow. "Since Ike has the energy to converse with his comrades, he will be first to duel today."

Knots clenched Ike's stomach together. A training blade was thrust in his hands. Within moments, the other twenty-five Squires, Captain Katya, and Asim surrounded him.

"Captain Katya!" a voice called from the gate into the courtyard. Every head turned to see Li Quan, a graying fisherman. "New merchants are asking for permission to come up for the festival."

"Templar Asim," Katya said, "Carry on for me." Captain Katya exited the circle of Squires and made her way out of the courtyard with Li.

A slash of pain and the cracking of air alerted Ike to his surroundings once more. Templar Asim had unveiled his whip and struck Ike across the foot. "Your attention is here, Mr. Ryder! Stance!" Asim shouted as he whipped the dirt just near Ike's ankle, causing him to jump. When he landed, Ike spread his feet and readied the blade in his hands. "Ms. Alanforth, go!"

Adrianna grabbed a rapier from the weapon rack outside the circle and darted toward Ike. Sweat had already caused the blade in Ike's hand to slip. The girl's charcoal eyes stared through him. She lunged the tip of her weapon forward, straight for his heart. Ike parried but was moved back. She pressed him with three more jabs of her slender blade. With two hands on his broadsword's hilt, Ike drove each strike away. Steel clattered together and cut through Ike's heavy breaths. Ting, tang, ting.

The last parry threw Adrianna off balance. She was open for a strike. Ike raised his sword and his gaze caught the girl's dark eyes. Something had replaced the vapid coldness behind them. It was fear. Red hot pain slashed across Ike's back, causing him to fall onto his knees. "She was open," Asim called out with the whip dangling at his side. "Ike Ryder, the gentle oaf." Snickering broke out among the Squires.

Ike held his head low and watched sweat trickle onto the dirt.

Another streak of pain tore across Ike's back, causing him to double over. Asim's voice sounded low and firm. "Why didn't you hit her?"

"She was too fast," Ike muttered as he fought off the tears pressing against his eyes.

"Too fast? I see," Asim began as he wandered the open space between Adrianna and Ike. "Does everyone hear that? Mr. Ryder is blaming his incompetence as a fighter instead of the fact that he was born without a cock between his legs."

Anger rose Ike up to his knees. His face flushed with blood, and his eyes fixed on Asim, who merely smirked.

"Do you have something to say?" Asim asked him. Nothing came to Ike's lips. The Templar wanted him to explode, any reason to punish him further. Still glaring at Asim, Ike clenched his teeth into his tongue.

"Ms. Alanforth is smaller and quicker. Still, with your size, a single well-placed strike would tear her in two," Asim elaborated while darting throughout the circle, as if the scene was unfolding in his mind's eye. "You lack conviction, courage, discipline. Do you disagree?"

"I-I," Ike could not force himself to speak.

Asim froze. "Nathan Abara," he called. Flynn led Nathan stiffly by the arm to the center of the circle. Within a moment, a training blade was passed into his hand. "Mr. Abara is blind," Asim began. "He'll never participate in true war. In a battlefield setting, he would be quickly overwhelmed, but in a controlled environment, he is an effective threat." Ike had risen to his feet. He knew what was coming. "Mr. Abara can feel the air being cut by steel, knows your movements by the sounds of your toes brushing up dust. He can predict and react, but most importantly…" Asim looked up at Ike, but the boy had never felt smaller. "He is a better fighter than you."

The whip cracked the space of dirt between Nathan and Ike. They readied themselves in mirrored stances. "He's six paces in front," Asim instructed Nathan. The boy with caramel skin and wavy hair advanced. Adrianna and the other girls batted their eyelashes at him.

He can't see you, Ike heard himself think.

Nathan knew the length of Ike's reach, but also, he knew that Ike had never struck first in a fight. Quickly, Nathan would move in and attack the legs. Ike was aware of this. He had spent hundreds of hours sparring with Nathan over the years.

A wide, horizontal slash reached out for Ike's knees. He countered with a low wave of his blade. Nathan had to use broad attacks, but the longer the fight drew on, the more precise he became. Four more wide arcs were intended for Ike's hips. Methodically, Ike threw the attacks away. A nick caused a drop of blood to splat onto the dirt from Ike's thigh. "Counter!" Asim yelled as he whipped Ike's back. The large boy staggered forward and fell into Nathan, who held him up.

"Just hit me," Nathan whispered into Ike's ear.

"I'm trying," Ike affirmed with a tinge of agitation.

Ike's cheek tore open with a hot snap of air. Nathan and Ike tumbled onto their sides, both clutching their faces.

"I thought perhaps you lacked the stomach to hit a girl," Asim mocked, "but now I think you may be sweet on the blind boy."

Dirt balled into Ike's fist. Fury tightened his gut and his eyes locked onto a space far away from the courtyard.

The two boys rose up. Asim's whip snarled against Nathan's back. "Hit him!" he commanded. No sword in hand, Nathan jabbed at Ike's jaw while tripping over his own feet. They tumbled to the ground once more, Nathan straddling Ike with his fist still raised. "Yield," Nathan huffed.

"I yield," Ike sighed.

Two cracks of air echoed through the courtyard as Asim struck Nathan's back. The lieutenant's cold voice was rattled and furious. "Do you think I can't see the hesitation? Do you think I cannot perceive the pitiful mercy guiding your hand? This is war; there is no place for restraint on the battlefield. Finish the fight."

Nathan began to retort, "But—"

Another slash stripped away flesh from Nathan's back.

"Do it," Ike whispered.

Nathan's head twitched at the words. He sent his left fist barreling into Ike's cheek. Pain burst in a web from the impact point, and Ike's head flopped against the dirt. A right punch cut across Ike's jaw, and another left hook left his head spinning. The barrage continued, leaving Ike spasming in agony underneath Nathan. Soon Ike felt his body lose the strength to react. His face went numb, and swelling closed his left eye.

The onslaught paused. Ike willed his right eye to swivel toward Nathan. Captain Katya held his fist. "Dismissed!" she shouted to the circle of Squires. Feet began to scurry out of the courtyard and passed out of Ike's field of vision. A desire to be anywhere else suddenly bloomed in Ike's heart. Not existing at all would be a better fate than lying on the courtyard dirt humiliated.

When the murmuring of the exiting Squires faded to silence, Captain Katya finally released Nathan's hand and uttered a single word, "Explain."

Templar Asim was quick to respond. "Duels held under the League of Tenshi must be carried out until one or both participants are unable to batt—"

"This is not a duel," Katya interrupted. Her tone was controlled and focused. While she spoke, her gaze never left the blood clinging to Nathan's knuckles. "This is a training exercise ordered under my command, not yours."

"How dare you speak to a Templar of Tenshi in that tone," Asim retorted. He loomed over Katya like an outstretched cobra.

Captain Katya swallowed her pride and bowed. "Forgive me," she said unconvincingly. "Somerset is under the jurisdiction of Templar Ol'dog and Templar Tempest. They have given me full command of its operations." Katya raised herself up tall. "Full command. As you know from years of working beneath me."

Neither Nathan nor Ike dared to move. Ike remained planted on the ground, his body feeling both empty and incredibly heavy. Asim's face appeared unreadable and vacant.

"Am I dismissed?" Katya finally asked.

Asim nodded and marched off through the main gates. Katya strode forward, close on his heels. As she passed by, her gaze paused on Ike. He felt analyzed, dissected by her watchful eye. There was no sympathy in her stare, only a cold observation that left him overcome with shame. Ike watched their boots trot off into the village.

Finally alone, Ike squirmed out from under Nathan and stood. The swelling in his face left him feeling off-balance and top-heavy.

"Ike?" Nathan said.

"Yeah?"

"I don't know where I am," he said quietly. "Disoriented." Ike reached down and took hold of his arm.

☼☼ V ☼☼

Alina stood at the front of the boat, staring off at the horizon. So much sea was stretched out before them that it seemed there was no end. Somerset must have been close by, yet the familiar floating island seemed unreachable. For a while now, she had been replaying a memory in her head. The day, if she recalled correctly, happened five years after Alina fell from the stars, an event she could hardly remember. Absal was visiting from the war front, and he took Ike, Bridget, and Alina into Somerset's woods to train. The children stood in a line wearing loose training clothes. Ike fastened his white belt tightly around his blue gi. Alina's training gi was yellow, and Bridget's was pink. From above, they must have looked like spring flowers.

"I already warmed up with thirty laps around the island," Alina joked to Ike.

She combed a handful of hair behind her ear while Ike said, "I remember when I stopped at thirty. My mom hated it because she had to change a wet diaper."

"So, it was last week?" Alina responded.

Ike snorted, knowing he'd been outdone. Alina smiled. She liked making him laugh.

"Ike, focus," Absal told him. "After this, I'm going to have you do some laps for real." Absal patted Ike's stomach. Immediately Ike's face flushed with color.

"Listen closely. Today I begin passing on the knowledge our Great Spirit once bestowed upon me," Absal announced. "There is energy all around us. It moves and flows through all living things." He produced a tiny yellow fire over his left palm. "This is ki, the energy of life."

"Wow," Ike muttered next to Alina.

Absal nodded to them and said, "Fledgling ki-wielders usually learn to produce heat before anything else. Fire is a specialty of the Knights. I will teach you all to awaken your ki just as the Great Spirit taught my brothers and me. I know the gift is within you. I can feel it." He scanned the children locking eyes with each one. "How else do Knights use ki?" Absal questioned them. "Bridget?"

"Um," Bridget mumbled. She elbowed Alina, who whispered in her ear. "To make their bodies stronger? And faster?" Bridget asked.

"Good job, Alina," Absal said. "What else?"

"Well…to make light?" Alina said, unsure. "And…"

"Some people can move things with their thoughts like this," Ike declared before going cross-eyed staring at a rock. Absal shoved the boy's head and knocked him over.

"Some use ki to connect with nature, broaden their minds, perform sorcery," Absal told them. "Not us. Knights use ki for war. We use our strength to kill, without mercy. That is our way. And it is the only way."

Those last words remained with Alina as she inspected her boat in the present. She couldn't decide if Absal's lesson held merit or truth. Was mercy a weakness? If so, Alina had certainly demonstrated her frailty as a Knight. When faced with utter destruction, she had chosen to flee with whoever she could save. Absal would have expected her to fight until death.

There was a silver-haired girl with brown skin hunched over under the mast. Alina knew her as Hanali, a fellow Knight she had met only a few months ago. She appeared depleted; sweat drenched her from head to toe. They were so cramped in the vessel that Hanali's legs became entangled with Commander Julian's while they slept. It was a surreal feeling to be this close to Markus Julian. Six months ago, Alina had been assigned to be one of his five hundred soldiers. Despite that, they had never spoken a word to each other. Now they were stranded in the Aged Sea, almost all hope of survival lost. How long before the Marauders found them? Absal's words returned — *And it is the only way.*

In one hand, she clutched a tiny leather pouch. Alina had found it wrapped in fabric against Julian's chest while tending to his wounds. She recognized the leatherwork from her time training in the capital city of Whitecrest. They were used to store drugs. Tentatively, she opened the pouch and pulled out a little black crystal. Light beamed off its sides and created a low, ominous glow.

A ragged voice startled her. "You —" Julian's grumble trailed into a cough.

Alina dropped the crystal into the bag and spun around. Quickly she hobbled through the tight space to be at Julian's side. Before reaching him, Alina stuffed the leather pouch in her pocket.

"Good morning, sir," she told him in a delicate yet formidable voice.

Julian began inspecting himself. Alina had removed his black jacket and chainmail, leaving him in a blood-soaked undershirt. The silver pendant of the numeral IV still rested against his chest, a sign of a Templar of Tenshi. He poked near the wounds in his leg and shoulder. If Alina had done the healing procedure correctly, Julian should have felt nothing except a knot of scar tissue. Spreading open the hole in his shirt, Julian stared at the raised blotch of white skin where the arrow rupture had once been.

"You healed me," he said to Alina. "Both of you are ki-wielders." The term ki-wielder referred to individuals who could perform fantastical feats beyond what an ordinary person could do. Spirits once trained ki-wielders to protect their homes. That was long ago, though. Now ki-wielders were weapons of war, not much else.

"Yes, sir. Healing is not my specialty," Alina responded with an eye examining the scar on his leg, "but I did an okay job." It was easy to be distracted by Julian's appearance. Even disheveled, bruised, and blood-soaked, he was handsome.

"What's her problem?" Julian nodded his head toward the silver-haired girl who was still doubled over under the sail.

"She exhausted herself," Alina explained. "You were out for almost a couple hours, sir. We're lost, and Hanali has been sailing—"

"The Marauders rolled right through us, but we couldn't have been their target," Julian announced as he got to a standing position. For a moment, it seemed like he might faint, yet he waved away Alina's outstretched hands. "It was a stroke of bad luck, had to be. No one knew our course except me." He put both arms on his head and took large breaths. "The only island worth mentioning in the southeast is Somerset. They must be headed there."

"Did you say, Somerset? I'm from—"

Commander Julian cut her off. "What's your name and rank?"

Alina was taken aback by his rudeness. She tried to collect herself under the pressure of her superior. There was an itching inside Alina's head like the hundreds of fallen soldiers were all crawling against her skull. Standing up tall, she tried to refrain from shaking. Her home was in danger. Julian began to rummage through his discarded jacket and barely glanced in her direction.

"Alina Starchild, Apprentice Knight of Tenshi assigned to serve the Green Guard," she told him.

"Starchild?" Julian uttered in shock while still digging into his jacket's pockets. "You're Absalom Ryder's Starchild?"

The question made her uncomfortable. There was never an easy answer. She stammered for a moment and then said, "I don't belong to Absal. He just found me."

"That guy is a piece of shit underneath all the spectacle," Julian said with a shrug as if he hadn't heard her at all.

"Could be worse. At least you aren't his brother's kid." Alina thought of telling him to mind his own business but didn't. He was her commander, one of the legendary Templars of Tenshi. Only twelve individuals could hold the title; they were the most formidable ki-wielders in all of Dawn.

"She's an Apprentice too?" Julian asked, pointing at Hanali.

Alina nodded reluctantly.

"How did two Apprentice Knights steal a Marauder cruiser?" he questioned and removed his blood-soaked shirt. The jacket and shirt were both dropped onto Hanali's legs. Finally, he turned to Alina, his torso now exposed.

Eyeing the open sea to avoid looking at Julian's body, Alina explained, "I was cornered on the western banks. They were coming from all sides. Just when I thought it was over, Hanali tackled me off the cliffside. Her people are masters of the wind. She used a gale to guide us down and—"

"All right, I got it," Julian interjected before taking a step closer. His eyes were kind but empty-looking. "You can really talk, huh?"

She scoffed, the first breaking of such polite etiquette. Her face twitched in response to the thoughts brewing inside her. He didn't even want to hear the answer to his own question. How could someone be so intolerable?

"Have something else to say?" Julian asked, releasing a quick tinge of what seemed like playful agitation.

Alina stood there and bit her lip. A small wave rocked them back and forth. It seemed like she may not say anything, but then Alina marched forward a step and said, "I guess I thought a Templar of Tenshi would be more admirable." She revealed the leather pouch and held it by the strings as if it were volatile to touch.

"Because your father is such a role model?" Julian responded sarcastically and stepped so close to Alina that she could see the hint of green in his hazel eyes. He was smirking and staring without remorse at every inch of her.

Instead of recoiling, Alina forced herself to look him up and down too. His body appeared incredibly toned with muscle and riddled with scars. Age lines he was too young to have had formed on his face from stress. In that moment, he did not seem like her commander or a famed warrior. He was just another boy masking pain with arrogance.

"You do not impress me," Alina said. She pressed the leather bag against his chest, and he caught her hand over his. His palms were rough and warm.

"Is that an invitation to try?" Julian asked.

"It's the opposite," she stated and pushed Julian away with a firm shove. Alina left the leather pouch in his hand, determined not to care if he kept it.

"Uh, guys," a wispy voice murmured. It was Hanali, her eyes slightly open and peering out to the sea behind them. "Who's that?" She pointed to a distant shape zipping through the water with great speed. How could it move so quickly? Did it have someone like Hanali as well?

Julian stomped toward the edge of the vessel, causing them to sway. "Can you get us out of here?" he asked Hanali with his stare locked on the small boat approaching.

A paleness had stolen the brown coloring in Hanali's skin. She shook her head loosely.

"Shit," Julian muttered under his breath. In a single swift motion, he turned and snatched the dagger sheathed behind Alina's back. "Hit the deck, Stargirl."

Grudgingly, Alina laid on her back and lowered Hanali, so she rested on her chest. "Is it Marauders?" Hanali asked her.

"Don't know," Alina replied quietly. Within a few moments, Alina could hear the water being torn apart by the racing boat. How could Julian make her hide? Hadn't he seen her usefulness?

A new sound accompanied the speeding vessel. Was it an accordion?

"What the hell?" Julian uttered above her. Alina peeked up and saw a tiny purple boat only minutely larger than their cruiser pulling up beside them. Outlandish faces were painted on the hull. They resembled masks of different cartoonish creatures and people. Glittery, yellow lettering sparkled on the side, reading *Marnie's Many Masks*.

On the foolish-looking boat near the single brown sail stood a frail man with balding brown hair. His skin looked very pale for someone traveling by sea, and Alina had never seen eyes so incredibly narrow. They appeared almost shut, like slits in paper, in what must have been an attempt at a friendly grin. Carefully he held an old accordion, which he squeezed back and forth cheerfully. "Greetings, friend!" the strange man called toward Julian.

"Um, greetings!" Julian shouted back over the annoyingly loud music. He flicked the dagger backward with a snap of his wrist. It stuck itself in the mast just above Alina's head. She quietly yanked the blade free and sheathed it.

"I did not expect to come across another ship so small in scale *waaay* out here," the frail man said. His voice sounded childish and brash like the instrument he played.

"Likewise," Julian replied. "What brings you so far out in the Aged Sea?"

"Oh, you don't know?" the man asked giddily. "The Spirit Festival begins today on the floating isle of Somerset. 'Tis a grand event, I am told. I'm heading there to sell my many masks."

"We need to go there!" Alina sprung up and shouted. "Marauder ships may be staging an invasion." Julian eyed her grudgingly, yet she ignored him. The mention of her home was too much to bear. "Can you take us with you? We're lost out here, and my friend is very dehydrated." She held up Hanali by the shoulders so the mask salesman could get a view of her.

"Oh, my goodness," the accordion-playing man declared. His tune went off-key for a single beat. Strangely, he did not look at Hanali. "You're a Starchild! I'd recognize that gorgeous hair anywhere. And those eyes are breathtaking! Of course, I'll help you."

Alina would have blushed if the man giving the compliment wasn't so bizarre. "No one has ever known just by looking at me," she told him.

"I know all the faces of Dawn, especially the rarest," he said and began to play a somber melody on his instrument. "Starchildren fall from the heavens in times of great calamities. They have protected the people of Dawn from the most incredible threats."

Julian caught Alina's arm and whispered into her ear, "I don't trust this man. He's playing at something."

"My Templar, we don't have a choice," she whispered back and nodded toward Hanali's limp body. Seeing Julian's stern grimace, Alina added a low, "Sir."

He exhaled and spoke even softer than before. "I didn't say we aren't going." Breaking away from Alina, Julian announced suddenly, "All right. Let's get a move on." He scooped Hanali into his arms along with his black jacket.

"How do you sail with no wind?" Alina inquired as she hopped from their cruiser to the humorously-colored boat. Looking down, she spotted piles of wooden and clay masks, which cluttered the interior. "Are you a ki-wielder?" she added to her question while avoiding stepping on their rescuer's products.

"Heavens no!" the man laughed and finally placed his accordion in a storage space underneath a trapdoor. "I spent my youth like many others, trying to unlock the hidden energy within me, my ki. I never had much luck, though! At one point, I became quite desperate and tried to study under the spirits like ancient times. What a disaster that became!" He roared with laughter. Julian and Alina glanced toward each other uneasily. "Now I travel and collect faces with my dear companion."

A ball of yellow light rose out of the storage space and hovered near Alina's nose, almost blinding her. She stammered back a step and nearly crushed a clay mask with her heel.

"That is Echo, a nymph of a distant meadow," he told them. "She has so politely asked the sea spirits to guide us toward Somerset. They certainly prefer her over me."

"Then guide away," Julian stated as he placed Hanali down in the boat.

"You heard the Templar, Echo," the mask salesman said delightedly.

The orb of light shimmered brighter for a moment, and then a great current swept the boat forward. They traveled onward and left the Marauder cruiser in their wake. Maybe the memories of the battle would remain with that pitiful ship, Alina thought to herself. Home would soon be on the horizon. Beth, Ike, even the pastry shop near the temple would be waiting. Could she really return to that life? Sea air passed over Alina and whisked up her tangled hair. Deep inside, she knew that the Somerset of her childhood was a mere memory. Nothing could be the same.

A particular mask caught her eye on the boat floor. Chipped black paint covered an old, wooden frame. Two bulging eyes gawked at her with tiny, yellow pupils. She retrieved the mask and brushed away dust from one of the massive eyes. The face filled her with a tremendous sense of foreboding.

☼☼ *VI* ☼☼

Inhabitants of Somerset packed into town square well before nine in the morning. No one ever missed the Spirit Festival's opening ceremony. Children darted through the street carrying powdered doughnuts and wooden swords.

Shop and restaurant owners had opened early in preparation for the ceremony. Most everyone dressed in formal attire, which meant collared shirts for men and sundresses for women. It was summer, and the heat forbade any extravagant clothing. Girls often spent months sewing airy and beautiful dresses for the Spirit Festival. Ike knew this from years of watching Alina and Bridget order specific fabrics from merchant ships. They'd then spend hours designing the perfect ensemble. On the last Spirit Festival Alina attended, she wore a beautiful white dress with golden detailing like traces of stardust.

A peculiar sight brought Ike back to reality. Knights of Tenshi in bloodied leather armor strode through the massive crowd. People shuffled apart to create a gap for the group to pass through. Some onlookers applauded, and the others stood in silent observation.

There were about half a dozen Knights, and the man in front pushed a wheelbarrow ahead of them. Ike observed the severed limbs and rotting heads piled in the barrow. This was a kind of ritual the Knights performed nowadays. They'd dismember their enemies and flaunt their slaughtered bodies in a display of power. The sight sickened Ike and turned his stomach. Flies circled the mound of dead flesh and began to feast. Ike's eyes drifted to the back of the Knights, where a young girl with honey-colored skin was led by a rope fastened to her neck. The eyes of the Knights were cold yet intensely proud.

"Ike," Flynn called, "This way. We have to stand with the Squires." Ike reluctantly pulled his attention away from the group of Knights and followed Flynn's eye line. The swelling made half of Ike's vision a blur, but his familiarity with the festival filled in the murky details. All Squires on the island stood in front of the Temple to El, the one true God. It was a far different structure than anything else on the island. A massive white stone had been cut and shaped into a towering sanctuary. Blue stained glass formed an ornate circular window at the very top. All people who were not Knights of Tenshi or Squires gathered in a massive semicircle around the white temple.

"You go, Flynn," Ike told him. "I'm just a shepherd." Since training ended, Ike had washed the blood from his face and changed into his formal attire once more. For some reason, the garments felt unusually large on him now.

Flynn grabbed his arm and tried to drag him toward the temple steps. "You're going to be a Knight of Tenshi. You endured the training like everyone else." Ike wasn't budged by Flynn's attempt to pull him, but he continued walking anyway. "Protecting our livestock is an important job. Plus, when they hear that you're—"

"Quiet!" Ike snapped.

They had to squeeze through the growing crowd to finally make it at the front. Lined up before the temple were Ike and Flynn's companions, the youth who would soon be declared Knights of Tenshi. They had spent their lives training on Somerset to join the Knighthood. Many had already left to join Absalom Ryder's war. About half of their class remained on the island, twenty-six in all, but the Spirit Festival had been chosen as this year's day of initiation. After the celebration, Ike would have to leave his home.

A hand fell onto Ike's shoulder. He looked to his right and saw Templar Asim. The wounds on Ike's face throbbed more intensely. "Where are you headed, Mr. Ryder?" He asked Ike in a slippery and bitter voice.

"Up there," Ike said and pointed to where his fellow Squires stood.

Asim's hand gripped his shoulder once more. "I'm sure you'd like to join your comrades for the ceremony," Asim told him, "but unfortunately, you have some business to tend to." He gestured with his head toward a pastry stand where a small sheep was nipping at the ankle of a baker.

"Peeko!" Ike shouted before darting through the gathering islanders to reach his sheep. The unruly animal must have slipped through the gate again. Peeko's victim was a middle-aged man with a thick mustache. Ike couldn't recall his name.

"I'm so sorry, sir," Ike said while trying to wrangle Peeko off the man's leg.

"This is a pest!" he screamed and kicked at the sheep. "He should be put down! I know some butchers in need of mutton."

Finally, Ike wretched Peeko from the baker's pantleg and tossed the sheep up onto his shoulders. Reaching into his pocket with one hand, Ike tossed four silver pieces onto the pastry stand and took a single sweet roll. "Keep the change, sir," he told him. As the baker waved him off, Ike knocked over a jar of candies. "Oops," Ike said with a shrug. When the baker leaned down to retrieve the jar, Ike scooped up his money and walked off.

With Peeko hung on the back of his neck like a scarf, Ike journeyed to the very edge of the crowd. Taking a bite of his sweet roll, Ike spotted a familiar face. "Wha' tha hell?" he said with a full mouth. Nathan stood beside Adrianna in newly fitted leather armor.

Ike rushed down the main road, and as he neared, he shouted, "Nathan!"

"You like it, Ike," Nathan said with a smirk.

"I couldn't find you after I cleaned up," Ike recalled. "What happened?"

"We've been made Knights ahead of schedule," Adrianna said. Both of them seemed to brim with pride. "Templar Asim made us part of his personal guard. We get a special rite in the capital, and then it's off to clear villages in the Great Sands."

"I can't believe that asshole is a Templar of Tenshi," Ike said with a firm bite into his pastry. "Every Knight is under their control. They're in charge of keeping the peace. Asim is just a killer and a thug."

"I'm going to look for my family," Adrianna announced and took a step away from them. "You have Nathan?"

Ike gave a thumbs up to Adrianna.

"I don't need to be watched," Nathan groaned. "I know my way around this island better than anyone."

"Humor me," Ike said. "I'm sorry."

"For what?" Nathan asked.

"That you have to go to war with Asim," Ike stated. He felt compelled to add, "Who knows what barbaric tactics that jackoff finds humane."

Nathan scoffed. "I thought training on this floating shithole would make you grow up."

"And I thought being asked to raid villages in the Great Sands would make you see the bigger picture," Ike countered. "You've been called to butcher peasants."

"This is the life we were dealt, Ike," Nathan stated. "You think you're noble because your hands are clean. That's the sentiment of a child. This is war. Cities burn on both sides. You either die in the flames or be the one lighting the match."

Ike gripped Peeko's leg so tightly he squirmed. Templar Asim and their captain were headed up the temple steps. The ceremony would begin soon. Ike decided to hurry through what he had left to say. "Your brother went to the Great Sands, and he never came back," he asserted bitterly.

"His ship was sunk by Marauders off the coast of Fairspell. He's either dead or a slave."

"You'll end up the same," Ike heard himself say.

"And you'll end up being nothing at all," Nathan replied quietly.

A *bang* echoed throughout the town square. One of the Squires—Ike knew him as Quentin—had slammed the ceremonial gong with a hammer. Furious at what Nathan had said, Ike took a step away from him. He couldn't abandon the blind Knight completely in a crowd like this, no matter how badly he suddenly wished Nathan had never been given that armor.

Captain Katya stepped forward from the line of Squires, Asim on her right side. "By nightfall, the Squires behind me will become Knights of Tenshi and join their comrades fighting for our honor in the Great Sands," Katya boomed her voice over the large crowd. Some of the Squires gave each other self-indulging smirks. Ike found their pride amusing as the most talented in their class had long since been deployed. The remaining Squires were the bottom of the barrel, himself included.

"But now, we gather here to reflect," Katya continued. Chatter reduced to complete silence. "The world of Dawn was forged thousands of years ago from dust and vapor by the *Deathrid*." Asim was handed a large crystal cube from a Squire. Clutching it with both hands, he seemed to be entering a deep concentration.

A flash lit the box with white light, and it began projecting an image above the crowd. Gasps of amazement and anticipation erupted as four glowing figures appeared overhead. The features were indistinguishable, but each mirage emitted a different color: red, green, orange, and blue.

"The Deathrid were immortal, powerful beings," Katya went on. "They were unrivaled by any god in the Old World and unmatched by any natural force. Yet despite their incredible power, the Deathrid grew lonely and wished to share their glory." Katya gave a pause and then spoke with even more authority, saying, "The Deathrid brought humankind to Dawn, their new paradise, and taught us the art of ki-wielding." She opened her palm, and a brilliant, rose-colored flame sparked into life. "Humans learned to harness this energy hidden within all living things. Bodies were strengthened by it, minds were expanded, and nature became intertwined with our souls. For a time, there was peace. But the gods of the Old World grew jealous of Dawn's prosperity."

Overhead, the image shifted to become a golden, winged woman. She held a masculine figure in a lover's embrace. The male image only had a faint, pale shimmer. "The old gods, long outcast from the heavens, made Dawn their new home," Katya said. "They mingled with the humans and became closer than lovers. Feeling threatened by these incredible deities, the Deathrid waged war against the old gods."

Golden creatures flew above the crowd carrying flaming swords. Cheers and applause spread throughout the town square. Ike and Nathan half-heartedly clapped, as they had been witnesses to this display many times over. Perhaps they weren't as sentimental as the majority of Somerset.

"Generations lived and died in bloodshed. In the aftermath of the First Great War, the gods' physical bodies were slaughtered, leaving them phantoms of what they once were. Their broken forms became known as spirits." The winged deities fell limp from the sky and rested just above the islanders' heads. Standing tall over the murdered gods were red, green, orange, and blue figures.

"Dawn was laid to waste, and the Deathrid planned to begin a new world. In doing so, the remaining humans would be massacred." The dead deities shimmered into hundreds of small human figures. They climbed over each other toward the Deathrid floating above.

"Our island was pulled from the Aged Sea by the Great Spirit in the days of the Second Great War. It was here the Storm Paladins and Starchildren battled the Deathrid and slew them." As the rising humans reached the Deathrid, all parts of the projection burst away to raining drops of light. Roars gushed out from the people of Somerset.

"Under guidance from the Great Spirit, the four kingdoms of Dawn formed the League of Tenshi to keep everlasting peace!" Katya screamed over the cheering crowd.

The Squires standing behind Katya stomped one foot and in unison cried, "We give our shield!"

"And on this day, we ask that the Great Spirit break her ten-year silence! We ask that she choose a new champion while her earpiece, the Templar Absalom Ryder, wages her just war against the filth that raped our homeland. So now, I call forth our guardian, our light in the deepest darkness, to select the worthiest among us!"

Uh oh, Ike thought. Captain Katya slid her feet into a fighter's stance and thrust a fist forward. From her knuckle came a searing jet of fire. Islanders in the front row ducked their heads as the stream of flame coiled up in the air and took the form of a fiery dragon.

Asim had rid himself of the crystal box and now mirrored Katya's stance. He motioned his hands toward the fountain planted in the center of the town square. Water rose out of its large basin and swirled into the sky. Now twin dragons danced overhead, guided by Asim and Katya's steady motions. The beasts emitted droplets of rain and flashes of intense heat as they circled each other in a kind of courtship. No one made a sound. Every islander was fixed on the spectacle above. Even Ike, who had grown cynical of ki-wielders and their lavish displays, couldn't help but stand in wonder.

Grunting with the effort, Katya and Asim thrust their fists up and toward each other. The twin dragons swirled around one another to a height far beyond the temple's peak. With a mighty crash, the two beasts collided. Heavy steam exploded forth and poured down from the impact. It fell over the town square and dampened Ike's hair in a warm fog. Peeko's wet fur stuck to his neck. "*Baa,*" the sheep moaned quietly in discomfort.

Silence remained for what seemed like an eternity. People shifted on their heels. Children tugged at their parents' arms and asked, "Is it happening?" Expressions of fervent hope faded to utter disappointment.

"Another quiet year," Nathan sighed under his breath. Was he talking to Ike or himself?

A woman near them uttered, "I knew she wouldn't pick anyone."

The man at her side said, "There are no worthy fighters left to choose from."

Ike agreed and wondered if the nymph he had seen was real at all. Maybe he had been asleep still. That was perhaps possible. Searching through the mist, Ike saw Flynn in front of the temple, anxiously darting his eyes in all directions. Flynn would leave here thinking that Ike had fooled him. Relief settled over Ike. He wasn't chosen after all. Smiling, Ike stuffed the last bite of sweet roll into his mouth.

Another voice called out, "Oi, let's go! Start the party!"

Katya remained still for another moment and listened intently. After a while, she said to the restless crowd, "It seems another year of silence is—"

Boom! A deafening crack of thunder trembled the clear summer skies. The massive congregation standing before the temple let slip an almost simultaneous gasp of fear. Hands were held over ears, sobs bellowed out from infants, and all eyes scanned the clouds for danger.

Whoosh! The wind howled through the streets and whisked away the layer of steam still lingering from the dragons' ritual. A name rattled through the rushing gust.

"Ike Ryder."

The hairs on Ike's neck stood on end. Panic began to beat against his heart, provoking a fierce desire to flee the scene entirely. Slowly, heads began to swivel about the crowd. Faces found him near the back, and their mouths opened in abject surprise. Ike realized that the last bite of his pastry had yet to be swallowed. *Gulp.*

Murmuring began. "The Ryder boy?"

"Him?"

"He's lanky…"

"Bottom of the class…"

"He's just a shepherd…"

Nathan nudged Ike with his elbow and whispered, "You have to go."

A path became clear through the crowd as people diverged to offer Ike passage. Hesitantly, Ike trekked through the town square toward the Temple to El. Every eye followed his movements in continued disbelief. Nervous sweat pooled under Ike's armpits and wool cap. His footsteps up to the temple overshadowed every prying whisper. *Tap, tap, tap…*

A foot reached out to trip him, yet Ike managed to catch himself before falling. Although Ike didn't acknowledge the taunt, a few laughs trailed out from the bully's direction. He was nearly there, the white stone steps now under his boots. Asim's expression appeared to be somewhere between puzzlement and delight. "Be cautious now, Mr. Ryder," he whispered. "The Spirit has been known to blind the weak-willed and drive them to madness."

Taking a quick breath, Ike lowered his head and proceeded past him. He came near Flynn, who was in the midst of telling Pauline, "I had to keep it a secret all morning. I knew the whole time — Oh — "

Ike set Peeko down near Flynn's feet without a word and turned to face Captain Katya. The twelve Squires were at his back now, and all of Somerset stood before him. Somewhere out there was his mother. Desperately, he wished to see her.

"What now?" he asked quietly to Katya.

She looked at Ike differently than any other islander that morning. The curl at the corner of her lip let Ike know she was pleased. "Your journey starts within the Temple to El," Katya said to him alone.

Ike nodded and proceeded back toward the large oak doors.

"And Ike," Katya called for his attention once more. He stopped and looked over his shoulder. "If you show any sign of weakness or fear, the Spirit will claim your sanity." She stepped closer so he could observe the earnestness in her eyes. "You'd be better off dead than suffer that fate."

He wasn't afraid; however, Ike lamented her lack of faith in him. Not bothering to respond, Ike continued through the line of Squires and pushed open the temple's massive doors with a single shove.

☀☼ *VII* ☼☀

Alina poured a sip of water into Hanali's mouth. "I can do it myself now," she told her and took the waterskin from Alina's hands. Color had finally returned to Hanali's cheeks after over an hour of rest under the sail's thin shade. The mask salesman sat near the rudder with his accordion in hand. An irritating jingle played out on repeat from the instrument.

"The Crystal Pass is up ahead," the mask salesman said merrily.

Leaning over to look around Julian's back, Alina spotted jagged crystals jutting out from the sea in all directions. Blinding sunlight bounced off the minerals, making it difficult to surmise where the clusters of crystals began and ended. Julian, wearing his Templar jacket over an exposed torso, held a hand over his eyes to block some of the harsh light. "How do you plan on getting through that?" he asked from the front of the ship. "We'll get torn apart."

"The sea spirits will guide us onward," the mask salesman declared. "I would worry more about the beastly leviathans that roam these waters." He gave a wink at Alina and Hanali. They smiled politely but gave each other an uncomfortable glance.

Silence poured over the boat. With a widening of his narrow eyes, the mask salesman had stopped playing his tune. Echo, who had been floating near Hanali's ear, darted inside the mask salesman's pocket. Julian stood firm and shouted, "Something's coming!"

Seawater burst into the air from behind their purple sailboat. Out of the ocean came a small sea vessel. Its top was covered by what resembled a wooden beetle shell. As the boat landed on the rising waves with another splash of white foam, the wooden shell separated into two and slid down into the sides of the hull. On the now exposed deck stood two Marauders clad in crimson leather armor. Both had brown skin, braided black hair, and red war paint framing their eyes. One was male, and the other was female.

"Stealth ship!" Julian yelled.

Hanali hopped to her feet and shot a fist toward the brown sail of their boat. Wind dumped itself into the sail and propelled them forward in a flash. "How'd they find us?" she asked just before sending another gale toward the sail.

Julian had maneuvered himself to the center of the boat and clutched the mast. "Concentrate on the wind," he told Hanali. Alina stood on her feet now too. She watched the man behind them move his arms in a long, sweeping motion. Water sprayed from the sides of the Marauders' boat in response to his efforts. Then the stealth ship shot toward them with incredible speed. Alina gritted her teeth. He could control the water with his ki.

"Can the sea spirits go a little faster?!" Alina shouted at the mask salesman, who now controlled the rudder with his grip.

"They're temperamental as it is!" he said with little concern.

Alina, Hanali, and Julian nearly fell overboard as their boat swerved left to avoid a huge crystal spike. The stealth ship appeared on the other side of the obstacle. Both vessels diverged from each other to avoid another mass of crystal.

"I need a bow!" Julian screamed at the mask salesman. "Or knives! Anything I can throw!"

"I have masks!" the narrow-eyed gentleman replied.

"Not helpful!" Julian shouted furiously. "Look out!"

Alina squinted to see through the reflecting sunlight. A multitude of protruding crystals guarded every possible angle they could take. The mask salesman turned the rudder sharply, steering them through a tight passageway. "Where are the Marauders?" Alina asked as she scanned the sea of razor-sharp gemstones. At that moment, the stealth ship soared over a low heap of crystals and landed with a crash at their side.

The two Marauders seemed calm and focused. Their ships were close enough that Alina could see the woman grinning. Hanali sent more wind into the sail, but the Marauders matched their pace with ease.

Steadying herself enough to draw a long breath, Alina concentrated on the flowing energy inside her. She spoke a meditative command and sent ki racing to her palms. "*Ree.*" A ball of ginger fire formed between her hands. "*Ka!*" The fireball erupted from her outstretched arms and expanded to a flurry of ginger flame.

Laughing eagerly, the male Marauder wafted his hand upward, creating a wall of seawater. Alina's attack smashed into the rising wave and produced a cover of steam. "No!" Alina screamed in frustration.

"Conserve your energy!" Julian said. "You're low on ki, and they have the advantage in water! We defend, not attack!"

She ignored him. Summoning the remaining ki in her gut, Alina waved a hand over her head and formed a long whip of burning fire. She sent it hurtling down toward the Marauders' boat. The flaming whip smashed across the center of the stealth ship, practically breaking it in two. Alina smirked triumphantly. They'd sink within a moment.

The male Marauder threw a wave onto his ship that extinguished the fire. Immediately, the female stomped her foot, and the flooding water froze to solid ice. She had mended the boat together in an instant. Now swathed by a layer of frost, the stealth ship continued forward gracefully.

Alina shot Julian an apologetic expression. He glared at her impatiently. "Don't act like you knew they could do that!" she shouted at him.

"You can't escape judgment, Templar!" the female Marauder bellowed. She threw a hand forward and caused a javelin of ice to shoot out from the sea. Julian held Alina against his chest to shield her. She instinctively shut her eyes and waited for the rod of ice to pierce them both.

No pain greeted Alina. Instead, there was a horrific, guttural shriek. Already knowing the source, Alina forced herself to look at her friend. Hanali had jumped in front of the mask salesman. He cowered behind her with tears trickling down his cheeks. The spear tore through Hanali's stomach and remained lodged there. Two spiked ends poked out from either side. Alina helplessly watched as Hanali collapsed onto the deck. Sobbing, the mask salesman held her there and stroked her silvery hair. Blood stained the melting ice with crimson.

Both ships slowed to a stop. The two parties were rocked back and forth in a sea of serrated crystals. A hand slid down Alina's back. She nearly slapped Julian, but then she realized he had unsheathed her dagger.

"*Dajo* bitch!" the male Marauder cheered. "I'm surprised those animals bleed red." Julian whirled his body around and snapped his wrist toward the Marauders. Alina's dagger spun through the air for less than a second before jamming itself in the man's neck. He coughed a spoonful of blood and fell backward into the ocean.

The remaining Marauder stood expressionless. She gave a single glance to where her companion had once stood before saying, "That was my brother."

"Then I regret granting him a swift death," Julian said coldly. "You will not be so lucky."

"Is that so?" she retorted. Sucking in a tremendous breath, the Marauder stomped her foot and thrust both hands forward. Ice sprawled out and consumed the water underneath the mask salesman's boat. Instantly, an enormous platform of ice appeared and hugged the multitude of surrounding crystals. Alina looked out in all directions. The ice stretched out for what must have been at least three hundred yards. How could a lowly pirate have this much power? "Let us fight with honor, Templar," the Marauder announced. "We'll settle this the old way. Just you and me."

"You speak of honor yet ambush my fleet in the dead of night," Julian said through a rattled voice. "You speak of honor yet kill without mercy." Alina once again recalled Absal's first lesson from years ago. *We use our strength to kill, without mercy.* It seemed Templar Julian did not share Absalom Ryder's values. Perhaps she had passed judgment on him too quickly.

"Life is different in the Great Sands," the Marauder said as she stepped out onto the thick sheet of ice. "We greet death as a dear friend. You Templars and Knights of Tenshi have shown us that there are fates far worse than dying."

Julian didn't glance in Alina's direction. He climbed over the boat's side and muttered, "Tend to the girl."

She wanted to follow him, but that desire passed quickly. Her friend needed a healer. Alina knelt by Hanali while taking her hand. It felt rigid and unusually light. "Will she live?" Alina asked the mask salesman.

"The ice is stopping the blood flow," the strange man told her. "When it melts, she will bleed out."

"I'm cold, Alina," Hanali murmured. Her sky-blue eyes were fogged over. Alina had to heal her. She tried summoning ki to her fingers but almost fainted instead.

"You are nearly emptied of ki," the mask salesman told her. For once, he seemed intensely serious. "If you try to heal her, you will fail, and the effort will kill you."

Alina choked back tears. If she relaxed her face, sobs would surely gush out. Julian had been right. She was reckless and wasted all the ki left inside her. Now Hanali would die because of her mistake.

"There is something we can try," he said suddenly and pointed a finger toward a multitude of massive crystals.

"Those minerals have healing properties. If you bring me one, I may be able to save her."

She'd have to make it across at least five hundred feet of ice to reach the nearest crystals. Would the Marauder see her and attack? How would she get a piece free if she made it there? "Okay," Alina said before stepping onto the ice. "I'll be right back.

✺◯ *VIII* ◯✺

Julian met the Marauder away from the boats. The bizarrely-colored ship he rode was a distant sight. They stood on the sheet of ice about thirty feet apart. He would need to close the gap quickly to survive.

"What is your name?" she asked abruptly.

"What does that matter?"

"I'd like to know the name of the man who killed my brother." The woman fretted through red war paint yet remained mostly composed. He knew she would be well trained and cunning. That was evident.

"Markus Julian," he reluctantly told her, "Fourth Templar of Tenshi."

She giggled but did not smile. "I've heard rumors of you. Drug pusher turned Templar. Most Knights think you cheated in the Trials. They say you're not even a ki-wielder."

He said nothing.

"Would you like to know my name?" she motioned her hand down, and a slender sword erected itself from the ice. It had intricate detailing that demonstrated years of careful practice.

"No," Julian replied.

"Tamara Ucan," she stated anyway and grabbed the blade of ice. "That is the last name you will ever hear. And it belongs to the last face you will ever see."

Calming his heart, Julian began his meditation. He emptied his mind of all thoughts, every fear. Nothing remained except the echoing motion of his own breathing. "Come on, then."

Tamara closed her fist, and the ice underneath Julian crumbled. He hopped onto solid footing then advanced. His opponent was ready. She raised her hand and produced a large block of ice from the frozen sea. A kick sent it hurtling toward him. Julian rolled onto his side and scarcely dodged the attack.

These conditions weren't favorable. The ice between them began cracking and shifting. Tamara controlled the terrain, and he was without a weapon. He would die if the distance between them wasn't closed soon. A spike of ice jutted out at his left. Julian moved fast enough to avoid a fatal blow, but the pointed tip grazed his ribs.

"*Ree-Ka!*" she cried before sending a blast of dense frost at him. Dropping both shoulders, Julian slid forward on his knees and felt the tip of his nose burn from the intense cold.

Finally, he was close. Tamara raised the ice sword over her head and threw it deftly. Feeling the ki flow and breathe around him, Julian avoided the blade and snatched its hilt from the air. Two hops across broken ice brought him face to face with her on stable ground. Not pausing for a moment, Julian slashed at Tamara's chest. Instantly the blade melted to a splash of water.

She punched him with frosted knuckles, and pain shuddered throughout his jaw. Still reeling, Julian's body acted instinctively. The meditation he had spent years perfecting allowed him to sense her energy shift and change directions. Ki flowed from her body into the ice below. Julian saw flashes of Hanali impaled and the frozen spike that cut her torso. Tamara was going to erect another spear of ice to pierce him. Her energy flowed to a spot just behind Julian.

As he concentrated on the coming attack, time seemed to slow. His body knew its course of action without a thought. Julian spun around Tamara's back as the spike of jagged ice sprouted toward him at a slanted angle.

The spear remained connected to the frozen sea like a deadly talon. Tamara turned to face Julian, which left her back to the spike. He caught her next punch and sent a jab at the middle of her neck. She croaked and grabbed her throat. With a firm kick, Julian thrust Tamara onto the spear of ice. It pierced through her gut with ease and glinted in the morning sun like one of the many crystals. Julian slid back on the rough ice below him. Slowly he lowered his foot and drew a steady breath.

Blood dripped from Tamara's mouth, complementing the red war paint around her eyes. Skidding her heels on the ice, she struggled to stay upright. "I—I didn't—think," Tamara said. Her voice sounded coarse and weary.

Julian wrapped his arms around Tamara and pulled her body from the spike. She squealed as her torso was freed from the jagged spear. Carefully he laid her on the sheet of ice.

"Even in the Great Sands," she told Julian quietly, "my mother would tell us stories of the Templars. She'd say they could move mountains and burn cities with a single glance." Tamara settled her fading eyes on Julian. "Your power is different, though. It's quiet and precise. I should have struck you down, but you saw through me—you saw through me."

He took her hands and placed them down on the wound. The massive platform of ice began thinning rapidly. "Are the Marauders headed for Somerset?" Julian said.

"Yes," she moaned. "The sun will rise only once more on that wretched place. And then we will come when the moon is at its highest peak. Or perhaps some are already there…watching…waiting."

"Enjoy hell," Julian said as he stood, "and give my regards to your brother. Soon the rest of the Marauders will be joining you two. I'll see to that personally."

"No, my people will avenge me. My brother and I will wait for *you* to join us, Markus Julian. When I don't return…the Marauders won't rest until Somerset is ash," she laughed and spat blood. "None are righteous here." Tamara grinned and displayed yellowed teeth coated with fresh blood. It was a display of immense, uninhibited elation. And the expression remained as her final exhale huffed out dimly. Julian stared for a moment at the deep, brown eyes. *None are righteous here.* Just after he turned back toward the mask salesman's boat, Julian thought that Tamara had been rather beautiful.

✵✪ IX ✪✵

Alina gripped a tiny fragment of crystal and pulled hard.
She was bent over against a sprawling deposit of massive,
translucent minerals. If only she could dislodge a small piece.
Her arms ached with the effort, and she screamed in
frustration. Hanali couldn't die like this. That morning, the
silver-haired Knight from the Dajo Wind Tribes had saved
Alina's life. And now she needed to return the favor. *You're a
Starchild*, Alina thought, *aren't you?*

Fatigued, Alina pulled away from the piece of crystal and
stared helplessly. It was only the size of a finger. If she used
just a little ki, that would be enough to rip it free. Alina
gritted her teeth and tried to force away the mask salesman's
words: *The effort will kill you.*

She concentrated on the energy flowing inside herself.
Only a thin, wispy trail of ki crawled throughout her body. If
that was depleted entirely, would she really die? Sweat
dripped from her forehead onto a clenched fist. Alina
commanded ki to flow into her right forearm. Her vision
became mottled, but the muscles on her wrist bulged, and the
veins pressed against her skin. Not wasting a moment, Alina
grabbed the crystal shard and ripped it free with ease.

Crippling exhaustion tempted her entire body to collapse
on the ice. She rose and trekked back toward the purple boat.
*Crack…Crack…*Was the ice getting thinner? Alina saw a
magenta blur ahead. Someone was standing there also. A
mirage of blond hair and tanned skin watched her approach.
He shouted something that she couldn't hear.

Suddenly Alina became very cold. The ice had broken, and she fell beneath it. Air squeezed through her nose and rose in tiny bubbles to the surface. She couldn't help but find humor in drowning. Just a short while ago, Alina had saved a Templar from the clutches of the sea. Now she was powerless to save herself.

An image of a round, black mask took hold of her vision. Two enormous, gaping eyes searched her fading heart for fear.

✴☼ ✗ ☼✴

Ike's footsteps echoed throughout the empty temple. The throbbing pain in his face had taken his mind elsewhere, to a memory from two years past.

On the weekends, Ike, Bridget, Alina, and Nathan would take a little rowboat to a tiny island off the coast of Somerset. It had a beautiful little beach hidden behind a cluster of rocks. Nothing else occupied the island except a patch of grass and a single palm tree. They called it the Cove. This particular evening, Ike found himself sitting alone on the Cove's white sand overlooking the Aged Sea. The village was miles away now, merely a collection of wooden and stone spires poking over Somerset's jagged earth. Ike emptied his mind of any and every thought. The afternoon's training had left his face and ribs bashed in. Blood still dripped from his nose. Perhaps that was why Ike recalled this day. Maybe pain connects all memories.

"You aren't going to see me off?" The voice came from Alina as she rowed a small boat up to shore. She wore tight-fitting leather armor, padded pants, and black boots.

"How'd you find me?" Ike asked.

"Every person has ki," Alina said, taking a seat next to him on the sand, "a distinct energy. I followed yours."

"I'm not a ki-wielder, though," Ike told her. "I didn't inherent the gift from my parents."

"That doesn't mean you don't have ki," Alina said. Both of them drank in the sight of the Aged Sea for a few moments. A cool summer breeze brushed back Alina's multicolored mane of hair.

"Was my mother hard on you?" he asked.

"Not as much as Bridget," Alina said quietly. "Not nearly as much." She stared at the setting sun. "Even Beth can't keep you from this, Ike. Everyone in Dawn will fight soon enough. That's what it's come to."

He nodded. That thought was what kept him on this tiny island. His mother would try to protect him, but his time would come. Dolphins swam through the waves. They watched them wordlessly.

"You better save the world for me," Ike said, breaking the silence. "I expect big things."

"Do you?" she replied, unsurprised.

"Not because you're a Starchild," Ike said. "Because you're…you know…you're you." Ike spoke so genuinely he couldn't bear to look at her. Out of the corner of his eye, Ike thought he saw her blushing.

"I'll try not to disappoint," Alina said, leaning closer. She placed one thumb on his forehead and another on his chest.

"What are you doing?" Ike's face became hot, and he recoiled a bit. She came so near that he could see the freckles dotting her nose.

"Healing you, dummy. Asim really let you have it today." She breathed warm air onto his neck and shut her eyes. A sensation poured into Ike. From her two thumbs came a flowing heat that circulated up to the top of his head and back down to his chest. The feeling was as if Alina had hugged him so tight, they became one. Ike became intoxicated by the closeness and caught himself staring at Alina's full, pink lips.

She opened her eyes and lowered both hands. "How do you feel?" Alina asked with a faint smile.

Feeling the burning heat dissipate inside him, Ike realized his swollen eye had opened completely. The aching and pressure in his face had totally subsided as well. He raised a palm and felt his now smooth features. "Better," he managed to say.

They both looked out to the horizon. An orange veil was spreading across the sky, signaling sunset. "Will you take me to the docks?" Alina asked.

He thought of telling her everything right then. He opened his mouth, and all the words almost came tumbling out. The truth that he was hopelessly in love; that she was all he had ever wanted; that every time he saw her, there was a horrible pain in his chest.

Instead, he said nothing. Because the truth was Alina didn't feel the same way. How could she? They had been raised almost like siblings; his fate was to die on this island, and hers was to save all of Dawn.

The memory faded away. Ike found himself standing before the Temple to El's altar. Swelling made his face throb and ache. Needing to ground himself in the present, Ike reevaluated his surroundings. Sunlight arched and stretched through blue stained glass like lightning. Rows of wooden pews led up to the stone altar. Above it, glistening on the white wall, was a sword. A strange gray metal made its blade and hilt. As he got closer, Ike noticed thick black wrappings that wound up to the cross-guard. That must have made the grip superbly comfortable. Still, the blade appeared much too small for a person of Ike's height.

Something changed within Ike during his brief solitude in the temple. Alina was no longer by Ike's side, ready to ease the pain in his wounds. He could still see the ceremony's aftermath, the doubt brooding in every islander's eyes. No one believed him capable of reaching the Spirit. Escaping the call no longer seemed like an option. Ike wanted to prove Somerset wrong. He'd bear the agony in his cheeks as an emblem of pride.

A loud creak echoed behind him, followed by a trail of white light from outside. A figure dressed in a long, black jacket approached him. She had brown hair that rolled down past her shoulders and intense gray eyes like thunderclouds. Underneath the Templar jacket, thin silver armor caught rays of blue light and reflected them in all directions. The large oak doors rested shut again, leaving Ike alone with the gray-eyed woman.

"Dreamblade only appears in the temple on the day of the Spirit Festival," the approaching Templar proclaimed with a gesture toward the gray sword. "It was forged for the Storm Paladins before their battle with the Deathrid."

"Has anyone tried taking it?" Ike asked her.

"Many have," she affirmed with a smile, "but only a warrior with Storm Paladin blood is able to call upon its strength." The woman nudged Ike with her elbow. "No matter where they are."

"Don't look at me," he laughed. "It's much too small."

"Legends say its shape changes for the wielder's needs," she affirmed. "What do you need?"

"I don't know, Mom," he said quietly.

"Let me help, son," she said after wrapping Ike into a fierce embrace.

"I don't know what's happening," Ike told her. "What would the Spirit want with me?"

"The Spirit hasn't spoken to anyone since your father left," Beth said as she let Ike go. "From what I know, she chooses champions to fight for her. When she sees something as unjust, someone is chosen to correct it. Champions also act as counselors… They share what the mortal world has come to. Help the Great Spirit make choices for us all."

Ike took a step away from his mother and looked at the gray sword. "Do you think I could do something like that?"

Beth joined Ike in his admiration of the weapon. "Do you want to do something like that?"

He recalled how fierce Alina looked two years prior, ready to face all of Dawn if it meant securing peace. For a brief moment, Ike felt compelled to speak honestly. "I don't want to do anything."

"That can't be true."

"What do you want me to say? That I want to study at a university and teach literature and the sciences? That I want to marry young and watch my kids grow old?" Ike's voice trembled, but he kept his frustration in check. What he had said were his deepest fantasies, dreams he could never indulge. "There is nowhere for me to go. There is nothing for me to be. All of Dawn has been swallowed by this war."

Beth seemed to settle on those words and let them wash over her. "You're gentle, Ike," she finally said. His reaction must have told her that he took the comment as an insult. "It's true," she persisted, "and it's your greatest strength. You aren't a fighter like Bridget or Alina."

She put a hand on Ike's cheek and stared into him deeply. "I have tried so fiercely to keep you from your father's war. It's my greatest regret that I couldn't protect you children in the end." Tears crept into her stormy eyes, but Beth held them back. "Leave," she said firmly. "Leave this island today. Don't see the Spirit. Don't be deployed with the other Squires. Find a life that is your own."

Ike struggled to understand her words. "How can I?" he said blankly. "Everything I know is here. I've given my life to the Knights."

"And it's broken you," Beth stated. "I can't stand to see you so — so horribly unhappy."

Feeling exposed, Ike dropped his shoulders and head.

"It's taken years," his mother went on, "but I have gathered enough supporters in the Great Sands and our capital to propose a truce. Almost every Templar supports your father, but with the nobility on my side, they'll have no choice but to listen." She grabbed Ike by the wrists. There was a fearful urgency behind her gray gaze. "This war is the Templars' responsibility. It is *my* responsibility. And I will end it. You have a destiny all your own to find."

Yes, that was what he wanted. Deep inside, Ike's heart raced in anticipation at the thought of planting his sword in the earth and fleeing to a new life. "They could execute me for desertion," Ike said. "And wherever I go, the war will be there."

"The Knights won't find you," Beth promised him. "And soon, you won't need to hide." She looked certain and unafraid. Then again, that was how Ike's mother always appeared.

"All right," he said, "I'll go. But not until I face the Spirit."

"Why?" His mother tilted her head in fearful uncertainty.

"The Great Spirit made my father begin this war." Ike's voice was rising, and so was his heartbeat.

"It's not that simple—"

"That's what everyone has always said!" Ike shouted. "She's responsible for everything. So, I want to hear what kind of murder she needs from me now. I want to seek her out and tell her something no champion has ever said—"

"And what's that?" Beth clenched her jaw and searched his frantic stare.

Ike calmed himself and spoke a single word. "No." He suddenly felt steady and composed. "I won't fight for her." As Ike spoke, his true intentions rose to the surface. "You said she could use me as a counselor. I have a chance to make her understand what the war has done to us, to all of Dawn. The corruption, the raids, the killing… What if I can convince her to stop it? The Great Spirit began the war. She can end it.

If she is just, then she will search my heart and know that I am bearing the truth."

Beth gave a cautious smile, one someone might see before a funeral, and plucked Ike's cap from his head. "I understand your pain," she said and ruffled his matted hair softly, "but she has power like you've never seen Ike. She could kill you in an instant, and if you show any trace of fear, you'll lose yourself completely."

"My mind is made up," Ike declared. Even his mother didn't think he had the strength to reach the Spirit. He held his chin out firmly and hugged his mother one more time. "After I do this, I'll leave."

"The past is like a weight on your heart, son," Beth said. "If you let it crush you, there will be no hope for a future. Your father left long ago. It can't be undone."

"My mind is made up," Ike repeated. "I can do this. I can make her see how far we have strayed."

"You carry Storm Paladin blood," Beth whispered. "She is obliged to hear your council. This island belongs to us before any else."

An unknown voice resounded through the temple, saying, "Ike Ryder." Pulling apart from his mother, Ike saw a woman dressed in blue silk robes near a doorway behind the altar. "Come with me. I will illuminate your path."

He took one fearful breath and then walked toward the woman in ornate robes. Feeling a draft pass through his hair, Ike realized his wool cap remained missing. Beth had almost reached the massive oak doors when he called, "I need that hat!"

"No, you don't," she responded with a mischievous glance over her shoulder. His gray hairs uncovered, Ike trailed the woman down a dimly lit hallway.

"What's your name?" Ike asked her. The poor lighting made it difficult to make out many features. She was older, perhaps past sixty, with very dark skin.

"Damini," she responded serenely. "I'm the high priestess."

"I've seen you many times during worship," Ike confessed, "but I never heard your name."

"We are all one body here, Ike Ryder," she said just before stopping at the end of the hallway. They stared at an old, cracked stone door. Two symbols were carved into the corroded surface. One was a diamond separated into fourths by an X. The other Ike had never seen. It was a circle with a thick dot in the center like an eye.

"I know the diamond is the symbol of the League of Tenshi," Ike said. "That circle, though. I've never seen it."

Damini pushed the heavy door ajar with her shoulder. "It's the symbol belonging to the Deathrid named Sephas," she divulged while struggling to open the passageway.

"Why would that kind of thing be here?" Ike asked. "Humans fought the Deathrid on this island during the Second Great War."

"Yes," she stated and gave the door one last push, "but a Deathrid did build this temple long before Somerset rose above the sea."

"Really?"

"Sephas prayed to El, the creator of all, within this very temple," Damini recounted as the door spread open. "He prayed for control over the beastly, untamable strength within himself. In answer, El bestowed upon him the Powers of the Storm."

Glancing past Damini, Ike saw what looked like a lovely spa. Steaming water rose from a round pool in the center of the stone floor. Lanterns floated in the air and emitted warm, yellow light. Different colored flowers and patches of grass had been planted into areas of dirt surrounding the pool. Distracted from their previous conversation, Ike wandered into the room and felt a pleasant humidity open his pores.

"Enough stories. It is time to listen, young Ryder. You will venture into the woods to meet the Great Spirit," Damini stated and walked into the bathing chamber, "but not until your body and mind have been cleansed."

Ike knelt to place a hand in the hot water. His fingers were enveloped in a soothing warmth, much like a soft kiss. "Cleansed?" he asked.

Damini strode to a small altar at the back of the room. Ike realized that the stone table was levitating above the ground. "Purged of fear," she said wistfully and with relentless wonder. "The Spirit's presence maddens those who are afraid. You must release all worry and remorse before approaching her." An intimidating enthusiasm beamed off her wrinkled face now. Ike recoiled from the water, watching her cautiously. "Meditate within the pool. Its water was taken from Kokoro Pond and carries the grace of our Spirit within it. You will see what you must remember. What is important now will be shown…the darkest depths of your heart."

Her words passed through Ike and left him with more questions than answers. Despite his uncertainty, Ike threw off his gi, sword, and pants. He remained in his underwear and stood before the water. "You have to be bare," Damini commanded. Uncomfortable, Ike stared at Damini until she rolled her eyes and turned around.

Completely naked, Ike descended into the pool. Steam piled into his nostrils and felt hot against his throat. Sweat already spotted his brow, yet the sensation was rather pleasant. Damini confronted him once more and spoke the instruction. "Meditate, Ike Ryder. Face your fears and release them. Or else you will lose yourself entirely."

A frightening calmness took hold of Ike. Every thought and worry fled from his mind with the rising steam. He felt completely unburdened, void of identity, concern, and shame. The water beckoned Ike onto his back. Closing his eyes, he sunk beneath the surface.

And then he was falling again, the morning's dream resuming. An endless vacuum of black sky stretched around him. Stinging pain alerted Ike to his right hand. There, a symbol had appeared in burning blue light. It was a circle with a thick dot placed in the center. He stared into the blue eye, and the pain grew fiercer.

"I'm going to kill you now..."

The voice trailed into his ears from somewhere very far away. Ike fell with greater speed. His burning hand, body, and vision faded to nothingness. The image that remained was a horrifying black mask with gaping, round eyes.

Part 2

Days Past

** I **

Ike rushed out of his home into the green pasture. Bridget ran at his heels and shoved him over. He tumbled onto the ground and felt like screaming at her, but a hand reached down. Golden, auburn, and ginger hair curled around the face of a little girl above him. Looking into her bluish-green eyes made his stomach burn. He was only five years old.

"C'mon, Ike," Alina said and pulled him up.

They lived just outside the village on a large plot of land. The Ryders' home was larger than most. It had two stories, large round windows, and a fresh coat of light blue paint. Ike didn't yet understand the privilege he was born into by having two Templars of Tenshi as parents.

A large figure burst out of the door behind them. It was Ike's father chasing after the three of them. "You can't run from the great sea beast!" Absal shouted as he tossed off his shirt, leaving him in wool swimming trunks.

Bridget and Alina squealed before darting toward Kokoro Pond. Ike followed close behind. They wound down a small path behind their home and found the small body of water within a couple of minutes.

Kokoro Pond was a shallow pool of brilliantly blue water just beyond the beginnings of the woods. Crystals larger than Ike's father were lodged in the earth all around the pond.

They vividly reflected the forest around it like multifaced mirrors. Ike counted seven of them. His mother once told him that the crystals had special healing properties.

Alina sprinted into the water and dived as soon as it was deep enough. Bridget belly-flopped into the shimmering pool soon after. Ike tripped and fell over into the mud. Burly arms scooped him up, and Absal carried him into the pond. When he was waist-deep, Absal tossed Ike forward into the pool. Opening his eyes, he saw Alina waving underneath the surface with her thick hair branching out like a halo. She looked otherworldly...and beautiful. They both swam up for air.

"Dad! Do the thing!" Bridget shouted out nearby.

"No, Mom doesn't like it," Absal told her.

"Do it! Do it!" all three of them chanted.

"All right, back away a bit," he finally said.

Bridget, Ike, and Alina shut their mouths and swam back.

Ike's father held his hands close together. He breathed in a long breath through his nose and exhaled. A speck of bright yellow light formed between his palms.

"It looks like sunlight," Alina told him.

Absal placed the dot of sunlight underneath the water. The pond became warmer and glowed a fantastic yellow. "The Great Spirit taught me to take in the sun's energy. One day, you'll learn to do this too," Absal said to all of them. Ike smiled at Alina, but she didn't see. Her eyes were shut, and she floated on her back in the warm sunlight. In between her hands shined a speck of light smoldering with the color of fire.

That night, Ike lay in bed listening to his mother hum a gentle melody. She sat next to him in a rocking chair and polished a thin silver armor breastplate while singing. The tune made him think of rolling waves and drizzling rain. Three lanterns floated in the room, emitting a very faint glow. Beth's concentration held them up. Telekinesis was a talent held by most well-trained ki-wielders.

"Mom," Ike interrupted the song. "Is Dad going to leave again?"

"No," she said quickly, "after we found Alina, he decided to stay for good."

Beth resumed the melody, and Ike settled into the soothing rhythm. Not wanting to sleep yet, Ike asked, "What's this song about?"

"It's about our ancestors," Beth said while rubbing her thumb against a stubborn smudge on the armor, "the Storm Paladins. They watched over Dawn long before Templars and Knights of Tenshi."

"What were the Storm Paladins like?"

"They were a clan of powerful ki-wielders," she said wistfully. "One of the Deathrid, Sephas, created Storm Paladins to be protectors of the innocent. Sephas taught them the Powers of the Storm that he learned from praying to our God, El."

"I thought the Deathrid were bad."

"Not always," Beth explained. "Sometimes people change. They were once kind, benevolent rulers."

"What happened to the Deathrid?"

"They became greedy and cruel. Battle and hardship made their hearts cold as stone. During the Second Great War,

Starchildren fell from the sky to save Dawn from the Deathrid. The Storm Paladins and Starchildren worked together to defeat them in a great battle."

"Alina is a Starchild," Ike stated.

"That's right," Beth confirmed. She set the breastplate down and combed Ike's hair with her fingers.

"Are you a Storm Paladin?" Ike asked his mother.

"Yes," she told him, "one of the last."

"I'd want to be a Storm Paladin too," Ike said through two big yawns. "Then I would be like you."

Beth placed a kiss on Ike's forehead and whispered, "Say your prayers to El." Ike fell asleep that night imagining himself defending Somerset from a humongous dragon. He stood tall on the edge of the island wielding a sword as big as his body. Alina stood at his side, shooting blasts of fire from her fists.

Ike wanted to stay right there, basking in his dream, yet the temple's water took him deeper. His heart ached and raced as the next memory drifted into focus.

** *II* **

"I know you're leaving for good. You disappear for weeks and sulk back here like I'm too stupid to figure it out!" Beth yelled downstairs. Ike and Bridget sat at the top of the staircase, listening. They were holding hands. Alina crouched further down the hallway with her head buried in her arms. He had turned seven only last week.

"When were you going to tell me about the army you've been raising with your brother? When it sailed up to my doorstep? After you took our kids?" Beth shouted.

"Just—just shut up! I need to think!" Absal yelled back.

"I know all about the life you live while you gallivant around—"

"The Great Spirit demands this war!" Absal told her.

"I've let you come back here time and time again for our children," Beth said. Her voice was calmer, but it sounded broken. "But I won't let you sweep them into this life you're creating."

There was silence for a while. Bridget cried and gripped Ike's hand so tight it felt numb. "Goodbye," Absal finally said. Footsteps headed for the front door.

Pulling away from Ike, Bridget ran down the stairs. Ike jumped up and watched her meet Absal at the door. He held the two bags he always traveled with. The same black cloak covered his frame. A diamond separated into fourths by an X was imprinted on the back. Always Ike would remember the absent expression on his father's face.

Bridget grabbed his legs. "Don't go," she murmured through tears. Suddenly Ike realized he was crying too.

Absal picked her up with one arm and asked, "Where's your brother and Alina?" He opened the door and picked up his two bags with a single hand. "Son?" Absal called.

Ike took a few steps down the stairs to be in clear view. Absal smiled, but his eyes were wide and vacant. "Come here. Let's go," he said in a hushed voice. With Bridget held against him, he took two steps out the door.

"Dad?" Bridget cried and kicked her feet.

Suddenly Ike ran toward his sister. He grabbed her hand and tried to pull Bridget free. Instead, he felt himself being hauled out the door by his father's strength. "No! No!" he screamed. The tears were flowing so heavily he could hardly see.

"Put her down," Ike's mother demanded. She stood tall before them in the entryway to the kitchen with her hands clenched. Intense, bewildering anger consumed her gray eyes. Ike peered up at his father. He seemed afraid. Absal set Bridget down next to him. Thunder boomed outside in the night. Beth stepped forward and thrust her fists in Absal's direction.

A fierce gust of wind crashed through the kitchen windows far behind Ike's mother and shot straight toward his father. It impacted him in the chest with force great enough to send him flying out the doorway and past the porch. He landed with a thud on the front lawn.

Lightning crackled against the sea behind Ike's father. Rain surged down the roof and onto the porch steps. Absal lay on the grass, looking up at their home. Beth waved her hand, and the door slammed shut. Ike and Bridget stood where they were, the great rush of wind having passed over their heads. Their mother engulfed them in a hug. Alina sat on the stairs above them. She wasn't crying, Ike observed. Instead, she stared past him like her mind was traveling somewhere a million miles away.

Ike followed Alina's gaze and sunk further within himself.

** *III* **

Ike walked through town with Bridget and Alina. Nightfall crept over Somerset and left a shadow of twilight on the floating island.

He was ten now, and on his way to meet Absalom Ryder for dinner. Years had passed since they last got a moment alone with him. Excitement almost managed to overshadow the haunting memory of his departure. Every face they passed seemed to be beaming and overcome with elation. The Knights had just secured a port near Fairspell with no casualties. At least that's what the report said.

"What was it like?" Ike suddenly asked Bridget.

"Huh?" she muttered as they walked.

"Finding your ki. What did it feel like?"

"Oh," Bridget spoke as if the whole ordeal was rather dull now. "I don't know. I guess I kept imagining chasing this little light. Like when the fireflies come in summer, you know? It looked like a bright, hot ball of light. All I had to do was reach inside, and..." She snatched something invisible with her hand. "...grab it."

Ike scrunched his nose in confusion. "Okay," he said, not knowing what else to offer.

Alina departed from Ike and Bridget to ascend the temple steps. "Bye, guys," she said gloomily. "I can come over for dinner tomorrow." For a few months now, Alina had been made to stay with the priestesses in the Temple to El. Ike still did not understand why. His mother had explained that

Starchildren did not belong to any one family but to all of Dawn.

"See you soon," Bridget told her with sunken shoulders. "When we go to the Cove tomorrow, tell me everything." She reluctantly looked away from Alina and kept walking.

Ike remained frozen for a moment. Were they hanging out without him? Was it because he wasn't a girl? Or possibly Alina never wanted him around in the first place. She moved out and could finally be rid of him. His heart dropped so low it felt like he might sink through the earth. Maybe it was because he wasn't a ki-wielder.

Eventually, Ike held up a hand to wave goodbye, but his palm just hung in the air, unmoving. Alina smiled dimly. She then went into the temple.

"Hurry, Ike," Bridget said from up ahead, "Dad will be pissed if we're late."

They found their father standing outside the small hotel called Somerset Inn with two men Ike didn't recognize. One had greasy pale hair, and the other was bald. Both had broadswords on their hips and unkempt stubble.

Laughter roared out between gulps of ale. As Ike and Bridget neared the three men, a strange stench reeked off the group. "Dad?" Bridget said.

Absal spilled a little ale as he turned to them. "Bridge!" he exclaimed. "These are my kids." Ike's father burped and then gestured toward the two men. "And these are my Knights." The two Knights snickered, and the bald one managed to say, "Hey, runt."

A fog seemed to shroud Absal's dark eyes. He didn't see Ike or his sister at all. "Let's go to the ship," Absal suddenly said while wrapping an arm around Ike.

"I thought we're going to the inn," Ike said, confused.

"C'mon," he yelled in a hushed voice. "It'll be much more fun."

Ike and Bridget shot each other panicked stares as Absal put a hand on each of their backs. He moved them forward toward the edge of the island. An old freight elevator brought them hurtling down to the docks, which rested on the brutal Aged Sea. Somerset's docks stretched out in a wide arc underneath the easternmost part of the island. About a dozen ships were anchored against long rows of rotting, aging wood. At the very end rested Absal's battleship, the *Black Sun*.

An hour passed, perhaps more. The ship was incredibly volatile. Ike and Bridget sat in a lounging area located inside the massive cabin. Young women wore tiny dresses and sat on some of the Knights' laps, drinking shots of a clear liquid. Another group of female Knights lying on rows of blankets had started smoking a black herb. Games of cards were being played, and a small fight had broken out over two missing silver pieces. Laughter, screams, and the indistinguishable music of several drunken bards bombarded Ike's eardrums.

Underneath those chaotic sounds of pleasure was another noise. It emanated from beneath Ike's feet. He peeked through a narrow gap in the floorboards to trace where the faint yelps of pain originated from. His eye caught the hand of a Knight stabbing a very thin blade into a potato sack. How would that make so much noise? Ike leaned down further to get a better angle. Then he saw the gaping eyes of a black man who sat tied to a chair. Blood polluted the dark sack he wore as clothing, and Ike darted his glance away when he heard another shriek of agony.

A sunburnt woman with tangles of mud-covered hair rounded Ike's chair. She jerked a leash and murmured, "Good boys get treats. Don't you want off the chain?" Ike leaned over to get a view of the animal being towed. Instead, he saw a scrawny older boy crawling on all fours. He had tan skin with long, red scars dashing across his exposed back. Only a loin cloth provided a hint of privacy, and a crude wooden mask veiled his face. A cartoonish smile had been painted cheek to cheek on the splintering wood, and thin slits gave passage to the boy's agonizing gaze.

Two desperate eyes fixed onto Ike's. There was a silent exchange of understanding, a meeting of prisoners locked within differing cages. The image of the boy burned into Ike's mind, along with a damning sense of weakness. He could not help him.

Slam! A severed head was slapped onto the table Ike and Bridget sat at. It had skin darker than Nathan's and wild, black hair. Rotting eyes stared blankly at Ike. He couldn't force himself to look away.

The boy who placed the head must have been no older than seventeen. He was missing an ear and had massive pupils. "Look at this shit," he said to an elder crewman and snorted something off his sleeve. "I gutted the bitch after he sliced my ear. The prick was laughing like a savage." The boy pinched the head's severed lip and made it jiggle up and down. Bridget and Ike held hands underneath the table.

"Do you see Dad?" Bridget whispered.

Ike shook his head.

"I'm going to be a good Knight," Bridget said abruptly. "Dawn needs Knights that are better than those people." She nodded at two men puking into the same saucer.

Womanly fingers scratched Ike's hair. He and Bridget both swiveled in their seats and saw a delicate girl with long red hair. She was stuffed in an extremely tight dress a tavern waitress might wear. Her face looked beautiful but worn. "Ignore 'em," she told Ike and Bridget sweetly. "Children shouldn't see such things."

"Have you seen Absalom Ryder?" Bridget asked quickly.

"Oh, you're Absal's kids!" she exclaimed eagerly. "I've always wanted to meet you. Your father and I first shacked up almost six years ago, but he had lots of girls back then. Most of 'em come and go, but I stick around to work the kitchen. I'm Jubilee, but I'm sure you've heard all about me. Absal and I met at the port of Skell'ig…"

Jubilee kept talking, but Ike stopped listening. Absal had "lots of girls" six years ago? That couldn't be right. His parents were together back then. She had to be mistaken. Bridget tugged on Ike's arm and pointed toward a blond man locking lips with one of the scarcely dressed girls. It took Ike a moment to realize that it was his father.

Hurriedly, Ike left the table and approached Absal Ryder. "Absal!" he screamed out over the commotion in the ship.

Absal came up for air from the girl's lips and looked to Ike callously. "Ike! You should be in bed," he scolded through slurred syllables.

"You never showed us where they are," Ike explained. "I want to go home."

Absal's face contorted in a way Ike had not seen before. He pushed the girl in his arms away and stood directly over Ike like a looming predator. He spoke stiffly, saying, "No, you're staying. We're sailing out tomorrow. After my Knights take Somerset under their control. Tuskan Ol'dog and your mother have stayed out of this war for long enough." Absal's expression flipped between resentment and sadness.

"No, I don't want to leave," Ike stated, feeling his heart's rhythm increase to an erratic hammering.

Scoffing, Absal knelt down and said, "This is living. Knights do good and can have anything they want." He grabbed Ike by the forearms so tightly that it stung. "If you come with me, you can have the world."

Ike felt his eyes grow heavy with tears. The ship suddenly seemed very quiet. "I don't want the world."

Those words seemed to have frozen his father. Absal stared at Ike as if he had never seen him before. The girl who had been sucking his father's face slid her arms around his neck. "Absal, I'm coming down. Where's the *crystal*?" she mumbled.

"Find your sister and go to bed," Absal instructed and stood up with the girl.

He had just wrapped his hand around her hip when Ike heard Jubilee scream, "You never told your kids about me!" She marched over from Bridget's table with an arm held behind her back. The tight dress made her move in an awkward waddle. Absal looked like he was about to say something, but before he could, Jubilee jammed a butcher's knife into his shoulder.

Absal shrieked and staggered back into a table. The flimsy knife only went in halfway and wobbled in his flesh like a pendulum. "I hate you!" Jubilee howled as she sent a frenzy of drunken fists into his abdomen. "Die! I hate you!"

Ike pushed through a swarm of Knights and crew members, all of them leaping up and darting toward the scene. He managed to reach Bridget. They locked hands. Together they fled the ship and darted onto the docks.

"Hey!" Absal shouted at them. He sprinted across the *Black Sun's* deck with incredible speed. Bridget yanked Ike onward. They ran fiercely, but he was down the gangplank and nearing their backs. *It's over*, Ike thought, *he'll take us*. Slowing his pace, Ike looked behind him and saw his father within arm's reach.

BOOM! Thunder roared into the night. A bright flash sent Absal flying backward onto his back. From the clouds, she descended. Beth landed on the wooden docks with a mighty crash. The diamond symbol marked her back and lingered before Ike like a shield. She gave a glance at Ike, and he saw the fury in his mother's gray eyes. "Go home," she uttered.

A hole burning in his shirt, Absal hopped to his feet with a single movement and tossed the garment off. His chest should have been destroyed, yet there was only a scorch the size of a fist. "Get out of my way!" Absal screamed. "Somerset is mine!" He thrust both hands forward and sent a beam of twisting, yellow light toward Beth. She pulled wind together by crossing her arms and formed a barrier of hardened air. Intense yellow energy slammed against her forcefield and created a halo around Ike's mother.

Bridget pulled on Ike's arm again. He forced himself to turn away, and they ran. Absal's Knights were leaping up from ships all around them. At the distant elevator, Bethany Tempest's reinforcements had arrived, launching arrows, flames, and bursts of wind. Ducking under a ray of fire, Bridget stumbled and slipped off the dock. Ike dropped down and searched for her in the dark water. "Bridget!" he shrieked.

Something felt strange, as if Ike's memory had gone out of focus. A crack of lightning illuminated the Aged Sea. In Bridget's place was Ike's own reflection. He appeared older, perhaps eighteen. The leather armor of a Knight gripped firm muscles. No gray spotted his hair. Heaps of blood dripped down his cheeks in its place.

Ike screamed. He cowered back. Everyone else on the docks had disappeared. Even the boats vanished. Instead, wooden gallows drifted behind Ike on the quiet waves. The bodies of Knights hung limply from nooses, twelve in all. Their faces were bloated and burdened with terror. In blood, on all their armor, a single word was written: *Deserter*.

Someone placed a hand on his shoulder. Ike's reflection stood at his side, both hands covered in blood. He had written the words and hung the traitors. Without even a breath, the reflection unsheathed his father's broadsword and held it out for young Ike to take. A choice became clear: the gallows or the blade.

Wake up, Ike told himself. Fear tore into his heart and made his head swim. *Wake up*. The reflection grew restless and pressed the steel to Ike's neck. Blood flowed free.

Alina's voice echoed from somewhere far away, "Ike, wake up!"

Part 3

Revelations

✳☼ I ☼✳

Steam hissed and permeated the air in a thick, white fog. The entirety of the spa evaporated, leaving Ike lying on warm stone. He was awake now, or perhaps he had never fallen asleep. Methodically, he rose to his feet, not caring that his naked body was exposed. An intense shaking spread throughout Ike's limbs as he tried to calm himself. Every wound he entered the pool with was healed, yet a much deeper pain ached inside his gut.

Damini stood somewhere in the room, yet Ike could perceive nothing except a pervasive, hot cloud. *"Ike Ryder,"* a silken voice rattled out, like a cobra displaying its scales.

"Who's there?" Ike murmured. Moisture clung to his skin and slipped down his forehead in thick beads.

"Your heart is heavy with dread. You failed to let go." Through the steam, Ike caught a glimpse of bright flames. Damini's body had been transformed. Her face appeared young and vital. Silk robes now hung loosely from her shoulders, revealing smooth, dark skin. A wave of fire danced atop her head in the place of hair. And the most frightening feature of all was the priestess's gaze. Two black eyes speckled with twinkling stars stared ahead.

"You're —" Ike lost the will to speak.

"*I've watched you since your first breath, child,*" the Great Spirit said through Damini, "*and I await your last. Come to me.*" The fog sunk to the stone floor in accordance with her words. "*Seek my dwelling place.*"

Ike began to shiver uncontrollably. "What—" He struggled to speak through clattering teeth. "What do you want from me?"

"*Everything,*" the Spirit said. She waved her hand toward Ike, and he felt himself plunge beneath the stone floor. "*We have much to discuss.*" All around him was rushing water. Ike sunk further and further into the island's depths. He fought to catch a breath but could find no air. Then a wild current sent him hurtling upward in a heap of twisting limbs. His scream was deafened by the roaring water crashing against his body. Then without warning, the current released him.

He floated within a familiar pool. Images flooded Ike's mind as he rested there. Alina's bluish-green eyes and bright smile. A teenage boy on all fours, his face concealed by a mask. Mom sitting in the dark. His father lying on the front lawn. Alina. His father. Alone. Ike was alone in a tiny room resting above an old tree. Sheep cried beneath him.

Ike swam upward. Breaking through the surface, he found himself surrounded by large crystals planted in the dirt. Somehow, he was treading water in Kokoro Pond. How was that possible? Growing tired, Ike lowered his feet and realized he could comfortably stand. It had been a while since he swam here.

"Hey," a lovely voice called out. At the other end of the pool was a green-skinned young woman with brunette hair dotted by flowers. She moved gracefully toward him, her eyes gleaming above the water. As the nymph drew nearer, he saw that she was naked. Ike recalled that he swam without clothes as well. Flustered, he covered his privates with both hands.

The nymph stopped just before Ike and poked her shoulders above the pool. He desperately tried to look anywhere besides her bare body. "Sorry I was so formal this morning," the nymph told him. "My mother is fond of spectacle and tradition." She rolled her head back in exasperation.

"It's okay," Ike stated quickly. Feeling her emerald eyes linger on him, he added, "I mean, you did really well, I thought."

"Really?"

"Yeah." Ike let himself look at her eyes but nowhere else. "You were very...whimsical."

She grinned and said, "I like that."

"A little frightening too."

"Oh..." Her smile wilted, and she sunk into the water.

"But in a good way!"

The nymph popped back up and said, "I had some trouble with the entrance—"

"Didn't even notice!" Ike reassured her.

She smiled and said, "My name is Lotis."

"Ike." He raised a hand and held it above the water. Lotis took his palm gently. "I guess you already—"

"Shh!" Lotis cut him off and placed a finger over his lips. Ike felt a growing heat below his waist. He tried to fight off the sensation. "The forest is telling a story."

A faint breeze passed through the surrounding trees. "I don't hear anything," he whispered.

"Close your eyes," she said quietly. Her fingers walked up Ike's cheek and softly shut his eyelids. Wind hummed over Ike, making him shudder. Somewhere within the breeze, he found the words:

In the beginning, women and men walked with the divine in paradise. Secrets were whispered to them, and gifts were given. All was shared with the children of Earth, except for two trees planted by the one God above all others.

Tempted by fear and greed, the first humans betrayed the divine and claimed the fruit of the first tree, which was forbidden:

Knowledge of Good and Evil.

Out of sorrow, the divine uprooted the second tree so humanity could never rival their power.

Years bled into centuries. Forgotten were the days of the first men and women.

Lost were the mysteries of the stars.

Then four particular children of humanity went searching for the gift long forbidden and forgotten.

They scoured the Earth and all places that were known to them. Time wound their lives to a close without their quest ever completed. As each of their hearts ticked to a stop, the four humans realized that their journey had taken them to the one place they had not explored: Death.

And it was there the last gift was hidden. Beyond the veil of death, they seized the second power of the divine that was forbidden to them:

Life everlasting.

The four humans were resurrected and created a world in their image.

This is the legend of the first Deathrid and the creators of Dawn. Promised was their return.

Stillness took hold of the forest once more. Ike opened his eyes and found Lotis walking out of the pond. He saw the back of her figure before turning away. "I didn't know the Deathrid were humans," he said. "People speak of them like gods. Evil gods at that."

"The forests know many stories that are long forgotten," Lotis stated. Risking a glance, Ike saw grass and vines spin up the nymph's body to clothe her. "You should learn to listen." She strode toward a sheathed blade resting against a crystal spire. Ike knew it as his sword. "My mother is waiting. You meditated within the temple for a full day. It's morning now. Better be going."

"Right," Ike agreed. Had he really been in the Temple to El for an entire day? The whole experience felt so fleeting.

Moving through the water, Ike felt an unusual weight on his body. A brilliant gray gi had appeared, covering his torso. Its material felt soft yet almost metallic to the touch. He was reminded of Dreamblade, the sword displayed in the temple. White wrappings covered his wrists, and a similarly colored sash tied itself to Ike's waist. Coming out of the water, Ike whisked moisture from his lustrous gray pants and stomped his white boots.

"Wonderful," Lotis cheered, "the forest has clothed you."

"Where do I go from here?" Ike asked.

"If you've truly abandoned all fear, follow me," she said. The nymph's form flickered into a small orb of emerald light.

It floated toward the forest's depths. *You failed to let go.* The words returned to Ike. He wouldn't be stopped here, no matter the risk. His father abandoned fear and made this journey. So would he. What did he have to risk? His life? That was something Ike didn't mind gambling. Settling his frantic heart, Ike took up his sword and followed.

✳☼ II ☼✳

Far from the shores of the Aged Sea in the capital city of Whitecrest, Bridget Ryder led a befuddled peasant by the elbow. She strode down a long hallway and lugged the feeble old man along. The floor, walls, and high ceiling were comprised of nothing except polished white stone. Finally reaching the end, enormous oak doors swung open by their own volition.

Passing through them, Bridget's boots stomped down in shallow, golden water. The thin layer of liquid blanketed the entire audience chamber, which was massive in scale. A vaulted ceiling was painted with sprawling nebulas that glimmered and shifted above them. This design matched the black stone walls on all four sides of the chamber.

Perhaps the most impressive sights were the twelve golden pillars arranged in a circle. They stretched almost to the ceiling, and in the center of each was a numeral, beginning with I and ending with XII. Every pillar's tip formed what resembled a throne. Only the seats labeled I, II, and III were occupied.

Bridget had to drag the beggar by the sack he wore as clothing to keep him moving. His bare feet slid in the gilded liquid, and he yelped, "Unhand me! You filthy Knight! Disgrace! Disgrace to the League of Tenshi! Disgrace!"

When they reached the center of the twelve pillars, a gust of wind blew away the golden water at their feet. The liquid withdrew to outside the pillars and left a circle of white stone. Engraved in this circle was the symbol of the League of Tenshi, a diamond separated by an X.

The woman at the throne labeled III boomed her voice down. "You've been summoned here for the crime of disrupting the peace."

Each figure above them wore a black hood that masked their face. The beggar shook off Bridget's grip and swatted away dirt from his garment. "Templars used to do battle with giants," the old man said loudly. "Knights used to protect the innocent! Not drag them off the street!" Gray hair spun down to the beggar's neck in thin tangles. His skin was pale and blistered from the summer sun.

"What do you say to this crime?" the Third Templar asked sharply.

"If preaching the truth is a crime," the beggar shouted, "then I am guilty! The spirits are whispering, speaking on the breeze. We have a right to know what they prophesize! No matter the cost."

"Tell me," the Second Templar called down, "what have you heard the spirits foretell?"

"Ah," the beggar wheezed, "take off that shroud, and I'll tell ya, Ryder."

Absalom Ryder, Bridget's father, removed his hood. Even from this distance, Bridget thought her father looked older.

His blond hair had grayed near the ears and seemed rather unkempt.

"You're the guilty one here, boy," the old man proclaimed. "Knights of Tenshi used to be powerful and wise ki-wielders. You turned them into a horde of mindless brutes! Fighting a war for you...for *you!*"

Absal laughed and said, "This is a poor use of your time, my friend. Right now, my interest is the only thing preserving your life, and I'm about to depart for the Great Sands." He waved a finger like a pendulum. "Tick, tock."

"Fine, fine, you want to know? I'll tell anyone who will listen," the beggar said with a newfound clarity in his murky eyes. "The spirits speak of a prophecy, an ancient one. It is to be fulfilled tonight with dusk's fall."

Absal shifted his head toward the man who had not spoken, the First Templar, who merely raised a hand to his chin as if in thought. "Which prophecy is this?" Absal inquired.

"The greatest of all," the beggar cried out with a grin. "The Deathrid! The Deathrid will return in a thundering quake of fire, lightning, and ash!" Teetering between complete madness and absolute serenity, the old man continued, saying, "On the Great Spirit's night, they will return to Dawn and reclaim what is theirs! They will walk among us and grow in strength. Many will take sides out of awe and fear, humans and spirits alike. Until...until..." He jetted a finger at Bridget's father and screamed, "Until the Starchild and Deathrid battle to decide Dawn's fate! This is her purpose! It will be a conflict that burns cities, breaks mountains, and leaves us in darkness."

Bridget looked up to her father, worry twisting her face. A prophecy about the Deathrid and Alina? Each Templar gave one another a single glance.

"Lock him in Whitecrest's dungeon," Absal commanded Bridget. "Alone."

She nodded and quickly took the old man by the shoulders.

"No! No! Get off!" he squealed like a ripe pig being readied for slaughter.

Tired of his resistance, Bridget slapped him with enough force to knock the beggar unconscious. Sending ki to her muscles to strengthen them, she threw the frail man over her shoulder and trekked toward the oak doors.

The Templars conversed behind her. She attempted to overhear their murmuring.

"Many more will talk," the Third Templar said, "no matter if it is true or not. I, too, have heard the spirits conversing about this…prophecy."

"The Deathrid are a myth," Absal sighed, clearly annoyed. "It's just a story."

Bridget heard a new voice speak, the First Templar. "For a champion of the Great Spirit, I thought you'd have more respect for her kind's wisdom…*brother*."

Absal grunted, slightly amused.

"For now, we wait," Bridget's uncle, the First Templar, announced. "We wait for destiny to arrive."

✳⚙ *III* ⚙✳

"We're here," someone whispered and nudged Alina's shoulder.

She blinked away harsh sunlight, and the image of a silver-haired girl became clear. Sky-blue eyes and a warm grin greeted Alina as she awoke. "You're okay," Alina murmured.

Hanali's armor had been removed, leaving her in a tight-fitting wool undershirt. Alina observed the massive tear over her gut and the sprawling bloodstains. However, Hanali's flesh looked perfectly healthy. The pigment seemed slightly lighter where she had been impaled, as if the skin was freshly grown.

"The strange man healed me," Hanali said and pointed at the mask salesman, who whistled playfully on the familiar dock. He unloaded masks from the boat into a rather large purple wagon. Echo, the nymph, danced in accordance with the salesman's tune. "He forced me to swallow some kind of crystal. I nearly choked on it, but then my wound closed itself."

Alina huffed out a sigh of relief. "Wait," she uttered, "who saved me?"

Hanali gave a nod toward Julian. The Templar waited impatiently near the mask salesman. He was shirtless again, leading Alina to realize that his black jacket was draped over her. Embarrassed, she bundled it up in her arms.

"I'm glad to see you," Alina said to Hanali.

"You've been mostly asleep for our entire journey. The sun set and rose again," Hanali announced and helped Alina up. "Your island is very strange. What makes it float?"

"The Great Spirit," Alina informed her.

"That gives me goosebumps," Hanali said, shivering. "I am using that word correctly, right? *Goosebumps?*"

"Yep," Alina said just as she stepped onto the dock.

Behind her, Hanali said, "If we see any ghosts, I am coming right back here and waiting for the Marauders to take me."

Alina didn't respond as she was flustered by Julian's gaze shifting toward her. "Thanks," she said and thrust the jacket into Julian's chest.

He pushed his arms through the sleeves while saying, "We're even."

"Starchild!" the salesman shouted. He held a clay mask over his face. Yellow fur frayed out from the mask like a mane. Alina twitched at the sight of intensely sad eyes, rosy cheeks, and pale paint.

"You've done so much for us, sir," Alina said politely and gave a slight bow.

"Nonsense," he laughed and lowered the mask to display grinning, sharp teeth.

"If not for you, we'd certainly be dead," Alina insisted.

"I wouldn't go that far," Julian chimed in. He took a step toward the mask salesman, but Echo zipped in front of him defensively. Mildly amused, Julian halted and said, "However, I will see that the League of Tenshi rewards you generously for your service."

"Assisting a genuine Starchild in a time of peril was award enough," the salesman replied. He tossed a final mask into his wagon, which was now piled comically high with a menagerie of faces, and started lugging it down the empty docks.

Alina exchanged befuddled stares with Julian and Hanali before following the salesman to the distant elevator.

"Lots of boats but no people," Julian said quietly.

"It's our biggest celebration of the entire year," Alina explained. "Everyone is in the town square for the party. It lasts for three full days."

"I'd be interested in that," Hanali exclaimed. "I mean…just to experience the culture."

"We're finding whoever is in charge and preparing for an invasion," Julian stated. "Beth Tempest lives here, doesn't she?"

"That's right. Beth raised me," Alina said. She felt a childlike giddiness when imagining their loving reunion. "She hasn't had a regiment of Knights for years, though. Captain Katya oversees things on the island."

"What Templar does this captain belong to?" Julian asked hurriedly. They were stepping onto the elevator now. A feeble old man grunted and began to crank a rusted lever. Screeching gears signaled the start of their ascent.

"Katya belongs to the Eighth Templar, Tuskan Ol'dog," Alina recalled.

"That *savage*?" Julian muttered. "Well, let's hope she's more sensible. You," he gestured at Hanali. "Let's go find the captain. Alina will inform Tempest."

Humming alerted Alina to the mask salesman behind them. He clutched a peculiar orange gem and admired it longingly. Curious, Alina took a step back and inspected the item. "What is that, sir?"

He displayed it between his thumb and forefinger. Inside the crystalline body was a tiny flower bud. "A suwanne gem," the salesman said blithely. "They grow near the meadow Echo once called home." The yellow nymph sparked a shade brighter. "Life can be preserved inside. This flower will bloom, live, and perish utterly protected from the world." The narrow-eyed man placed the gem in Alina's hand.

"Seems like a sad life," Alina stated and offered the gem back.

"Better than many," the salesman insisted. "Keep it. Something to remember our short-lived travels."

Feeling obligated to demonstrate gratitude, Alina said, "It won't be safe to roam the streets tonight. More Marauders are coming—"

"I don't fear any man or woman," the salesman giggled. "The will of the spirits is all that matters in this world. And my collection of faces please them greatly."

Alina debated dropping her offering of appreciation yet forced herself to continue, saying, "Well, accompany me to my home before you make your sales. At least then you will know of somewhere to take shelter if the island is overrun."

"I can't refuse such a kind gesture from you," he stated with a humble bow.

"By the way," Alina said, "is your name Marnie?" She looked at the familiar mustard paint on his wagon that read *Marnie's Many Masks*.

"Oh, no," the mask salesman chuckled madly. "No, it isn't!"

A squeal of grinding metal interrupted their conversation. They had arrived on Somerset. "Happy Spirit Festival!" a bright-eyed Squire shouted from beside the elevator. He went pale white and bowed to Julian upon spotting the Templar jacket.

The mask salesman wheeled his wares onto the road and began giggling incessantly at the sight of the town less than a mile away.

Hanali tailed him. She scanned the many palm trees, lush grass, and fluttering birds. "It's so green," she said in awe.

Julian took Alina by the elbow as she tried to exit the elevator. "I don't want you alone with that man," he said firmly.

"He's treated us with nothing but kindness," Alina retorted while shaking her arm free. "And why do you get to choose my company?"

"Because I'm your commander and Templar," Julian stated. "Or did you forget?"

Oddly, Alina had forgotten. Their brief time spent together had washed away the barriers between superiors and subordinates. Julian's flirtatious demeanor only aided in that regard. "He may be odd, but we'd be dead without him, *sir*," she said defiantly. "And I can protect myself. Regardless if my commander is there or not."

Slightly fearful of what Julian may do, Alina marched onto the road. "Stargirl," Julian said behind her. Sighing, she turned. His hazel eyes were tired and unfocused. "I'm making you Captain of the Green Guard. Han—the other one there is our lieutenant." Alina froze, genuinely stunned for a moment. Julian seemed to recognize the expression of delight and shock on her face because he said, "Seeing as there are only three of us left, the promotions are kind of necessary."

"I'm honored," Alina managed to say.

"As I said, there's only three of us."

"Let's meet at the training courtyard near the old keep at nightfall," Alina told him as she took a few steps down the road. "That's where Katya would choose to gather the Knights and Squires."

After diverging from Julian, Alina heard him bark at the nearby Squire, "You! Where's your mommy? No, not your real mom. I mean your captain."

✳☼ IV ☼✳

Ike followed the orb of emerald light through dense foliage. He had unsheathed his sword and used it to hack away vines and bushes riddled with thorns. Squirrels darted up nearby tree trunks. A lone wolf eyed the prey from under the brush.

"When you meditated in the Temple to El," Lotis's voice emanated from the dot of light, "what did you see?"

"Memories I don't like thinking about," Ike answered. He neglected to tell her about the strange vision of hung deserters. Just thinking of the sight made his stomach sink.

In a green flash, Lotis's body reappeared. She flew backward, twisting herself through tight openings in the vegetation with ease. "The closer we draw to my mother," Lotis said, "the weaker reality's veil becomes. Your heart will unravel."

Chopping down a thicket of leaves, Ike added, "And if I show any fear —"

"It will become your reality," Lotis stated.

The Great Spirit's words echoed in Ike's mind: *Your heart is heavy with dread. You failed to let go.* Would he lose his sanity before the Spirit could kill him? This was Ike's chance to convince the Great Spirit to end her war. He had to make it. He had to at least try.

"This is as far as I may take you," Lotis declared. Ahead of them was a narrow clearing of grass that wound through a multitude of trees. "Stay on this path."

"See you, Lotis," Ike said. He attempted to appear courageous but felt his face tighten with uncertainty.

The nymph smiled and swung her shoulders bashfully. "It's been nice meeting you, Ike. I hope you survive." Her form retreated to the sphere of green light and darted through the many trees.

Pausing for a moment, Ike took in the sounds of the forest. Birds chirped soft melodies, creatures scurried through the shrubbery, and a frantic heartbeat drummed loudly within his chest. "No fear," Ike exhaled. He stepped onto the path and walked onward.

※☼ *V* ☼※

Trumpets, cymbals, and an old piano bellowed music near the fountain in the town square. Julian gritted his teeth and pushed through the crowd of islanders who laughed while stuffing their faces with pastries. Several of them danced with exotic masks obscuring their faces. The narrow-eyed creep must have sold a few masks on his way through the city. In the commotion of the town-wide festivities, Julian had lost sight of Alina and the mask salesman. Seeing as the

Starchild was a local, she had probably found a less rambunctious route.

"Keep up, Han...Haleelee!" Julian shouted behind him.

"I'll be faster!" the silver-haired girl said. She grinned relentlessly at the jubilant celebration all around them. A street performer put a finger to his temple and levitated the wide-brimmed hat atop his head. Claps gushed forth as the object traveled from person to person.

Islanders tossed coins into the hat merrily. Julian's companion began reaching into her pockets. He whistled at her and said, "Focus!"

In front of the massive white temple were two artfully crafted oak chairs. A woman and man sat in them. The female had brown skin, thick braided hair, and the meticulously crafted armor of a captain. Julian identified her quickly as Katya. However, he was taken aback by the man next to her. He was pale with long black hair and a gaunt face. A black coat draped down to his ankles. How could there be a Templar Julian didn't recognize?

Julian nearly toppled a man juggling flaming batons as he ran toward the temple steps. The woman called Katya vaulted to her feet upon spotting him. She seemed completely startled by his appearance. Julian began speaking before she could say a word. "Captain, prepare your island for invasion. About eight hundred Marauders in six ships will attack at midnight tonight."

Katya blinked rapidly. Perhaps she was hoping Julian would vanish as quickly as he arrived on the temple steps.

The man next to her rose elegantly with his nose shoved upward. "It's very uncustomary to ignore a fellow Templar," he proclaimed in a shrill, obnoxiously elegant tone.

Julian gritted his teeth. There was no time for customs or manners. Had this fool not heard him? "I don't know who you are," Julian snapped at him.

He sucked in his cheeks and said, "Betsalel Asim. I am the Fifth Templar of Tenshi." The man gestured to a silver pendant of the numeral V around his neck. "We haven't become acquainted yet."

Letting a scoff slide through his teeth, Julian uttered, "My apologies, I was much too busy fighting a war to attend the Trials." He focused his attention on Katya again. "My Green Guard was ambushed in the night, five hundred Knights of Tenshi killed. The Great Sands sent them to capture Somerset for the Empress. Evacuate the civilians and—"

"Tell me," Betsalel Asim interrupted, "how did a band of pirates slay an entire regiment of Knights? This seems very out of the ordinary."

"Well, my fellow Templar..." Julian's clenched jaw made his words slink out sharply. "We were outnumbered and ambushed. You may have missed that detail due to the constant self-praise rattling around that high-class skull of yours." Asim narrowed his black eyes. "Additionally, my dear comrade, the Marauders have laid waste to some of the most well-defended cities in history. And that was before they were supported by the wealthiest empire in all of Dawn."

"I'd like to speak now," Katya suddenly announced. She collected herself and scanned the enormous gathering of islanders as she spoke. "We'll cut the elevator and defend the island from above. That should give us time for reinforcements —"

"No," Asim cut in.

"With respect, sir," Katya said bitterly, "this island is still under my control. The Eighth Templar, Tuskan Ol'dog, entrusted it to me."

"That he did," Asim agreed. His pale lips slipped into a smirk. "Still, the Squires made Knights of Tenshi yesterday are mine. The League has also been kind enough to reassign four hundred current Knights to fill my personal regiment. Most have already arrived."

Images of the many docked ships passed through Julian's thoughts. Most of them were battleships. He looked out to the lively crowd filling town square. He spotted leather-armored Knights in the masses of partying islanders. "If we defend, the Marauders will burn our docks at the very least. That will leave Absalom Ryder's armies without a safe port in the Aged Sea. Such an outcome is unacceptable," Asim stated bluntly. "I'll take my newly formed regiment and meet these pirates head on."

"You mean to leave us defenseless?" Katya asked, bewildered.

Asim contorted his face with what must have been offense. "The island will have you, Bethany Tempest, and…this Templar as a last line of defense. Also, his girl there." He gestured down the stairs toward the silver-haired Knight.

"That's my lieutenant," Julian said defensively, "Hanali of the Dajo Wind Tribes." He shot a quick glance back at her to verify the pronunciation. She gave a short nod. "She is one of two Knights I have left. Listen to me," Julian's tone grew desperate. "Our only hope is to defend the island. If you sail out with only four hundred soldiers, they will die."

"Doubtful," Asim retorted without hesitation. "I've spent my entire life preparing to wear this jacket. I was groomed for battle in the capital, unlike *others* who cheat, lie, and steal their way to prominence." He nearly snarled in Julian's direction. "My power is great, and any Knight is worth at least fifty peasant raiders. We will return before dawn victorious, and this island will never be touched."

Asim's shoulder grazed Julian as he descended the steps. Out of options, Julian whirled around and said, "Let me join you." The Fifth Templar stared at him in delight. "I've seen them fight, and I have much experience at sea. We'll lead together."

"I'll pass," he chuckled. Giving one last glance at Julian, Betsalel Asim strode into the crowd. From his place above the celebration, Julian saw that many people had taken notice of him. They pointed and gawked in wonder. There he stood, one of the legendary Templars of Tenshi. How many people would die because they believed him worthy of that title?

"I should tell my people," Katya told Julian grimly.

"Not yet," Julian responded. She looked at him, confused. "Let them celebrate without any panic. The Knights will be gathered for the Fifth Templar, but you will tell your people that they are joining Absalom Ryder in the Great Sands." Katya folded her arms and remained exceedingly poised. "There are spies here. They are out there in the crowd… watching."

Julian scanned the sea of celebrators and saw nothing except a blur of laughter, dancing, and merriment. Finding a Marauder spy would be impossible, and that's why their enemies had certainly planted several among them. Cursing to himself, Julian acknowledged that he would have done the same. "If we reveal the threat too soon," Julian went on, "the Marauders will be tipped off to our knowledge. The Fifth Templar's ambush will be compromised. But if that elitist prick doesn't send word by midnight, we'll know he's defeated."

"Then the islanders will take shelter, and I will protect this place," Katya said and forced a thin smile. "I would be honored to fight alongside two Templars."

"You said they'd take shelter?" Julian repeated. "No, they need to evacuate."

"That would take days," Katya said calmly. "We have one elevator to the docks. And if my sources are correct, the Marauders control most of the Aged Sea. There's no place to flee, my Templar."

Julian rubbed his face and groaned in frustration. Thousands of civilians were roaming the streets, readied to be slaughtered.

"The Great Spirit offers Somerset the ultimate protection," Katya said to reassure him. "We float hundreds of feet over the ocean. No army can reach us easily. We *will* protect this place, my Templar. If we prevent panic and the islanders remain assembled in town, we could move them beneath the town's keep in under a couple of hours. I'm sure of that."

Nodding, Julian sunk a few steps lower. "We'll see," he murmured. Hanali watched him earnestly. She was waiting for instruction. "I'd like a couple of rooms prepared," Julian told Katya. "And order a blacksmith to meet with me. I need weapons." Katya gave a short bow before walking toward a Squire at the temple doors.

Hanali followed Julian back into town square. "What do we do now, sir?" she asked him.

"I'm taking a bath," he said frankly.

"Am I truly your lieutenant?" Hanali batted her sky-blue eyes. Julian noticed the feathers in her hair had been lost somewhere at sea.

"There's only three of us," he answered.

"*Anasgvti ayohuhisdi vtla galutsv.*"

"Huh?" Julian said. He wondered if extreme fatigue had contorted her words to gibberish.

"It is a saying in my tribe," Hanali revealed. "May death never come. My ancestors chanted this before war."

Julian said nothing. They broke through the hordes of celebrators and strode onto an open street. An old wooden building stood wedged between shops. Green lettering above the front doors spelled out *Somerset Inn*.

"Many have died for me to reach this place. I wonder why I still breathe." Hanali had spoken the sentence before halting in place. Julian stopped and eyed her while feeling shame. She said what he was too cowardly to admit. "If the Marauders come, I will fight to my last breath. That is on my honor as a Knight of Tenshi." Her blue eyes were clear and focused.

"Yeah, okay," Julian muttered. "Get some new clothes," Julian added, glancing at her torn, bloodstained shirt. "Blend in until midnight. Drink, sleep, do whatever you want. If the new Templar is defeated, which he will be, take shelter with the islanders."

"We aren't doing battle?" Hanali nearly shouted in surprise. She appeared furious, an emotion Julian didn't expect from her.

"It won't be a battle," Julian explained impatiently. "We have no army. It will be a massacre. An extermination."

"An honorable death," Hanali interjected. "Protecting innocent lives is an honorable death, my Templar."

"Let me rephrase this," Julian snapped. "This is a command. You are saving your own life, and the Starchild is too. Beth Tempest will see to Alina's safety. There's no doubt in my mind."

"Please," Hanali pleaded, "I want to fight."

Ashamed at his lack of courage, Julian turned away before saying, "You will say nothing to the islanders. No one will know of the invasion until we hear from the Fifth Templar. If you break this order, I'll have your Knighthood as reparation." He didn't bother glancing back at his subordinate. He knew she'd be devastated and hurt, but that meant nothing. She'd be alive. The Marauders had been known to spare ki-wielders if they were without ties to the Knights. Perhaps it was because of their respect for strength. Julian hadn't thought much about this phenomenon until now. Marauders would slay children in a heartbeat, but not an innocent ki-wielder.

"What if I find the spies?" Hanali said from behind him. "I could kill them."

"I'm serious. I'll take your Knighthood," Julian said once more as he strode into Somerset Inn.

✳☼ *VI* ☼✳

The blue paint on Alina's childhood home struck her as faded and chipped. She walked onto the porch and held her fist against the aged door. Two years had passed since she left Beth and Ike to join the war. Back then, Alina was arrogant enough to believe she could change the world. They'd surely be disappointed to see how far she had fallen. Captain Katya expected Alina to make lieutenant in less than a year. In reality, Alina never made it past Apprentice Knight. At least until her entire regiment was killed.

Behind Alina, the mask salesman hummed to his nymph, who zoomed around his body in flickers of yellow light. His wagon full of masks rested on the front lawn. The stack of faces was a little less mountainous, thanks to the walk through town. He began to sing lyrics and tap a beat on his knee. "The Deathrid come on the Spirit's day, upon darkness's fall! They live and die by their own restraint. What comes will bleed through all!"

Alina pressed her knuckle softly into the rough wood and prepared herself to knock.

"You know, the League of Tenshi made it forbidden to adopt a Starchild long ago," the mask salesman interrupted his tune to tell her. "They are supposed to be raised in temples. I'm surprised to learn of this place."

Gracious for the opportunity to stall, Alina pulled her hand away and said, "Beth and Absal stretched the rules. The twelve Templars control the League of Tenshi, after all. I couldn't call them mother and father, but I lived here until I was twelve." A memory flashed through her mind of Beth brushing her long hair after a warm bath. "Eventually, the other Templars threatened to take me from the island. Beth had me sent to the temple here so I could still be close. After that, I spent most of my time studying with the priestesses or training with the Knights."

Skipping up the steps, the mask salesman tapped a loud rhythm with his knuckle on the door. "Oh, I am very excited to see a Starchild's home!" he squealed. "And meet another Templar of Tenshi!"

"She might not even be here," Alina said. "Maybe we should go—"

The door swung open. Beth stood there in tan trousers and a white blouse. She didn't look a moment older than when Alina left her. Her gray eyes welled up with tears, and Beth threw her arms around Alina. They both cried into each other's shoulders. Alina dug her grip into Beth and held on tightly. "My little star," Beth whispered into her ear.

"Lovely," the mask salesman proclaimed. "Lovely, lovely, lovely...*Haha!*"

Beth let go of Alina and inspected the strange man beside her. "What are you doing here?" she asked Alina. "What's happened?"

"So much," Alina exhaled. "May we come inside?"

"Of course," Beth said. She took her by the hand and led Alina through the doorway. "Welcome home."

❈☼ VII ☼❈

Julian dried his hair with a towel and stood naked in front of the mirror, his ruined garments laying in a pile by the bathtub. A single beam of light fell through the one window into his suite. No lantern was lit, which left the chamber mostly in shadow. The large bed had been freshly made and tempted Julian to collapse into it.

He pulled on the fresh clothes delivered by a Squire earlier. His fingers would not stop trembling, and buttoning his pants and fastening the black belt felt abnormally challenging. Sucking in a rasping breath, Julian tried to focus on his reflection. But memories of the recent battle blurred the image reflecting back at him.

Fire. All he could see was the rushing flames tearing through his battleship. Faces screamed at him. They were people he knew, names that he said for months on end. And they were being gutted by blades and scorched by fire.

Kill. Julian had stood on Serpent's Edge and fired arrow after arrow. Every steel tip found its place, and Marauders dropped like rain onto the rocks below them. Julian had climbed onto a mound of bodies to gain a better perspective, his hands continuing to work feverishly. Arrows shot free from his bow, seemingly without end. And then he reached into his quiver and found nothing.

Live. He toppled down the mountain of corpses and ran. Knights screamed out for him. *Help me, help me.* Julian sprinted past a boy as a hammer bashed against the child's skull. Was that his Knight? Or was he an enemy? Blood burst and spilled from broken flesh. There was nowhere to run. They'd die here. *They'd die here.*

A knock on the door brought Julian back to his senses. "In a minute!" he shouted back. Julian grabbed his black jacket from the floor and dug through its pockets. He found a leather pouch and freed a single black crystal. Using the bottom of a candlestick on the dresser, Julian smashed the crystal into a powder. Bending over, he snorted the black dust in through his nose.

Shivers jolted up his body. His mind instantly emptied and cleared. Every step toward the door felt weightless. He yanked it open and found a small man standing there. In his tow were a cart and a younger woman. "Blacksmith?" Julian asked the dwarf.

"At yer service, Master Templar," the small man responded. He was mostly bald but hadn't shaved recently. Patches of gray stubble dotted his head and face. One of his eyes was lazy and drifted about the room like a loose marble in the man's skull. "Dildor. Call me Dildor, Master."

The woman behind him wheeled the cart into his room. A high bun kept ginger hair out of her face, which looked smeared with soot. Julian didn't mind her filth. In fact, it was comforting. The sight reminded him of the capital's slums where he grew up. Each visitor wore leather aprons filled with tools.

"What are you in the market for, sir?" the red-haired woman asked him.

Julian's high was mounting and making it difficult to remain still. He tapped his foot and scratched at his neck. "Show me everything," he said.

Nodding, the dwarf dug through the cart and held up various weapons. "This here issa curved short sword of my own making. Difficult to pierce with but better fer slashing." Julian didn't watch the dwarf display his wares. He instead darted his gaze between the woman and his bloodied clothing on the door. She blushed and combed a strand of hair back. "Ah, got ten throwing knives here…C'mon, Rosemary! This one ain't supposed to be here…Ah, I've heard stories of yer bowmanship, Master Templar, so I've got my finest bow here. Fifty arrows to start yer off with if yer choose. Ah, got a real fine dagger—"

"I'll take it," Julian declared. He had drifted to the dresser and poured himself a glass of whiskey from a bottle he had requested.

Dildor and the woman looked at each other uneasily. "Which item?" the woman asked anxiously.

"Leave the cart," Julian stated and downed the glass of dark liquor. He didn't bother to offer them another glance. After several quiet moments, Dildor and the woman began shuffling to the door. They were obviously saddened by the loss of so much inventory for no charge. *Such is the life of a Templar*, Julian thought. Everything in Dawn was free for the taking.

Finally, turning to see them go, Julian spotted a small chest under the dwarf's arm. "What'd you take?" Julian barked at him. The blacksmiths were almost through the door.

Dildor clutched the chest with both hands and cowered against the wall. "My apprentice brought somethin' by mistake. I ain't parting with this here. It ain't for sale."

Julian stepped close to the dwarf. Dildor's lip fluttered in fear. "Leave it with her."

"But…" Dildor shifted his one good eye in all directions, searching for an escape.

Julian peered down at the dwarf and grabbed him by the chin. "Go," he demanded.

Dildor tossed the chest into the woman's hands and darted into the hallway. Grunting in annoyance, Julian slammed the door shut. He then marched to the bed and sat down. The ginger-haired blacksmith stood frozen. Her fingers were locked around the tiny chest.

"Your name is Rosemary?" Julian asked indifferently.

"Yes," she murmured. "I did bring this chest by mistake. Honestly, I'm not sure how it ended up in that cart."

"Bring it here," Julian told her. Nodding, Rosemary walked across the room and joined Julian on the bed.

"It's locked," Rosemary said after Julian took it from her.

He slid a finger into his boot and pulled out a lockpick. As Julian went to work on the chest, he said, "Tell me what's inside."

"A powerful weapon," she explained. "Dildor spent years searching for it. He finally traded it off an old sorcerer near Nix'Apla. It was forged during the First Great War."

Click. Julian popped open the chest. Inside lay a strange contraption he had never seen. A metal tube was connected to a kind of gold handle. Where the two pieces linked was a small crystalline barrel filled with a glowing, red liquid.

"Betrayer, the Crimson Pistol," Rosemary said while they both observed the exotic weapon. "Legends say, Nero, the Deathrid of Destruction, had it forged after capturing the goddess Asteroth." She continued to tell the weapon's tale as Julian took the pistol into his hand. "For months, he kept her in his fortress. He ravaged her body and defiled her. And when Nero finally had his fill, he slit Asteroth's throat and let her blood fill the chamber of this gun."

"How does it work?" Julian asked. The gun's metal felt warm to the touch. He couldn't help but stare into the chamber's deep, red fluid.

"You point it and pull the trigger," Rosemary explained.

Power seemed to trickle into Julian's veins from the gold handle. He could swear it spoke to him. *Kill.*

"There is a reason these kinds of weapons were never brought to Dawn," Rosemary said. "Only death comes to those who take up the mantle of gunslinger. No happiness or joy can ever find you." Her fingers crept over his.

Julian placed Betrayer into the chest once more. He searched Rosemary's face. She was probably younger than thirty, yet the grime made it difficult to tell. The heavy apron covering her body left everything else to the imagination as well. "The dwarf called you his apprentice?" he asked.

"No," she said quickly, "I've been a proper blacksmith for five years. It's just expensive to open a shop. I moved here from the capital—"

"I'm from Whitecrest too," Julian interrupted. His shoulder and hers had drifted together.

"Where?" she asked quietly. Her eyes were managing to avoid his gaze.

"The slums."

"Maybe we knew each other."

"You know what's coming tonight? You're not a fool." Julian said suddenly. Rosemary didn't recoil from him. Instead, she kept her gaze steady.

"I heard murmurs of pirates," she said quietly. "And when I look in your eyes, I feel like I see the end times." Her hand fell on his leg.

"What would you do?" Julian asked. "What would you do with your last hours?"

"I wouldn't fight."

Their lips came together. Julian wasn't sure who advanced first. She pulled away for a moment to throw off the thick apron. It landed near the tub, on top of Julian's ruined clothing.

She was right. Fighting would be meaningless. A few ki-wielders could never destroy the Marauder fleet. And fleeing would mean his death at the hands of the other Templars. There wasn't a way out. He wanted to think of something else, anything other than the coming destruction. "Do you get high?" Julian asked in between kissing her neck. His hands began to inspect her newly revealed body.

"Yeah," she sighed in pleasure.

"The bath is still warm. Let's get clean."

"You smell clean already."

✳✪ *VIII* ✪✳

Beth placed a bowl of bread and a plate of dried meat on the kitchen table. Alina reached for the food and began inhaling it. She had spent the last ten minutes in a breathless retelling of the last day. Now the Starchild replaced her tears with heavy, shuttering breaths. A careful hand brought slices of meat to her mouth while she continued pacing back and forth.

Contemplating the Marauder invasion, Beth peeked out the window to gauge the sun's placement. Beth surmised there were only about five hours before dusk. Nine hours before midnight. "Rest here until nightfall," Beth told Alina. "We have no army, no defenses to prepare. Ki-wielding will be our only weapon, and that means you must be at your full strength."

Alina gave a weak nod, as if she hadn't really heard her. She appeared so fatigued that a simple breeze would knock her into a deep sleep. Beth had other concerns at the moment besides Alina's dreariness, though.

From the kitchen, Beth could see into the living room and entryway of her home. The narrow-eyed salesman sat on her sofa and hummed softly to a yellow nymph. Before the unkept fireplace was a mannequin that displayed her silver armor and Templar jacket. Concentrating on the man, Beth attempted to evaluate his ki.

No, he wasn't a ki-wielder. Beth could not sense the turbulent current of energy that people like herself and Alina emitted. Still, he made her very uneasy. Bright purple robes hid most of his frail body. One could effortlessly conceal a weapon or spellbook within them. Moreover, Beth had encountered several ki-wielders with the ability to suppress their energy. This talent made their power impossible to sense.

"I'm so tired, Beth," Alina interrupted her thoughts. Her exhaustion seemed to make it difficult to chew. The meat mushed against her molars while she spoke. "If I close my eyes, I'll fall asleep. But then I'll wake up to the Marauders on our doorstep." She shivered and dropped into a chair.

Beth rushed to Alina and rubbed her back tenderly. "I'm proud of you, Alina," she told her. "You've made it home."

Alina hugged her midsection. For a split second, Beth saw a little girl with unruly, thick hair. Bright bluish-green eyes looked up at her. "Will you help stop them?" Alina asked her.

"I will," Beth stated. What Alina had told her was inevitable. Years ago, when Absal set out for war, she knew this day would eventually come to be. "This island is under my protection from anyone who would do it harm." She shot the mask salesman a glance. He lay on the couch and swatted playfully at the nymph.

"I thought you'd be upset with me," Alina muttered suddenly. "You were harder on Bridget for joining the war. I thought maybe that was because — because I'm not your daughter. But then I realized it's also because everyone expects me to fight. Starchildren end wars. That's what all the books say. But I can't do anything." Tears rolled down her copper skin.

Shaking her head, Beth dropped into a seat next to her. She took Alina's cheek with a gentle hand and guided her eyes toward her own. "You are more than my daughter," Beth said plainly. "A Templar lives because of you. A friend is still breathing because of you. They weren't saved because you're an incredible fighter, which you are. They were saved because you are selfless. That's why I knew you would have to leave one day. I have to share you with all of Dawn."

Alina stared out the window in the same manner she did as a child. Her eyes looked to somewhere far away in the blue sky, somewhere only she could see.

"Stop thinking the world can be saved with your fists," Beth told her.

The Starchild's nose scrunched up. "I don't think that," she said.

"Such a lovely home," a childish, brash voice chimed in. The frail man had meandered into the kitchen. He examined pictures on the wall of Beth's children. His narrow eyes squinted so severely they looked completely shut. "I'm envious of these photographs," he said with a pout. "My village didn't have a camera, no. We were much too poor for that. Stories were all we had, yes. Stories of brave ki-wielders like your daughter here, the Starchild. She is wonderful indeed." A yellow light hovered above his shoulder. Beth felt that it was watching her.

"I've been meaning to ask," Alina said to the strange man, "did your stories tell of where Starchildren are from?"

"No," he said sharply. The man's thin eyes widened with the word. Beth saw something in that instant. Malice. "No one knows that. It's a secret the spirits keep for themselves and no one else. You hail from the heavens above. That is enough to know, yes."

Alina rolled her eyes and chomped into a piece of bread. She didn't seem to notice what Beth had witnessed. Perhaps Beth was just paranoid. Hearing of an invasion was enough to set anyone on edge. *Better to be cautious,* she thought.

"I'd like to see one of your masks," Beth asked him. Her gaze locked onto his.

The mask salesman twitched his lips and then smiled cheerfully. "You'd like to see one of my faces? What an honor," he sang before sprinting toward the front door. The nymph trailed close behind him.

During his absence, Alina sprang up and said, "Wait, where's Ike? Is he in town?"

"Well," Beth began, "he's been chosen. By now, he's probably near the Great Spirit's dwelling place."

Alina's jaw fell open. "Ike?" she murmured. "Ike was *chosen*? To be the Spirit's *champion*? Our Ike?"

"That's right."

Alina put both hands on her hips. "Well, I have to see him. He doesn't know what's coming tonight. I mean, if he makes it out of there. Will he make it out of there?"

"He will," she reassured her. *Please, El*, Beth thought, *bring him back to me.* "I've already told Nathan to wait for him by Kokoro Pond. That's where he'll return. Go get both of them."

"Nathan is here?" Alina yelped while already heading for the door. She combed a handful of hair behind her ear.

The frail salesman trotted inside with a clay mask in his hand. Alina almost rushed past him, but he grabbed her by the shoulder. She flinched and pulled herself free. "Where are you going?" he chuckled.

"I'll be back," Alina assured him.

"Go on, Alina," Beth instructed. "Your friend and I will be just fine without you."

Giving a single nod, Alina went out the front door. Neither Beth nor the salesman moved until the door swung shut. *Creak. Slam.*

Beth stepped into the living room. The mask salesman mirrored her every step toward the fireplace. His movements made Beth's skin crawl. Every swing of his arms was poised, defined, and purposeful. It was so different from his childlike trot just moments ago. Was he copying her?

"Take a look," he said while offering the mask. A disturbingly intense grin had manifested on his face. Alina would be far down on the path now. They were totally alone.

Not hesitating for a second, Beth swiped it from him. She glared down at the mask and was overcome with a strange sense of familiarity. A white face with empty eyes looked up at her. Something about the curvature of the nose and the point of the chin made her heart race. Warmth pooled against her fingers like she was holding human skin. A shift in the air seemed to darken the room as if light itself was retreating.

"That was made after your face," the mask salesman said. His tone had become low and manic. "I've handcrafted one for every Templar."

"What have you come here to do?" Beth asked him. She grabbed his robes with her free hand and yanked him close. A ball of yellow light zipped toward Beth. Before it could reach her, Beth blew a gust of air from her lips that sent the nymph hurtling against the wall. The dot of light dimmed and floated to the ground. Still staring at the man in her clutches, Beth shouted, "Who are you?"

For the first time, the man's thin eyes opened wide. His irises were abnormally small and almost completely black. The frenzied grin across his face grew wider and wider. "Let me show you."

Faster than Beth could see, the man slipped free from his robes and loomed before the fireplace. He squatted on all fours completely bare, like a prowling animal. The robes still held in Beth's hands began enveloping her entire body. Dense fabric restrained her arms against her chest.

The man held a hand to his face. He gripped his cheeks tightly and yanked on his skin. Just before the robes wrapped around her eyes, Beth saw the man pull away a narrow-eyed mask.

✿✿ IX ✿✿

Moisture clung to the air and felt heavy in Ike's lungs. He trudged down the thin path of grass in Somerset's forest. By now, he had sheathed his sword and begun to walk at a brisk pace. Nothing had disturbed his passage since Lotis left him alone. Maybe he really had let go of all fear. At the moment, he certainly didn't feel afraid. He was sweaty but definitely not afraid.

Ike stepped into a haze. The wind felt like static and blurred the world around him. Almost toppling over, he steadied himself against a tree. A figure ran past him. She had auburn, ginger, and gold locks of hair. "Alina!" Ike called out. He tried to run, but it felt like moving through water. A root caught his foot, and he fell flat on his face.

Looking upward, he shouted again, "Alina, wait!" Someone else stood several yards down the path. It was Asim, dressed in the training garments he wore as a lieutenant. "Weak," he spat. "Worthless. It would be better if you never existed."

Alina stood behind Asim, her back to Ike. She wore a white dress with tiny, golden stars as detailing. Something was wrong. Her feet were gently sinking into the dirt. Ike pushed himself to his feet. Slowly, Alina turned her head back toward Ike. She screamed an ear-splitting, frenzied cry of pain.

Blood spilled down her body in thin lines from wounds Ike couldn't see. Now she was sinking faster into the earth. Ike ran past Asim, yet Alina seemed to be getting farther away. The distance between them stretched out further and further with every stride Ike took. He sprinted as fast as he could, yet he wasn't getting any closer.

"Do what you're told," his father's voice said. Absal had replaced Asim and floated alongside Ike. A flimsy kitchen knife was stuck in his shoulder. "You're coming to join me."

More faces and voices bombarded Ike from all around.

"I'm going to be a better Knight than those people," Bridget said.

"You're a child," Nathan said. "I was never your friend."

"If you show any sign of weakness or fear," Katya stated, "the Spirit will claim your sanity."

Alina's neck sank into the dirt. "Help me!" she shrieked. "Ike! Please! Why won't you help me?"

Ike dove forward and reached out for her. As he landed on the dirt, the last traces of Alina's hair disappeared into the earth. "No!" he screamed. "Don't leave me! I'm sorry! I'm sorry!" He wasn't crying. Instead, Ike dug into the ground with his bare hands. She had to be down there.

A shadow fell over him. There was a low, creaking sound as if something swung on a rope. Ike settled his hands and glanced up. Hanging from a tree by a noose was his body. The face appeared bloated, purple, and rotten.

He shouted and crawled backward. All around him, dangling from every tree, Ike saw his own corpse.

Panicked grunts huffed from Ike's throat. *I'm afraid*, he thought. *I'm so afraid*. A rope shot down and lassoed around Ike's neck. It tightened and plucked him from the ground. He wheezed and spat as his airway was snapped shut. No breath could find his lungs.

Strangely, the sensation began to feel comforting. No more war. No longer would he live a life he didn't wish to complete. Relief washed over Ike, and he let his body relax. He wouldn't feel alone for a second longer. He wouldn't have to be anything. This is what he wanted.

The noose tightened, and Ike squealed a silent cry. A young man stepped before him. He held the other end of the noose, which was thrown over a thick branch. His grip looked firm and unwavering. Ike knew the face before him. It was his own. Like the many lifeless bodies swaying in the forest, the young man's face bore Ike's reflection. Except this double wore the leather armor of a Knight and had blood smeared down his cheeks like war paint. His hair contained no streaks of gray either. He appeared vital, strong, and enthralled by Ike's suffering.

Struggling to keep conscious, Ike watched the double raise his other hand. With it came a severed head dripping blood from the neck. Dead brown eyes looked ahead vacantly. Ike thought that perhaps it was his head, but now he could perceive nothing except a blur of colors.

The truth blossomed in Ike's heart as the specter before him yanked the noose even tighter. Death didn't scare him; what did was being killed by *him*.

He feared losing himself in the anger, feeling his blade slice through flesh, becoming like his father, finally letting go of the restraint that kept his sword from cutting down anything in front of him.

In training, Ike had felt the power in his swing and stance. He knew that he had the strength to knock down Nathan or any Squire, to become the warrior Absal Ryder yearned for him to be. He resisted the call to Knighthood out of fear, a fear that he would lose his soul. A fear that he would abandon himself on Somerset and become the shadow of his heart.

The double released the noose's tension enough so Ike could draw a single, shallow breath. He watched the young man motion his eyes to a spot on the forest floor. Ike looked to the dirt and saw where Alina had sunk beneath. In that moment, the shadow of Ike said something to him. Nothing was spoken aloud, but Ike understood the feral gleam in the double's eyes, which said, *I won't forgive you for losing her.* He dropped the head, unsheathed a familiar sword coated with dried blood, and pressed the steel to Ike's neck.

Feeling the noose begin to tighten again, Ike summoned the strength to kick his double in the gut with both feet. Both of them landed in the dirt with a thud. Ike gagged on his own breath while struggling to throw off the noose. The double jumped up and raised his blade over Ike, who had barely gotten to his knees.

Ike's mother had called him gentle. He knew it was untrue. A part of him yearned for revenge. Adrenaline poured into Ike's veins, and he felt an uncontrollable rage at the thought of being struck down here. Ike looked at the double and saw himself, his father, the war, everything he hated and could not control. Pushing hard off the ground, Ike grabbed the double around the waist and drove him forward into a nearby tree. The double's head bashed against the bark, and he barely held onto his blade. In a single motion, Ike drew his own sword and held it steady against the young man's throat.

Kill him, a voice Ike did not recognize spoke within him. Snarling as he did it, Ike pressed the steel into the double's neck and watched him wince and gasp in pain. He'd kill him; Ike would tear through his fears and rip them apart.

But then something changed. When the blood began to flow down his blade, Ike witnessed agony and terror overwhelm the face before him. He pulled the sword away from the young man's flesh. No part of him wished to cause anything such pain. The anger faded from Ike almost in an instant. He sheathed his sword.

Upon seeing an opening, the double brought his own blade up and swung it down toward Ike's chest. A strange calm cleared Ike's senses. He grabbed the double's wrist to block the attack and punched him in the throat, hard. As the double choked and lost hold of his sword, Ike grabbed his collar with one hand and bashed his other fist into the young man's nose.

Bone shattered, and blood sprayed onto Ike's knuckles. He let the double slide down the tree to the forest floor. Ike stood tall over him and realized that his mother had been partly right. He was gentle; fiercely so. And perhaps on occasion, this was what compassion looked like.

He kicked the double's sword a few feet into the nearby grass before giving a passing glance to the defeated reflection. Ike left his shadow in the dirt and continued on the forest path. A thought formed in Ike's head and rang in his ears: *I don't fear you.*

Without warning, the bodies vanished, and the haze lifted. Ike suddenly remembered what his purpose was in Somerset's forest. He had nearly gone insane just now. As if his thoughts were heard, a voice spoke on the breeze. *"You were almost lost to me, Ike Ryder."* The wind came from just ahead, out of a doorway in a massive hollow tree. Branches and trunks fused together and stretched high above any other vegetation to create the peculiar cavern. Most of the hollow tree was in shadow. The late afternoon sun could barely cut through the dense leaves.

"You feared the past," the Spirit's voice said. *"You feared what it could do to you…How it could change you…There is so much left for you to lose."*

Ike walked toward the voice emanating from within the enormous tree. Perspiration drenched his entire body. Dots of light floated toward the entrance as he approached. *You've made it,* Ike thought. No one had believed him capable of reaching here, yet he had made it.

His foot stepped into the grotto. Lush grass and a multitude of flowers grew throughout the tree's interior. The ground felt incredibly soft, tempting him to collapse and fall asleep. Perhaps Ike would have if he hadn't seen the strange figure before him.

In the center of the hollow tree, kept under a veil of shadow, loomed the shape of a woman. She stood incredibly still. For some reason, it was difficult for Ike to focus his eyes on her. A sharp static tore through his vision whenever his glance lingered on the sight.

There was no turning back now. Ike continued walking toward her.

Multicolored lights poured into the cavern from behind Ike. They swam in the air toward the womanly figure. The many nymphs shined brighter and lit the hollow tree with a wondrous glow. Now he could see the shape clearly. There, in the very center of the tree, was a wooden statue of a woman. Strangely, it did not appear to be carved. Rough bark and traces of leaves suggested that the statue was naturally grown. Instead of feet, the figure's legs withdrew beneath the earth like roots.

Ike stood several feet from the statue and waited. A dizzying power radiated from the wooden shape. That was her. He felt sure of it. Just then, the eyes of the statue opened. Black ovals dotted with stars focused on Ike. Fire bloomed on the figure's head and rolled down her shoulders like locks of long hair. The mouth opened, and for the first time, Ike heard the Great Spirit's voice from her own lips. "I am glad you've found me," she said. Her true voice was airy, elegant, and incredibly lovely.

He stared into her eyes and suddenly felt like retching. Gripping his stomach, Ike collapsed onto his knees.

"You'd do well not to look at me for long," the Great Spirit said. "The many warnings are true. My presence can be maddening for mortal beings."

"It's like I can see the whole universe," Ike panted. "In your eyes…there's everything."

"Steady yourself, young Ryder," she said. "We do not have much time. I must bestow upon you a heavy burden."

This was the moment. He fought through nauseous breaths and slightly shook his head. Summoning all his courage, Ike said, "No." The floating nymphs dimmed their light a shade. Cracks of fire from the Spirit's mane filled the brief silence.

"No?" the Great Spirit asked. Her wooden face contorted with visible frustration.

"I came here to say no," Ike said louder. He stood tall and raised his head. *No fear.* "My entire life was shaped by the war you burdened my father with. Knights take slaves, destroy cities, kill without restraint…all in your name. I've *seen* what they are like." Ike forced himself to stare into the Spirit's maddening gaze. "You picked the wrong champion. I won't call my people to battle. So, kill me if you must. I'm at peace. But I am done with your burdens. If you have a shred of morality within you, please, you will end this war. End it and save your people. Kill me if you must, but save them—"

A surge of fire erupted from the Spirit's head and shot toward the veil of leaves above. Ike fell backward in surprise. The nymphs scattered in the air to avoid the lapping flames. "Young Ryder," the Great Spirit boomed, "I have seen the birth of stars and witnessed the death of worlds. Do not test your wisdom here."

Ike shielded his face from the intense heat. Then as quickly as the fire swelled, the flames retreated. "You stand there and speak of death because you don't fear it. That is what makes you weak," the Spirit said furiously.

Shivering and sweating profusely all at once, Ike barely kept his knees from shaking. "Listen well, son of Absalom," the Great Spirit continued. "Your father betrayed me! The night this island was nearly destroyed was also the night of your birth. Did you know this?"

Petrified by the Spirit's raw power, Ike said nothing. But this was known to him. However, the fact had been rarely ever mentioned in his family.

"Your father stood where you are now, an infant in his arms," the Spirit continued, "and I told him to resist bringing justice to the Great Sands. I foresaw that in four years' time, a curious star would fall to our island. A star that needed his protection."

"Alina," Ike heard himself say.

"The winds of fate foretold her arrival," the Spirit said somberly. "And the Starchildren's return meant another prophecy, the *Great Prophecy*, would soon come to be. So, I instructed your father to stay here, to never leave. But Absalom could not quell the call to battle. He left this place despite my warnings. And he used my name dishonestly to rally Dawn to battle."

"Why?" Ike couldn't help asking. "Why did you need him here?"

"Because of this day," the Spirit's voice echoed throughout the hollow tree. "This is the last sunset my eyes can foresee. It is a day of reckoning, one which will return this realm's creators to their world. Yet, someone has come to interfere. He means to bring about my doom and bury our home beneath the waves."

The air around Ike felt awfully thin. He couldn't seem to take a full breath. "Who?" Ike asked.

"Mako." The Spirit spoke the name with absolute revulsion. "Mako the Face Stealer."

$$*\text{☼} \; \chi \; \text{☼}*$$

The mask salesman's robes swaddled Beth so tightly she could hardly breathe. He remained in front of her still, but he did not engage. Instead, the strange man chanted a ritual in some language Beth had never heard. Whatever he was preparing, she could not let him finish.

All the attention the mask salesman gave to his ritual left his binding spell vulnerable. Summoning ki to her muscles, Beth fought against her restraints and raised both hands to her mouth. She tore the fabric apart enough to see and gasp for air. The man slouched over on the floor appeared drastically different than before. He was massive in size with gargantuan muscles. Most of his head was shaved except for a row of red and purple dreadlocks in the center.

He ceased his chanting and smiled at Beth. A familiar grin spread across the tanned skin. Gritting her teeth, Beth tore at the robes around her once more. This time she ripped them in two and tossed both pieces to the side. "Is that your true face?" she asked him.

Laughing, the man picked up a narrow-eyed, pale-skinned mask from the floor. "I have many faces," he said. "But they all belong to Mako." Still grinning, he bit his thumb hard. Blood spurt from the wound and he began drawing symbols on the hardwood floor with the cut finger.

Beth raised a hand to the sky and focused on the clouds. Just before she could call down a bolt of lightning, the man called Mako tossed the narrow-eyed mask at her. Reacting instinctively, she caught it. A horrifying image spread throughout her mind. Beth saw the same frail, pale-skinned figure she knew as the mask salesman. However, he was different. There was no crazed smile or childish humming. Instead, he shrieked at her through the mask she held, "Free me! Free me!"

She staggered backward, and Mako took advantage. He chanted one more phrase, "*Krushna Sunyata!*" His bloodied palm pressed into the symbols on Beth's floor. They flashed a baleful, deep crimson.

Suddenly, Beth's surroundings were swallowed by a black void. She stood in shallow, muddled water stained with the color of blood. Above her were murky, yellow clouds that emitted a weak light over the endless void. The only other sight Beth could see was Mako. He stood up in the ankle-deep water and gestured toward Beth. A piece of his purple robe flew out from the liquid at his feet and bound itself around him like a toga.

"Where have you taken me?" she inquired calmly.

"The Endless Night," he giggled. "It's a realm just outside our own. I've had it ready in case I ever had to meet *you*."

"What do you want?" Beth asked.

He tilted his head playfully like a confused toddler. "I'm a collector," Mako laughed.

"Of what?"

"Faces," he said. His eyes grew familiarly narrow.

"I see," Beth stated. "It's Alina's you want, isn't it? She is the first Starchild in over five hundred years."

"Yes, collecting a Starchild is something I've really wanted to do," Mako murmured. His voice settled into a low pitch. "But I didn't come here for her. Our meeting was by fate's design. I came all this way to take the face of your Great Spirit."

Beth shuddered. "You mean to steal the power of a god?"

"Mm-hmm," he hummed. "Getting the Starchild to a good spot has really made things difficult, though. The other Templar suspected me as well. Echo is always telling me to mind my greed. But the rewards will be terrific." Mako widened the stone-cold eyes of his new body and displayed his teeth in a snarl. "I'll take your face, your child's, and the Great Spirit's. And when I'm done, I'll leave this place to rot at the bottom of the sea."

"You won't touch my daughter," Beth said. "I'll kill you where you stand." She called on the wind and rose above Mako in a spiraling tornado. Bloodied water spun into her cyclone and showered Mako in the color red. The spectacle should have been much larger. Why did she feel so weak?

"Impressive!" Mako shouted over the rushing wind. "But this place is much different than Dawn. The air is thin and weightless. The clouds never boom with thunder. Your power here is a shadow of its full potential, Storm Paladin!"

"That's enough to deal with you!" Beth focused on the yellow clouds and drew them together in a spiraling heap. Thunder cracked throughout the Endless Night. Then Beth sent streaks of lightning bounding down toward Mako.

He moved incredibly fast. Mako contorted his limbs and danced across the water. Four lightning bolts slammed into the earth one after another. Red steam rose from the shallow sea. Out of the mist came Mako, completely untouched. "I think this will be fun," he laughed.

Mako grunted in a rough, vile tone. The muscular form he currently occupied began to transform. His entire stature grew larger, and his skin became stone-like. Jagged rocks formed an insidious smile within Mako's jaw. Two red and purple dreads remained hanging from the armored skull.

Beth felt sweat slip down her cheek. What kind of atrocity was this man? She commanded a hurricane of wind to bombard him from above. The red water was parted by the intense gust revealing slick, black rock underneath. Mako held a stone arm before his eyes and remained planted on the ground like an immovable pillar. He laughed hysterically against the powerful storm, *"Hahaha! Hahaha!"*

As soon as the hurricane began to dissipate, Mako launched himself off the ground in a monstrous leap toward Beth.

☼ XI ☼

"Mako means to claim my power as his own," the Great Spirit told Ike. Her tone had become increasingly earnest. Nymphs raced about the hollow tree in a passionate frenzy. "His story has been told on the sea winds. Born into the Shadow Tribes on the outskirts of the Great Sands, the Knights of Tenshi slaughtered Mako's people and took the young into servitude. Upon escaping your father's armies, the boy sought after his tribe's ancient, horrific witchcraft. With every face he claims, Mako's power and fury grow."

"What—" Ike stammered and felt his head grow heavy upon his shoulders. "What will happen if he steals your face?"

"When I am taken from this tree, our island will fall out of Dawn." The fire emanating from her head dimmed slightly with the words.

"You're speaking as if this has already happened," Ike managed to say.

"As dusk approaches, my fate becomes clearer," she said softly. "It is doubtful any life will survive what is about to unfold."

"If you told us sooner, we could have done more," Ike said hesitantly. He readied himself in case the Spirit erupted with rage again. "We could have fled. Everyone could have been saved." His voice carried no anger. There was only panic and sorrow.

"I have seen every outcome, every possibility, young Ryder," the Great Spirit proclaimed. "There is but one hope."

The midsection of the wooden statue stretched open. Blinding blue light poured forth from inside the Spirit. Ike covered his eyes and felt static race up his spine. It was more than light. The Great Spirit's body was filled with lightning.

"The Deathrid named Sephas sealed me within this forest during the First Great War," the Spirit said. "When this was done, the Deathrid also placed within me a piece of his knowledge…one of the Five Powers of the Storm. Years ago, your mother journeyed to me and studied this ancient secret. But like all Storm Paladins, she could only comprehend a sliver of its majesty."

Something blossomed out of the ground at Ike's feet. It resembled a jar but was formed out of many interlocking twigs. "Mako will be unstoppable if he claims my power and that of the Deathrid," the Spirit said. "Take this knowledge from me and protect it at all costs. There is a prophecy, one which is known to Mako and many. When the sun sets on this day, the Deathrid will return. This is the last truth my eyes can foresee. Return to the Deathrid this knowledge so that Mako may be destroyed by it."

Ike plucked the wooden jar from the grass and held it tightly. "I'm sorry," he murmured. "I thought the Deathrid was a horror story told to children. How can this all be happening now?"

"You ask many questions," the Great Spirit said grimly. "Grip that flask tightly."

His head spinning, Ike clutched the container with both hands. The lightning racing inside the Spirit's body surged outward toward the flask. Ike slid back on the grass as the electricity slammed into the wooden jar. Lines of static flashed against the walls of the hollow tree. Nymphs dodged the electrical storm as Ike fought with all his might to not be thrown over. Gradually, the light inside of the Great Spirit grew fainter. The last bolt of electricity poured into the flask, and the top sealed itself shut.

"This is your task," the Great Spirit said as the hole in her torso closed. "The Deathrid smote me when I was at my most powerful. We once had our…differences, but their might is our only hope to slay Mako if he acquires my face."

Wiping sweat from his eyes, Ike let a quiet sigh slip through his heavy breaths. Moments ago, he had refused the

Spirit's call. He had been prepared to die here if that meant protecting Dawn. The flask vibrated intensely in his hand. Ike's head felt heavy, like he had been flipped upside down.

His father began the war despite the Spirit's orders. For years Absalom Ryder lied and claimed his battles were honoring the Great Spirit of Somerset. Absal's ego and vengeance destroyed Ike's family. His rage killed thousands upon thousands. The Great Spirit was never to blame.

Ike gripped the flask tight. This quest, the one he planned to reject, was to save lives instead of ending them? "If I was able to do this, where would I find…the Deathrid?" he asked.

"He will come to claim what is his," the Great Spirit said. "You must go now and protect the knowledge you carry. My dwelling place is no longer safe."

Nodding, Ike turned and began to walk toward the large archway. He witnessed the Spirit's fear and knew it to be real. His mother, Nathan, Flynn, and so many others roamed the streets of Somerset in ignorance of the coming threat. He could not let his home be destroyed. No wants or needs passed through Ike's mind. All he could picture was the Floating Island of Somerset crashing into the Aged Sea. Nothing mattered now besides the flask in his grip.

Just before Ike stepped into the familiar forest, he halted. He spoke with his back to the Great Spirit and her many children. "Why would you choose me to do this? I'm not sure that I can."

"In time, you will understand why," the Great Spirit whispered on the wind. "But know this…The Face Stealer will destroy all of Dawn with my power. Mako cannot be allowed to leave Somerset with my face. Whatever it takes, whatever sacrifice is required, he must be defeated. I entrust you with this message and purpose." Glancing over his shoulder, Ike saw that her eyes had closed and her mane of fire had extinguished. "Goodbye, Ike Ryder."

✳☼ XII ☼✳

Alina wandered down the path behind her childhood home. Her body desperately craved rest, yet she gained a second wind at the thought of seeing Ike. Why would the Spirit choose him to be her champion? If she was honest with herself, Alina felt a tinge of jealousy. The Spirit's champions were supposed to be the most skilled warriors on the island. That certainly was not Ike.

Too much time had passed since Alina left Beth. Looking at the sun, she still had about four hours before nightfall and beginning battle preparations. That didn't seem like nearly enough time. Alina didn't feel able to face Nathan, or Ike, or the Marauders. For a while, she had stayed slumped against a tree, knowing that Nathan was probably up ahead. This may be the last time she had to speak with him. War would consume Somerset in less than eight hours. Nothing she could say seemed like the right last words.

A branch snapped under her foot. "Who's there?" someone asked from up ahead. Alina looked forward and realized she had meandered farther up the path than she intended. Sitting tall on a tree trunk was Nathan. New leather armor made him seem ready for battle. The League of Tenshi's symbol was stitched over his heart, and a familiar red strip of fabric covered his eyes. All the anxiety Alina felt washed away as she took in Nathan's appearance. She decided to approach him as if this was an ordinary day, a sentiment Alina needed to indulge for just a moment.

Alina tiptoed toward Nathan. A meadow of flowers sprawled out before the stump Nathan sat at. She attempted to remain stealthy while also avoiding trampling any of the dahlias and lily buds.

"I can still hear you," Nathan said calmly. His caramel skin looked darker from months at sea.

Feeling that her ruse was futile, Alina hung her shoulders and said, "Can't you just let me scare you?"

Nathan stood up quickly and leaned his ear in Alina's direction. "Is that...?"

Alina ran forward and hugged Nathan. He flinched at first but then settled into the embrace.

"Alina?" he asked her curiously.

"What're you doing in that armor?" she said while reluctantly pulling away.

"I've been made a Knight. I'm actually leaving already," he said anxiously. Since Alina had last seen him, Nathan's features had grown sharper and more defined. He had always been exceedingly handsome, yet Alina did not expect him to look so mature. "Marauders are attacking tonight," he went on. "Asim is the new Fifth Templar. He means to defeat them at sea."

"What?" Alina shouted. "He'd need a thousand soldiers to pull that off! I fought them, Nathan. They're unstoppable on the ocean."

"Most ships have already sailed out," Nathan told her with a shrug. "Mine is the last to depart. It's for noncombatants and medics mostly. I need to get to the docks, but I wanted to say goodbye to Ike." He crossed his arms nervously.

"Do you think he…" Alina couldn't bear to say it.

"Ike is stronger than anyone thinks," Nathan stated firmly. "He'll be okay."

"I hope," she said more to herself. It was then Alina noticed how close they were standing. She also observed how rough Nathan's skin had become and the fresh stubble on his chin. As they grew up on the island, Alina found it hard to ignore her attraction to Ike's best friend. He was a little younger, yet he exuded this undeniable intensity.

"I'm glad I've gotten to hear your voice," Nathan said suddenly.

"Me too," Alina told him. She inched closer. "You've really grown up."

Nathan smirked and brushed his curly hair back. "I bet you have too."

"See for yourself." Alina took his hands and placed them on her cheeks. Nathan's fingers slightly trembled as he ran them over her features. The sensation was much different than when Julian was this close. She could only describe the contrast as a feeling of sincerity. "What do you think?" she asked him quietly.

"Good," Nathan mumbled. He pulled his hands away yet remained close to her.

"Good?" Alina echoed with a laugh.

"I mean beautiful," Nathan stammered. "You've always been that."

"Guys haven't been shy about making me feel that way," Alina sighed. Why had she said such a thing? The beating of her heart made it difficult to think. "You probably don't want to hear that." She stepped back slightly.

"No, it's okay," Nathan said quietly.

Alina kept talking despite her desire to stop. "It's just that people treat me differently because I'm a Starchild." She looked at the budding flowers to distract herself. Nathan's breath felt warm against her cheek. When had he gotten so tall? "Absal used to flaunt me like a trophy. My Templar made me his captain over my friend, and there was no reason for that." Thoughts she just now realized were spilling out. "People never really see you when they just look at what you are."

"I understand," Nathan whispered. He drew even closer now. Their hands slid together as an invisible magnetism forced them to intertwine. "My ship is leaving soon," he said even more quietly.

"Okay." Alina stared at his lips. This might be the last time she'd see him.

"Will you tell Ike—"

She pulled his head down and kissed him.

✳☼ XIII ☼✳

The sun sank deeper into the sky. Ike ran through the forest up a winding path of grass. How long did he have before sunset? There couldn't be more than three and a half hours between then and now.

As Ike sprinted onward, a green dot of light zipped up to his shoulder and expanded to the form of a green-skinned woman. "Hey, Ike!" Lotis said excitedly. She floated alongside him like a swimmer performing a relaxed backstroke.

"Hi...Lotis..." Ike huffed.

"Where are you going?" she asked and batted her emerald eyes.

Ike skidded to a stop. He turned completely around before staring at the wooden flask within his grip. "I don't know!" he exclaimed. "It just feels like a situation where I should be running!"

"You seem tense," Lotis said with a pout.

"Yeah, I guess I am," Ike wheezed. The power humming within the container made his skin crawl. Hurriedly, he managed to fasten a wooden loop at the end of the flask to his belt. "The sun is going to set soon, and I need to tell my mother about everything," he said to Lotis.

"That isn't part of what *my* mother told you to do," Lotis said rather crossly.

"Please." Ike put both hands on her shoulders. The green nymph's cheeks flushed pink. "People could still try to flee the island before this...Face Stealer gets here. The Spirit didn't say I had to keep everything a secret."

"Hm," Lotis hummed. "Good point. Where are you trying to go?"

"Well, I came from Kokoro Pond—"

Lotis tapped Ike's forehead, and suddenly he felt completely weightless. His body rose from the ground and shot upward through the trees. Branches snapped against his back as he rose higher and higher. A long, continuous scream bellowed from his throat.

He broke free from the tree line and was tossed forward in the air. Again, his body slammed against tree branches and leaves. His descent was slightly slowed by some magical force, but it still felt a great deal like falling.

Splash. Ike crashed into Kokoro Pond. Without relaxing for a moment, he swam to the surface and coughed up water. "Holy shit," he mumbled while scrambling for the pond's edge. Crawling onto dry land, Ike's hands slipped. He fell forward into the mud and laid there for a moment. *I wonder what Peeko's doing,* he thought, *that son of a bitch.*

Grunting with the effort, Ike got to his feet and ran down the dirt path toward his home. He had to be faster. Where was the Face Stealer right now? Could he be on the island already? People passed through his mind. Flynn, Katya, Nathan, the baker who wanted to slice up his sheep. *Faster.* Ike panted and felt a cramp twist his gut. If he reached his mother, she would know what to do.

Ike stopped running. He stared at something in front of him, something that should have been impossible. Standing in a meadow of budding flowers were Nathan and a girl with auburn, ginger, and gold hair. Alina's lips pressed tenderly against Nathan's. They drew apart and came together again and again. For a second, Ike wondered if he was back on the Spirit's path witnessing a horrible illusion.

Alina's eyes flashed toward him, and she pulled her mouth from Nathan to shout, "Ike!"

Ike willed himself to say, "Both of you need to get on a boat. Something's coming to sink the island. Tell everyone. And…I need…" Losing control of his legs, Ike wandered off the dirt path and into the trees. No thought could overcome the shock rattling his skull. He heard Nathan's voice from far away saying, "Alina, I have to go. I'm sorry — I have to go."

Ike stopped moving when the edge of the island came into clear view. Waves rolled in from the horizon. A hand came around his wrist. "Hi," Alina said in her elegant and ornate voice. "Why are you running off? And how'd you hear about the Marauders' attack?"

Marauders' attack? What was she talking about? Unable to look into her eyes, Ike pulled his hand free and marched closer to the island's edge.

"Ike!" Alina shouted again.

His heart dropping to his feet, Ike turned to her. She had somehow grown even more gorgeous. Her copper skin seemed to glow in the afternoon sun, and her figure was shapelier and more mature. The leather armor around her body appeared worn and was stained with streaks of dry blood.

"You're acting so strange," she said with bluish-green eyes searching him. "I know things are bleak, but aren't you happy to see me?"

Memories of two years prior floated through Ike's mind. He remembered how Alina had gushed over Nathan's name. She looked at him then the way every girl did, completely enamored. Inside, he knew that she had become taken with Nathan as they got older. That was a realization he had consciously ignored.

"Is this all because you saw me with Nathan? Don't tell me you've never seen two people kiss before," Alina said and rolled her eyes. "It was just a kiss goodbye. We have more important things to talk about!"

Ike clenched his fists and furiously wished that he could push away every feeling in his heart. He prayed quietly to El that his love for Alina would vanish and free him from this horrendous pain.

For two years, he had tried to forget the humiliating emotions he had for her. Nothing had changed after all this time. Looking at Alina, the sea breeze fluttering through her thick hair, Ike felt the same way he did at four years old. She was the most beautiful person he had ever seen.

"Oh," Alina gasped. Understanding washed over her face and made her stare go wide. "You're jealous."

Ike shut his eyes tight to avoid seeing her bewildered expression. How could Nathan have done this to him? He knew what she meant to him. *He knew.*

"I—Ike," Alina stammered, "I don't know what to say." Ike glanced at her and saw what must have been pity in her eyes. "You're like my brother."

The words crushed him. "I know," Ike said quietly.

Seagulls cried overhead. "The, um—pirates, Marauders, I mean, planning to attack," Alina struggled to say, "you were talking about them? Something coming to sink the island? Asim is attacking them with his army, but I'd bet my life he's going to lose."

"No," Ike said. "Something else is coming tonight. It's what the Spirit told me."

"What?" she asked anxiously.

"He's called…" Ike felt silly repeating the name. "Mako the Face Stealer."

"Face Stealer?" Her face contorted like she was contemplating the title.

"Yeah, he steals faces. He wants to steal the Spirit's face. Everyone needs to get off this island. The whole thing could fall into the sea."

"Why would we run?" Alina asked, slightly agitated. "Beth is here, so is my Templar and Katya. We'll deal with this guy while Asim is losing to the Marauders."

"He's too powerful," Ike stated frankly.

"Who says?"

"The Spirit says!" Ike shouted in frustration. "The Spirit entrusted me with something of hers. I need to protect it until after the sun sets. That's our only —"

"Did you get a description of the guy?" Alina asked and motioned to her face.

"Description?"

"Yeah, like, is he skinny? With really narrow eyes and a yellow nymph that follows him?"

"That is a very specific description," Ike said and marched toward her.

"Well, I met a guy, and faces are sort of his thing," Alina explained without meeting Ike's gaze.

Ike swallowed hard. "Where is he now?"

"At our old house," Alina said quietly, "with Beth."

"We need to go!" Ike exclaimed and took off toward the trees.

Alina strode in front of him and placed both hands on Ike's chest to stop him. He hadn't realized how short she seemed now. Her head was well under his chin. "Ike, we need to think for a moment," she told him calmly. "Beth is a *Templar*, one of the twelve strongest people in all of Dawn. If the man I'm thinking of is this…Face Stealer…then she's probably dealt with him by now. And if she's somehow lost, what could you hope to do?"

Ike nodded and calmed his breathing. It wasn't like him to rush ahead without a thought.

"I'll go and see what's happening," Alina announced.

"No, wait, Alina. I can't let you go alone!"

"You aren't a ki-wielder," Alina said bluntly.

Of course, she was right. He'd be useless in a ki-wielder fight. The Spirit entrusted him with protecting their last hope. Running into battle sword-first was a stupid notion. However, Ike had just been through more than she could know. Battle didn't scare him because he knew this fight was to protect his home. "No one needs to shield me," Ike stated. "I'm not a ki-wielder, but I have the training of a Knight… just like you."

"I thought you hated war."

"This is more than war," Ike said sharply. "It's saving our home and everyone on it."

"I'll be careful," she reassured him with a pat on the arm. Nothing Ike said seemed to reach her. "I could be wrong about all of this. Wait by the pond. If I'm not back soon, run into town and get Katya. My Templar is there too. You'll have to pass the house to reach the road, but if you're so tough now, that shouldn't be a problem, right? Just move fast and stay low." Alina smiled and took a step back. She was leaving again, just like before.

"I should have told you," Ike said without warning. Alina stopped and stared up at him. He couldn't read her expression. Her face seemed almost blank. "Before you left, I should have told you how much I care about you. But I knew what'd you say." She gripped her elbows and looked away. "I wish I didn't feel this way." Her eyes flashed back at him. "I'm sorry that I do."

"Don't be sorry," Alina said softly. She offered a frail smile before jogging into the trees.

☀ *XIV* ☆☽

Hanali wedged herself between two hollering islanders to see what the sudden commotion was about. Walking through the market street in two lines were over fifty Knights and Squires. Everyone had piled against shops and wooden stalls to give the procession safe passage.

Some people whistled and cheered for the deploying soldiers. Other islanders whispered to each other in fear and began drifting together to gossip nervously. Hanali couldn't join either activity, however. She locked eyes with a short young man, probably a newly inducted Knight. He had black hair and thin eyes. A solemn frown told her everything he felt. This might as well have been a funeral procession.

"They're really taking everyone, eh?" someone said to her. "That's the fifth group to go."

"Indeed," Hanali replied and darted toward a food stall to distract herself. Only a handful of ki-wielders would be left to defend this place. In the old ages, a few ki-wielders could decimate entire armies, but times had changed since then. Her tribe believed that the gift of ki-wielding was becoming more widespread and less powerful. There was only so much ki in the universe to share. Not many other cultures had such a cynical view.

A roasting skewer of lamb caught Hanali's attention. Rows of sizzling meat filled the stall she had wandered to. Licking her lips, Hanali reached for a chicken leg.

The middle-aged man cooking the meat slapped her wrist. "Money first, foreigner," he said coldly. A net held back dark, greasy hair, yet he left his bushy beard free.

"I spent all my money," Hanali explained as she motioned to the lilac tunic covering her upper body. It had little feathers stitched into the design and was laid over white tights. Purchasing new clothes was a necessity after the morning's battle.

"Keep moving then," he told her, "and that tunic's for boys."

Embarrassed, Hanali rushed through people waving sticks that sparked with light on the ends. She collided with the back of someone, a tall man with braided black hair. He turned only slightly toward Hanali and revealed a deep scar over his brow. As he drifted away, a sinking feeling replaced the hunger in Hanali's gut. That scarred man smelt like seawater…and blood.

Without thinking, Hanali tailed the man across the street. She watched him bump into a young boy with red hair who dropped a toy sword from the impact. Moving carefully, the scarred man retrieved the sword and placed it in the boy's grip. Did they know each other?

The boy darted away from the man and dragged a woman who seemed like his mother toward a line of children. They joined a red-haired gentleman who waited near the front, probably the boy's father. Following the line with her gaze, Hanali saw that it ended at a stall. There, a younger woman, probably about twenty-five, sat and painted a child's face to resemble a tiger. Hanali noticed that there were two empty chairs by the woman as well as another set of paints. She slid through the crowd to reach them. Just across from the stall, leaning against a shop, was the scarred man.

"You'll have to wait!" the face painter said quickly to Hanali. She pointed to the line of children winding down the street. They all twitched impatiently and yammered with each other. "My other girl is a no show."

"Well, I am a show," Hanali said with a thumbs up.

"Huh?"

"I can paint well," she stated clearly. "We can split the money I make. If you are willing."

The face painter patted the tiger boy and sent him on his way. Another child took a seat, this time a girl. As the woman cleaned her brush in a jar of water, she said, "Hm, you can do one, kid. If I like it, you can work the night."

Grinning, Hanali took a seat beside the woman and grabbed a brush from the stall.

"I'm Yuma," the face painter said, smiling. She had small eyes and silky black hair.

"My name is Hanali."

The boy with red hair plopped down. His mother kept a watchful eye on Hanali from the line of children. "You look different," the boy said to her.

"I'm from the Dajo Wind Tribes," she told him. "I can make you look like an eagle." Wetting the brush with blue paint, Hanali painted an eagle on the boy's wrist with a single, continuous stroke.

"You are good," Yuma affirmed.

The boy beamed and said, "Eagles can swoop down fast and — and grab little dogs. My brother told me."

"This is so true," Hanali responded while selecting the paints she needed. "The eagle is my Totem Animal. They are very strong." She began to paint a yellow beak over the boy's mouth.

"Do you believe the Marauders are coming?" the boy asked suddenly.

Hanali held her breath, unsure how to respond. He had spoken so quietly that no one else heard. She wasn't one to disobey orders and reveal the threat. To members of the Dajo Wind Tribes, loyalty prevails over all else. Her eyes wandered to the scarred man who still rested against the nearby shop.

"My dad thinks so, but my mom doesn't. We watched the Knights sail away."

"If they do come," Hanali said, "you'll need to protect your parents. Pirates are afraid of birds, and everyone knows this."

"But pirates have parrots."

"Besides parrots," Hanali said. Then she added, "I saw a man pick up your sword for you." The boy shot a look back at his mother, who now held the toy. Hanali sighed with relief that the boy didn't look to the scarred man himself. That would have given her away. "Did you know that person who helped you?"

"No," the boy said frankly. "I've never seen him before. He's not from here, I guess."

Hanali wet her brush with more paint and kept a single eye on the scarred man. Seemingly out of nowhere, a woman appeared at his side with dark skin and short, choppy hair. Something about her appearance reminded Hanali of the Marauder woman who attacked her in the Crystal Pass. They whispered to each other, and Hanali became certain that they were the Marauder spies. What were they planning? Did they suspect the Fifth Templar's ambush? Or maybe they intended to attack from the island while their forces invaded. She needed to watch them more, much more. Perhaps there were others to be exposed. And then, when Hanali perceived the opportunity, she'd kill them. For the first time in her life, Hanali didn't feel like obeying orders. She knew what a single Marauder was capable of.

To keep her cover intact, Hanali continued painting white feathers on her customer's cheeks. She imagined the little boy lying cold and still on the stone road. Piled high around him were the bodies of the islanders. Many of them still bore blissful, ignorant grins.

☀☼ *XV* ☆☽

Alina sent ki to her legs and felt them strengthen as she ran toward Beth Tempest's home. Trees passed by in a blur due to her increased speed. The image of Ike standing before the island's cliff wouldn't leave her mind. He had become very large, definitely much taller than Absal. His body had matured and slimmed down. And then there was the gray streaking through his hair. What had caused that premature change? She should have been focused on the Face Stealer, yet Alina wasn't sure the mask salesman could be this powerful foe. Forcing away her worries for a moment, she remembered the sensation of Nathan's hands against her cheeks. His lips still felt close to hers.

The blue-painted home came into clear view between thick branches. A massive hole on the roof caught her attention. She burst through the tree line and slowed to a quiet trot. Splintered wood was dispersed all about the lawn and surrounding grass. Thin plumes of smoke rose from broken windows. Her worst fears were true. Julian had been right about the mask salesman from the start.

Shutting her eyes, Alina attempted to sense the energy around herself. She felt the ki flow from the woods, the birds overhead, and Beth's home. The ki originating from the damaged house felt tumultuous, dense, and frighteningly powerful. Focusing on the presence was like being swept into a storm. That was Beth's energy.

She let out a sigh of relief and made her way through the front door, which held onto its frame by a single hinge. Beth lay face down on the living room floor. Her Templar jacket and silver armor had replaced the blouse and trousers she wore before. The ceiling above her was broken apart and provided a view of the clouds. Wisps of smoke originated from scorch marks on the living room floor.

"Beth!" Alina shouted as she ran to her side.

The Templar twitched and rolled over to look at her. Two gray eyes gleamed at Alina. "I'm all right, sweetheart," Beth said quietly.

"What happened here?" Alina helped Beth to her feet and patted away woodchips from her jacket.

"Your friend wasn't what he seemed," Beth grunted and held her ribs. "He was some kind of powerful ki-wielder. The man knew dark wizardry I've never encountered before."

"I'm so sorry I brought him here. I was stupid to trust him," Alina said soberly. "Where has he gone? Did you…kill him?"

"I couldn't manage that," Beth admitted and limped toward the kitchen. Alina held her arm and led Beth to a chair. "But I trapped him somewhere he can't escape. It was a realm outside our own that he somehow learned to summon. The League of Tenshi made such techniques forbidden centuries ago."

Setting Beth down at the kitchen table, Alina held her in a tight hug. "I don't know what I'd do without you, Beth," she said, feeling tears pool in her eyes. "I should tell Ike you're all right."

"Oh?" Beth said curiously. "You've seen Ike?"

Alina squeezed Beth tighter and nodded.

Beth kissed Alina's forehead and pulled away to observe her. "Something is wrong," she said, raising her eyebrow. "Your ki is restless. What's bothering you?"

Alina sank into a chair next to Beth. "Nothing," she said with a clenched jaw. "I'm just anxious to hear from Asim's army. We should begin preparing for the worst." Alina stood quickly.

"We have time," Beth responded and pulled her back down by the hand. "You don't want to enter a battle with a conflicted heart. Remember the story of Storm Paladin Ymir? She lamented waging war against her lover and —"

"She called down a storm so furious it killed her along with both armies," Alina recounted. "I know." Why was Beth so keen on pressing her? Didn't she care more about the impending Marauder attack? Something about Beth's words felt strange. It was unlike her to be so unfocused on the task at hand.

"Are you sure you're okay?" Alina asked.

Beth smiled kindly. "Talk to me," she said. "This may be our last chance, sweetheart." The gray eyes looking back at Alina were so warm and familiar that she abandoned her suspicions.

"It's... Ike," Alina said uncomfortably. "He confessed certain feelings for me."

"Oh?" Beth said with a laugh. "You've finally realized."

"You knew?" Alina exclaimed.

"I knew the moment he laid eyes on you," Beth said, shrugging.

Immediately Alina felt restless, so she stood up abruptly and paced through the debris-filled house. "I never thought to look at him that way... I don't want to die tonight with this distance between us. He means too much to me."

"Hm," Beth murmured. She stood up and strode to Alina, who had wandered into the living room. "Just be honest with yourself and him."

"Honest?" Alina repeated and eyed Beth attentively.

"How do you feel?" Beth questioned her. "Honestly?"

"I feel…" Alina struggled to sort through the torrent of emotions inside herself. "…confused. I think I might…" She couldn't finish the thought. Blood rushed to her face and ears.

Beth nodded and pulled her into another embrace. Alina settled into her shoulder, feeling a familiar comfort take hold. Then Beth squeezed her tighter and tighter. Her hands slid down Alina's back to her lower waist. Beth pressed her face into Alina's hair and sucked in a deep breath through her nose.

Forcing away the shock, Alina pushed her with all her might and shrieked, "You're—"

"*Hahaha!*" the imposter cackled, holding her stomach. "Oh, the look on your face…I want to save that forever and ever." Beth's voice had completely shifted. The tone sounded manic, childish, and very familiar.

Alina spread her legs to a fighting stance and let fire blaze on her clenched fists. She yelled at Mako the Face Stealer, "Where is she?"

Mako grinned through Beth's face. "She's right here," he stated casually. "All of her power, dreams, memories, and ki. I've taken it all."

"You won't reach the Spirit," Alina stated feverishly. Jetting her fist forward, a flash of fire shot for Mako. The attack slammed into Beth's silver armor, yet Mako stood there completely unfazed.

"Hm, how do you know about that?" Mako asked and tapped Beth's chin with a finger. "What did little Ike hear, I wonder? Doesn't matter. Who's going to stop me? You?" He wafted his hand toward Alina, and she was thrown off the floor by a tremendous force. Her body crashed through the wooden wall of Beth's home, and she landed with a thud on the grass.

"Poor Alina," Mako mocked her as he stepped through the newly created hole. "Never truly having a family, always burdened with so much purpose. Don't worry. I will set you free."

Alina crawled back on the grass, feeling a great deal of pain in her spine. Her instinct told her to fight with everything she had. Anger threatened to blind her from reason. No, she had to think quickly. *You can't save the world with your fists*, Beth had told her. She needed to run and get help. Julian, Hanali, Katya, anyone. Together, maybe they stood a chance.

Mako pranced across the grass toward her. She had to be fast. Alina got to her feet and formed a flame over her open palm. "*HA!*" Mako snickered. "That again? Do you really —"

Focusing on the fire, Alina channeled bright, white ki from somewhere deep inside her. The flame burst into a blinding light. Mako shielded his eyes and shrieked. As he recoiled, Alina sprinted toward the paved road that led to town. When she neared the stone pavement, an invisible weight took hold of her. Every step felt heavy and burdensome. Then she was pulled back as if a hand had taken hold of her collar. Grass and dirt sprayed from the ground due to her heels scraping against the lawn.

The invisible force turned her around, so she faced Mako. He had Beth's hand outstretched and looked oddly serious. Alina came closer and closer until her neck was in Mako's clutches. "I think it's destiny we met, Starchild," Mako told her softly. She could hardly draw a breath under his fierce grip. "Think about it. There's only one of you in the world and only one of me. Our boats just happened to pass each other in the Aged Sea. That's fate."

Saliva spilled from Alina's mouth as she fought to take in air. Her hands beat against Mako's arm, but it wouldn't budge. "Of all the faces I will take, the many spirits included," he said quietly, "yours will be my favorite." Immeasurable panic sent Alina's body into a frenzy. She kicked and squealed against her capture. Without a steady breath, it felt impossible to ki-wield.

Mako reached into Beth's jacket and produced an elegantly crafted clay mask. Alina recognized the copper coloring and full lips. He had even painted freckles across the nose. "You're mine," Mako whispered as he pressed the mask over Alina's face.

"No! *No!*" she wheezed while staring through the eye holes. Beth's gray eyes appeared to be consumed by immense joy. Alina felt the current of energy inside her being pulled toward the mask. As the ki left her, she became weaker and fatigued. Her kicking feet slowed to a halt. *This is it*, Alina thought. *I've failed.*

White-hot energy from deep within Alina rushed to the mask. The clay face burst into flames and caused Mako to drop Alina onto the ground. She fell limply yet immediately forced herself to stand.

Beth's face snarled at her. Mako tossed the flaming mask to the side and said, "Starchildren really aren't human. I'll need time to craft a mask that can hold *you.*"

The bright, mysterious energy still coursed through Alina. She had never felt so strong…and furious. Gritting her teeth,

Alina said, "Get. Away. From. Me." Power erupted from her body, an uncontrollable kind of ki. A shockwave boomed from Alina and pushed Mako back at least twenty feet. Light oozed off her copper skin. Alina's hair fluttered about her face and glowed with the colors of ginger and gold.

"*Haha!*" Mako laughed madly. "Now that is the power of a Starchild!"

"*Ree-ka!*" Alina shouted before blasting a massive wave of fire toward Mako. The explosive flames were the color of Alina's shining hair.

Still chuckling crazily, Mako held out a single hand and parted the wave of fire. It stretched out on both sides of him, searing the grass and blazing into the air. When the flames subsided, Mako remained where he was, a black burn on his palm and arm. "Impressive," he giggled. "If I wasn't wearing this face, you would have killed me."

He floated off the ground and rushed toward Alina on the wind. Refusing to surrender, Alina let loose all her remaining ki in one final attack. She expected to produce more fire but instead unleashed a beam of pure, white energy from her hands. Beth's frame was swallowed by the intense ki. That had to be enough. It was everything she had.

Her attack faded away, and Alina stumbled forward, completely exhausted. Mako took her wrist. She looked at him feebly. The blast had singed Beth's armor and burned holes in her black jacket. "That's enough," Mako said in Beth's lovely voice. "You don't have to fight anymore."

Mako twisted her arm and sent a strange sensation through her body. Something in Alina's pocket burned her skin. She collapsed onto her knees and reached for whatever it was that ailed her. "I thought your face might be difficult to take," Mako announced, "so I made a contingency plan. Echo recommended it." Alina pulled out the orange suwanne gem, the memento given to her by the mask salesman. It glowed brightly and liquified in her palm. The fluid spread down her elbow and over her armor.

Alina's vision became distorted and mottled.

Beth stared down at her. "Rest now," she whispered.

☀☼ *XVI* ☆☽

A beetle floated in the pond and fluttered its wings frantically, trying to free itself from the water. Ike stopped his nervous pacing and knelt down to scoop up the bug. He blew softly on the beetle's wings to dry them. After a few moments, the insect took flight and zipped among the trees.

The sun crept toward the horizon and left the forest in a deep auburn glow. Ike returned to wandering impatiently around the edge of Kokoro Pond. He couldn't wait any longer. Alina was wrong about him being useless. Still, the Great Spirit entrusted him with delivering the Power of the Storm dangling at his waist. If he ran to Alina and the Face Stealer was there, Ike would be putting their one hope in jeopardy.

"Screw it," Ike muttered to himself.

He picked a spot near the left side of the pond, in front of a huge crystal. Dropping to the dirt, Ike dug a foot-deep hole and stuck the wooden flask into it. Alina hadn't been gone long, but there was a sinking feeling in his stomach. The forest air felt dry and foreboding. Ike stood to kick dirt and leaves over the hole. After the Power of the Storm appeared well hidden, he took off toward his childhood home. He'd scope the scene, determine the danger, and then run to town on the road if Alina was threatened.

Ike's feet pounded against the dirt path he had taken countless times as a child. Within a minute, the back of his old house would be in clear view. Maybe all would be well. Alina would be sitting in the living room with his mother, dinner roasting in the kitchen's wood oven. This could all just be one long nightmare. Perhaps he hadn't woken up at all this morning. He found it harder to lie to himself as smoke piled higher into the sky.

Pausing at the tree line, Ike stood before a great fire swarming through his old home. Blue paint burned to flakes of ash while the second story buckled and collapsed. Ike walked out of the forest, unable to move his legs any faster. Black smoke clung to the grass at his feet and rolled through the pasture toward the front lawn. His heart racing, Ike rounded the blazing fire, searching for signs of life.

As he came around the roaring flames, Ike saw the back of a hooded figure standing on the front lawn. Alina laid awkwardly at his feet, a strange orange glow consuming her body. Her gaze caught his. Tears rushed down her face, and she called out to him weakly, "Ike…"

Without hesitation, Ike sprinted toward her. There was a flash of orange light that seemed to draw the black smoke to Alina. When the glimmering light receded, Ike stumbled to a halt. He couldn't grasp what was before him. Where Alina had rested, hovering over the grass, was an orange gemstone larger than his own body. Firelight reflected off its crystalline surface and made it difficult to see clearly.

The hooded man placed a trembling palm on the gemstone. A yellow nymph flew out from his black robe and hovered near his shoulder. Trembling, Ike walked toward the enormous gem. He saw the truth within a single step, yet he continued onward, hoping his eyes were deceiving him. Encased within the gemstone was Alina, her thick cords of hair flowing about her body. Both of her eyes were closed, and her armor had been replaced by a rolling, white dress. She appeared to be in a deep sleep, both hands held over her stomach as if offering a cup to drink from. There, between her fingers, was a flower bud.

Almost within ten feet of the man, Ike stopped again. Staring at his back left him with a crippling despair. As if the figure sensed him, he turned his head. Ike fell back on the grass. He looked onto the face of his nightmares — a black mask with gaping, horrifying round eyes. "There you are, little Ike," Mako the Face Stealer chuckled insidiously. The tiny yellow irises of his mask seemed to fix on him.

"Wha—" Ike couldn't speak. He crawled back on his hands, and Mako took sulking steps forward.

Mako the Face Stealer wore nothing save a tattered dark robe and a cloth around his waist. His skin was tanned and marked sporadically by deep red gashes. The man's build seemed thin, almost skeletal, yet he presented defined, vein-filled muscles from underneath the robe. As he got nearer, Ike could perceive the detailing of a faintly carved grin on the ghastly mask.

Heat from the burning house kissed Ike's neck. "What have you done?" he murmured.

"I've made her mine," Mako said and slouched his shoulders forward. "She'll be well kept in there until I'm able to take her face…a year, maybe." Both arms swung side to side. "*Ahh*," he sighed like a toddler on the verge of sleep. "It's been such a long and boring day. I've had to play so many parts. It's nice to feel my *own* skin…" Mako traced a scar with his grimy fingernail. "…even if it's repulsive."

Ike sprung up to his feet and unsheathed his sword. The steel blade glistened red from the fire's glow.

"*AHAHA!*" Mako laughed madly from behind the round mask. "Echo, did you see that?" The nymph hovered up and down, the motion of a nod. "I'd have ripped your guts out if I wasn't so curious." He flicked a finger, and the fire at Ike's back hurtled upward into the air. Ike's old home was freed from the flames, yet only a heap of charred wood remained in its place.

Staring into the sky, Ike watched as the vast fire Mako commanded took the form of a man's face. It had sharp, rat-like teeth that smiled wildly. When Mako lowered his finger, the face of fire dropped just above Ike. Sweat raced down his chest. "What. Did. She. Tell. You?" Mako questioned him in a playful but menacing tone.

"Who?" Ike whispered.

"The Spirit!" Mako screeched, and the flaming face erupted into hot, black fire.

Letting go of his fear, Ike said quickly, "Show me my mother."

Mako tilted his head. The black mask grinned fervently.

"Release Alina," Ike continued. "Do that, and I'll tell you."

"Liar!" Mako screamed. He flicked his wrist and smashed the black fire into the grass right beside Ike. It cracked the earth and sent dark flames exploding skyward. "Liar, liar, liar! Ugh! This is so boring! You want to see your mother? Fine."

The minuscule pupils within the mask's eyes flashed yellow. Ike's surroundings were consumed by darkness. Red water suddenly appeared underneath his hands and feet. Murky, yellow clouds rolled through the dark air.

A woman lay on her side before Ike. Leaving his sword in the water, Ike crawled toward her. He pushed away brown hair and turned her chin to face him. "No..." Ike moaned. "No..."

It was his mother's body. She wore her white blouse and trousers. Brunette hair rolled down past the shoulders. But her face was gone. Ike stared at where her gray eyes should have been. Every time he tried to focus his gaze, a kind of static prevented him from perceiving anything except a beige blur.

Tears fell from Ike's wide stare. He took his mother's hand and gripped it hard. She felt cold. Around her neck hung a silver pendant of the numeral X. Ike removed it from her carefully.

"I always despised you," Beth's voice said from behind. Ike whirled around and saw his mom twirling his broadsword. "You're talentless, weak, a disgrace to my heritage." She threw the sword at Ike's head.

He hurled himself to the side. The environment had shifted once again. Now he knelt next to Kokoro Pond.

Methodically, he placed the silver pendant in his pocket, as if the careful movement would keep time from progressing. His sword was stuck in a tree to the right of his head. Standing up, Ike pulled the blade free and readied himself in a stance.

Mako had killed her. He'd killed Ike's mother and taken her face. Darkness was beginning to fall over Somerset. No creature stirred within the trees. No sound broke the palpable silence blanketing the pond. His heart racing, Ike spun in a circle and searched for the Face Stealer. He was nowhere to be found.

Ike focused through his rage. If he kept Mako busy until the prophecy was fulfilled and the Deathrid returned, then the Spirit and his island could be saved. He was tempted to glance to where the flask was buried, but Ike resisted. Somewhere within the trees, Mako was watching.

"Come out!" Ike screamed. Birds scattered into the air. His grip on the sword was weak and shaky.

"*Hehe,*" Mako giggled against the back of his neck.

Spinning on his toes, Ike slashed at the masked man. He sidestepped to dodge and then ducked to avoid his next attack. Ike clenched both hands on the broadsword and lashed out wildly. Mako averted strike after strike with ease. A few times, Ike swore that his blade passed right through him. Mako was moved back by Ike's barrage, and he leaped over Ike to prevent himself slamming against a tree. Screaming with a desperate fury, Ike sliced through a chunk of thick bark with his sword.

His enemy behind him again, Ike turned quickly. Mako floated in the air and leaned back as if he were lounging.

"You know, I'm actually impressed, little Ike," he said, tapping his feet together. "Your form is refined. It's your will that's lackluster. None of those attacks would have been fatal. Don't you want to murder me?"

"Shut up!" Ike screamed. "You killed her!" His voice cracked and ached in his throat.

"Yeah," Mako admitted casually. A white-skinned mask appeared in his hand, one with fierce gray eyes. "But she isn't gone. I have her right here. Every memory and thought. Did you know that she wished you were dead?"

"Enough—"

"She'd bathe you and come close to drowning your fat, pathetic body in the tub."

"Stop." Ike's teeth ground so violently his entire jaw ached.

"The outsider...Not a ki-wielder...Not a warrior...An embarrassment to both parents who resented you." Mako laughed and rocked in the air. "Did you know that Alina believed me to be your mother and told me *everything* you said to her?"

Ike's entire face burned red. His legs felt heavy and useless.

"We both laughed! That was after Alina almost vomited, of course. Did you really think a Starchild could feel something for *you*? And she lived in your house, c'mon, little Ike! Did you ever consider going outside the family? Well, I guess no one else would even talk to you—"

"Stop it!" Ike bellowed. He hadn't blinked in so long, and tears began to leak from his dry eyes. "You've taken everything."

"Not yet," Mako chuckled. Dropping to the ground, he skulked toward Ike. "I will give you another chance to tell me what the Spirit told you." Ike slid his feet back in the dirt. All traces of light had nearly faded from the forest. "If you are honest with me, I will spare your life and give you passage from this wretched place. You can go anywhere, be anything, I don't care." The black mask peered at him from within arm's reach.

"But if you refuse my kindness, I will tear the answers out of you," Mako said and froze in front of him like a doll gone limp. "I could take your face and taste every memory you have…" Suddenly, Ike was thrust against a tree by the Face Stealer. Drool dripped from underneath Mako's mask as he clutched Ike's jaw tightly. "But who would want this mug? Honestly, Ike, I'd rather die than be in your skin. Ugh, it gives me shivers imagining that."

With buckling knees, Ike swung his sword at the black mask.

Mako the Face Stealer sunk beneath the earth and popped up ten feet away. "I was hoping you'd make this fun," he snickered. A long black blade slid out from his sleeve. It was slender and carefully polished. Black smoke leaked from the dark metal as Mako crept toward him. Ike watched intently and prepared himself to defend.

In a flash, Mako slid across the dirt and shoved Ike in the chest. He sailed backward and felt the world shift around him. Ike landed headfirst on a jagged stone. With his vision blurred and his head aching, Ike struggled to perceive where Mako had taken him. There was a white, shabby hut built atop a large tree. Shrieks of animals reverberated off his eardrums. Still reeling, Ike blinked hard and focused his eyes.

Blood flowed down the grassy hill in a thick, crimson stream. Ike got up and stumbled toward the demolished fence that once secured his pasture. Every sheep lay slaughtered, all forty-three. Wild tears in their flesh left gaping wounds that stained their wool red. One sheep's dead gaze seemed to cry out for him. "Peeko..." Ike whispered somberly.

He clutched the sword in his hand, and it felt unusually light. Suddenly the blade burst with black smoke and crumbled to dust.

Mako spoke on the wind, like a sinister spirit. "What else needs to die for you to loosen your lips?"

A hand took hold of his ankle. Ike looked down to see that a grimy, scarred arm had emerged from the dirt. It pulled Ike down into the soil and then yanked him back upward.

When his body sprung forth, Ike found himself hanging upside down. A thick, black rope bound his legs together and dangled him from a tree. The crystals of Kokoro Pond jetted out from the sky. Ike saw Mako near them. He was hunched over, the black robe thrown off, and he wiped blood from his blade with a bare hand.

Pressure mounting in his skull, Ike stared at the streaks of scars tearing across Mako's back. The sight made him remember a boy he once met on his father's ship. He wore a clay mask with a red grin. A knight had led the prisoner by a tight leash. "I know you..." Ike mumbled.

One gaping eye turned to see him.

"I'm sorry," Ike groaned weakly. "I'm sorry for what they did to you."

"I bet you are," Mako said as he floated toward him. The black blade came close to Ike's neck. "It was my time on your father's ship that taught me how to play a part. I hold no resentment—well, that's a lie. I am going to slaughter the Knights like I did your sheep, but I will do the same to the people of the Great Sands as well. I'll grow my collection of faces until it's completed. And everything I feel is unworthy of that collection…will be torn apart."

"What's the point of this?" Ike said to the black mask. "You don't have the right to wear my mother's face. You don't have the right to take Alina and whatever you want."

"*Haha!*" Mako laughed. "But I do. Power is all that matters in this world, Ike. That's a lesson you have always been too naïve to accept. Before Dawn, before the Old World, all ki belonged to one source…the God above all others, El. I will take it all back, every trace of ki from every man, woman, child, and the spirits. When I'm done, I will be greater than any god, even the Deathrid, and I'll shape this world to be whatever I want…Whatever I think is fun."

The tip of the dark blade poked Ike's hip. A flood of intolerable pain tore through Ike's body. He screamed a horrifying, raucous cry, a sound he never thought himself capable of.

"This sword was jinxed by my tribe," Mako giggled excitedly. "What you're feeling is the curse pouring into your nerve fibers. It's overloading the pain sensors in your brain beyond their capacity. If I delve the blade deeper…"

The metal scraped against Ike's bone. What followed was a mind-numbing agony that ripped into every shred of bone and muscle within him. A continuous howl bellowed from Ike's gut.

"...the effect is more severe," Mako laughed so giddily that the sword trembled inside Ike's flesh.

A ball of yellow light zipped up to Mako and bashed against his mask. He shook his head in surprise and yelled, "What? This is where you draw the line, Echo? I'm just having some fun like we always do."

The nymph bounced fiercely in the air, and Mako's mask followed the movements as if understanding the meaning.

"Whatever!" Mako shrieked. "I don't need you anymore. The Great Spirit's face is in my grasp." He slapped the speck of light with his free hand and sent it hurtling out of sight.

Mako yanked the black blade from Ike's hip, prompting another screech of pure anguish. "Okay, last chance, Ike," he sighed.

Ike dropped onto the ground, the rope disappearing from his feet. He scrambled to his knees and glanced up. Two bulging, round eyes stared at him mercilessly. Mako held the tip of his sword against Ike's collarbone. Shivers of pain coursed through him.

"What did the Great Spirit ask you to do?" His voice became frantic and yet oddly focused. "Tell me, and the pain will go far away."

Agony was all Ike could feel. Not able to move, he suffered stab after stab into the same open wound. Mako giggled and cut tiny lines across his ribs over and over again. Ike couldn't make sense of time or how long he'd been tortured. Soon he could not remember why he cowered in the mud at all. And why did he need to keep a secret? He would say anything to make this pain stop. Yes, all he had to do was give him the wooden flask. It could be over.

A massive, orange gemstone rose from the mud behind Mako. Alina glimmered inside of it. Ike remembered his purpose. He clenched his teeth and fought off a quivering lip.

"While we wait for your statement, little Ike," Mako teased, "why don't I give the people of Somerset something to *really* celebrate this Spirit Festival?"

Faces shot out from the earth all around them. Masks of varying sizes and colors danced in the air and zipped through the trees.

"What—" Ike coughed out. He couldn't force words through his throat. It was too hoarse from screaming.

"You think I've taken all you have, but really I've been very generous so far," Mako said coolly. "Every person on this island is next to be killed, far more gruesomely than your stupid sheep. Then, I'll hunt down those young little Knights you're fond of and pluck their eyeballs out. After that, your sister and I will have a lovely evening together, if she's still alive, that is."

The blade sunk beneath Ike's skin, just under his collar bone. Too weary to shriek, Ike spat drool and trembled all over. Something thicker than sweat trickled down his brow and chest. Drops of it landed on his balled fists. Glancing at the fluid, Ike realized he was sweating blood.

"Time to talk," Mako stated. Every mask froze for a moment, and then they all soared southwest through the forest, the direction of town.

Ike stared into the black mask's dreadful eyes and wrapped a hand around the blade in his chest. The edge sliced his skin and shook his entire being with pain. He didn't care. "You'll," Ike mumbled. "You'll kill them all anyway." Placing his other hand around the sword, Ike wrenched the blade from his flesh.

Blood splattered onto the mud. Ike thundered his voice, as much as his broken larynx would allow. *"Nothing!* I'll give you *nothing."*

"This just got boring," Mako yawned.

An invisible force constricted Ike's arms and legs tightly. His aching body rose from the ground and hovered above Mako.

"All of this was just to let off some steam," Mako sighed and stretched toward the black sky. Night had completely fallen. Wasn't the prophecy supposed to have begun? Where was the mighty Deathrid the Spirit put so much trust in? "When I take the Spirit's face," Mako went on, "I'll know everything she's ever said. Sorry to have overblown your importance, little Ike. I couldn't resist playing with you."

It had become difficult for Ike to remain conscious. His eyes flickered open and shut. The spot where he had buried the Power of the Storm was in clear view. Any moment now, the Deathrid would appear in a marvelous display, like Lotis had said that morning. The spectacle would be extraordinary, yet Ike knew such things were possible. Powerful, immortal beings destined to reclaim their world. That was what the Great Spirit put her faith in.

"I'm going to slam my fist against your chest with an excessive amount of force," Mako told him. "Your bones will cave, and your heart will enter into an irregular rhythm. Within sixty seconds, your heart will stop entirely."

Ike's head fell limp. He heard Mako's words, yet his mind couldn't hold onto their meaning.

"Hey!" Mako snapped his fingers to keep Ike's attention. "I'm going to kill you now."

The Face Stealer jabbed a fist into Ike's chest cavity. Bones crumbled, and a horrific vibration surged through his heart. He fell back onto the ground. Mako grabbed his collar and dragged Ike to the shallow end of Kokoro Pond. Snickering as he did it, Mako tossed Ike into the pool.

He landed with a splat, face down in the low water. His ears above the surface, Ike heard Mako's final words to him as he drifted into the forest, "Alina and I won't be missing you. Goodbye, Ike."

Blood slowed to a crawl within Ike's veins as the seizing jolts of his heartbeat spread further and further apart. Desperately, Ike pressed against the mud to turn his body. *Please, my God*, he prayed, *I want to die looking at the stars.*

Moaning with the effort, Ike flopped over and settled his eyes on the sprawling constellations. No one had come to save him. The Great Spirit was wrong. The prophecy had not come to be. He shot his eyes in all directions he could manage. Mako had taken Alina into the forest. She was gone.

Pain gripped Ike's chest and left a pervading numbness in its wake. The growing absence of his heartbeat left the inverse of an echo in the air.

Shadows webbed across Ike's vision. The Face Stealer held Alina in his clutches. A single throb of his pulse kept both eyes open. His mother was dead, her ki part of Mako's fury. Ike contracted his lungs to draw in a whisper of air. The

Spirit's power would be taken next, and his island would be buried beneath the waves.

Darkness was all Ike could see. His eyes had fallen shut.

He couldn't give up. This wasn't all he could be. *Don't give up.*

Silence stretched throughout Ike's body and left him void of feeling, sight, or sound.

Quietly, it ended.

Ike Ryder died.

Dawn Crusade

Part 4

Mortem

(☆ I ☆)

Ike fell through endless black sky. He plummeted deeper until the sensation overwhelmed his being.

Somewhere high above, Ike could see something bright and pure shining down on him. He had seen this door in dreams and felt its offering of rest.

No. He wouldn't rest, not ever.

The doorway faded and left him alone.

An eternity had passed since then. On and on, Ike fell. Nothing.

He was nothing, not even a thought.

Crash. Ike sunk into dark water until he came against a rock. Slowly the ground beneath him began to rise toward the surface. When it emerged, Ike found himself on a circular stone platform about fifty feet in diameter. Water poured off the sides as the large pedestal settled just above the sea.

There was only darkness for a long moment. Ike held himself and shivered. Then a white light rose from the ocean and then another. Soon a multitude of lights shot from the black sea and raced into the sky above. Ike watched them take their places, forming patterns and clusters. When the spectacle ended, a veil of bright, incandescent stars stretched across the void. Their illumination revealed another platform in the water.

Across the sea, what looked like miles away, laid the other pedestal. It looked larger than the one Ike stood upon, perhaps twice the size. In the very center stood a colossal golden tree. Fruits clung to its branches and began to glow a similar color.

Straining his eyes, Ike spotted three other platforms much like his own surrounding the larger one. He imagined lines connecting the smaller pedestals. The shape would have resembled a diamond.

Under the starlight, Ike struggled to perceive much detail. Still, he could faintly see figures standing on the bordering platforms.

Slowly, a fruit resembling an orb of magnificent golden energy rose from the tree. As it ascended, the sphere expanded in size until it was larger than the slab of stone underneath it.

The orb broke apart into four pieces. Each fragment became a different color: red, orange, green, and blue.

Humming with power, the pieces floated toward the bordering platforms. Ike marveled as the blue sphere eclipsed the stary sky above him. Just as it settled overhead, the orb began to compress itself. It imploded and condensed until the sphere was only the size of a fist. That did not make it less frightening. The orb descended toward Ike, pulsing with an incredible intensity. Flashes of fire and electricity sparked off the surface. It came to a halt close enough that Ike could reach it if he stretched out his arm.

Ike looked deep into the orb of pure energy. Staring into it felt like delving into an infinite, relentless storm. Gradually, an understanding took hold of him. This was ki, the energy inside all living things. It beckoned him to take the power for his own with a seductive, vigorous magnetism. Yet, Ike thought that he should resist the energy's pull. Reaching out for it felt depraved, unnatural.

Live. The word passed through Ike's mind as he contemplated the blue orb. *Live*.

He needed to return to Dawn. Whatever the cost.

With a trembling hand, Ike reached up. But something caught his wrist. Swiveling his neck, Ike saw a shadow of himself clutching his arm. Black smoke oozed off its body, and two murky yellow mad eyes gazed into his.

As Ike tried to shake off the creature's grip, two more hands came around his thigh. Another hand took hold of his left arm and then his shoulder. Shadows were rising from the stone underneath Ike and digging their misshapen fingernails into his body. He couldn't tell how many had taken hold of him. Dark faces were all around. They grinned feverish, savage smiles, reminding him of a dark mask he had once seen.

The shadows began to sink back into the stone beneath them. Their hold on Ike tightened as they attempted to drag him down. Screaming as he did it, Ike fought against the shadows' strength. He lashed out his limbs and pushed on his heels to keep from descending. His defiance was futile. Glancing down, Ike saw that the ground had become infested with clouds of darkness. Gradually, the shadows were pulling him into the black abyss. Fingers came around Ike's face and pulled his head back. He felt his shins pass into the dark void.

Images floated by Ike's vision:

Alina. His mother. Nathan, Flynn, Bridget, Katya. Somerset.

He wouldn't surrender. This couldn't be all he was. He hadn't given all of himself, not yet.

A shadowy figure rose close to Ike's nose. It hung out a distorted tongue and smiled. Ike smashed his head into the shadow's skull. The creature fell backward, and Ike disrupted the shadows enough to wrench his left arm free. Swinging wildly, he sent his fist barreling into a shadow on his right. He clambered over the dark figures and reached for the blue orb.

What felt like hundreds of hands came around his body. They pulled on him with all their strength. Ike's finger nearly touched the sphere. He shouted frantically and threw his shoulder forward.

Ike's hand clasped the blue orb, and it burst into a current of raw, pure energy. The power flowed into his palm and tore through his bloodstream. It felt savage and untamable. Every shadow surrounding him shattered into plumes of blue fire along with the darkness at his feet.

Liberated from the prying hands, Ike crumbled to his knees and felt every vein within him become overwhelmed with the raw, bewildering energy. A symbol had appeared on his hand in glowing blue light, a circle with a dot in the center. The platform beneath him sparked with a similar glow, and Ike saw the same symbol imprint itself on the stone.

Every emotion Ike had ever felt bubbled to the surface and evaporated from his mind like the passing of steam.

The worthlessness, isolation, and shame. All Ike Ryder was burned away as the fierce current of power took hold of him.

He knew what he was becoming. The forest's story returned to him: *And it was there the last gift was hidden. Beyond the veil of death…*

Five holes opened on the edge of his stone platform, all an equal distance apart. Something told him they needed to be filled. His power was not complete.

The blue energy pooled into Ike's heart and settled there. Methodically, he rose and clutched his right fist, the symbol shimmering up at him. Ike glanced upward and felt himself ascend toward the stars.

Three other figures rose with him in shrouds of orange, green, and red light. They sped past the shroud of constellations, death conquered and defeated.

(☆ *II* ☆)

Life rushed into Ike's lungs, and his eyes burst open to the night sky. Colors warped into formation from a dry blur. Cracks of air snarled into his throat as Ike felt blood slip into the veins of his toes. Nerves panicked throughout his back and sent his muscles into frenzied, incoherent tension.

I died.

Ike's eyes watched wind twist between the branches of the many trees above. Cold moonlight felt almost tangible against his skin.

I died.

The thought repeated against the thudding of Ike's frantic heart.

I died.

He rose from the water and saw a strange symbol glowing on his right hand. Feeling weak, Ike stumbled out of the pond before falling against one of the large crystals on the right side.

There he saw his reflection. The color gray pooled into both brown irises, like rain flooding soil. The gray streaks in his hair were overcome with tinges of blond. Spreading open his gi, Ike witnessed the wound under his collarbone snap shut, a blue energy illuminating the nearby veins. The face he looked upon was familiar yet entirely new. Blood and grime coated his entire body from the battle with Mako.

As the blue light faded from his blood vessels, the mark on his hand dimmed as well. In its place was a black tattoo of a circle with a dot in the circle.

What happened to him? The last thing Ike remembered was falling into a terrifyingly abysmal sleep. Everything faded away. And then there was darkness and a blinding blue light. That was it; the light had changed him, rearranged his insides. He had never felt so strong, so incredibly capable.

Ike focused himself and felt something incredible within his body. If he glanced at his reflection just the right way, Ike could almost see a current of energy flowing up and down. It climbed to the tip of his head and then raced down to his toes. There were seven pools along the way where the power settled, seven chakras. This was what Ike had spent his entire life training to understand: the energy of life, ki.

He recalled meditating in the keep's courtyard and chanting mantras, *Ra-Chi-Ro*. The memory of his father willing sunlight to beam off his fingertips followed. And then, the sight of his mother calling down lightning from above.

Lightning. Ike glanced behind him to where the Power of the Storm was buried. As soon as his eyes met the spot, a surge of electricity leaped from the ground and shot into the sky. It flashed in the clouds for just a moment before plunging back down and striking Ike in the sternum.

In his mind's eye, Ike saw a large stone platform with five holes on the perimeter. A crystalline pillar fell from the sky and crashed into one of the pits. Lightning raced through the pillar, and the symbol engraved on the platform's surface flashed blue.

Accept this knowledge…The First Power of the Storm, Lightning. The words came to Ike in his own voice. *It will fall with your command.*

Thunder crackled in the night as Ike felt the lightning mingle with the current of ki inside him. The static spoke to him and passed on understanding. Ike knew that the lightning would fall whenever he demanded. He realized how his ki could focus the storm like an anchor. It was his power to wield as his mother had before him. But his mother and her people only knew a shadow of this power's potential. Ike had drunk the storm in, made it part of his mind, body, and soul. The Great Spirit's quest was completed. Ike had delivered the Power of the Storm to its wielder.

Electricity jolted from Ike's skin and raced down his gi. Unable to suppress the energy inside himself, Ike thrust his fist forward into the crystal. Massive cracks exploded across the glassy surface. Seeing a dozen broken reflections of himself, Ike let his fury ignite a rush of adrenaline in his body. *Mako…Mako…* The name forced his expression into a snarl.

Ike departed from the crystal and walked into the forest. His steps grew faster and stronger. Dirt puffed out from the ground as he sprinted ahead with newfound speed. There were a thousand questions plaguing his mind. Who and what he was felt like an utter mystery. Was he still Ike Ryder? Or had he become the horrific legend feared by all? None of that mattered. Mako would taste his rage. Ike would unleash everything within himself, every shred of power. He'd come to know his strength, the might of a Deathrid.

❨☆ *III* ☆❩

Captain Katya stood upon the watchtower of Somerset, a telescope in hand. She scanned the horizon for any sign of activity. It had been hours since the first wave of ships set out for battle. Asim should have sent word by now. The Serpent's Edge was not far from Somerset's shore. As she thought this, her vision passed by a glimmer of fire.

"*Craw,*" a bird squawked on the ledge near her. The creature resembled a crow made of shadow and held a crumpled paper in its beak. Katya recognized the bird as Asim's Totem Animal and snatched the paper. As she did so, the crow dissipated to a shadowy mist.

Igniting a small flame in her hand to read the parchment, Katya stared down at a single sentence:

We've lost.

The paper burned to ash as Katya tightened her grip. There weren't enough ships to evacuate. Civilians would have to shelter, and the Knights would fight. Katya, Bethany Tempest, Julian, and his subordinates were the only ki-wielders left. How long would they last? Beth Tempest alone could sink twenty ships. With her, at least there was a chance.

She prepared herself to call the Squires below and ready the announcement, but something distracted her. A mask of a coyote's face bopped by in the air and circled down to the street below. Katya surveyed the town from atop the tower. Dozens of masks floated toward the town square and the bustling market street. They bounced on the wind in a kind of playful dance. Something about their intent felt strange, almost sinister. What was going on?

(☆ *IV* ☆)

Hanali finished the last stroke of paint on a little girl's chin. She handed the child a small mirror so she could inspect the work.

"I'm a tiger!" the girl shouted and jumped from the chair.

"*Rawr!*" Hanali said humorously and tickled her ribs. The girl giggled as her father slapped a gold piece into Hanali's hand. "I appreciate this, sir," she told him and crammed the gold into an already overflowing jar sitting on the wooden stall's shelf. "Who's next?" Hanali asked the winding line of children.

"Me! Me!" the kids chanted. By now, Hanali's line was over twice the size of Yuma's. Her employer had shot a few jealous glances but seemed pleased overall with the heavy foot traffic. She even gave Hanali a belt to use that had slots for three brushes and six small containers of paint.

Somerset's Spirit Festival had only intensified as the night went on. Musicians meandered through the packed market street and performed compositions ostensibly known by everyone. People sang in a native language Hanali didn't recognize. They danced together, cheered, and kissed under the bright stars.

None of that interested Hanali. She had been carefully observing the scarred man, her suspected Marauder spy. No one other than the woman with short, choppy hair had spoken to him since he came to this street. Hanali watched her return to him while she painted. The scarred man stepped away from his post against a rundown shop and took something from the woman into his hand. Was it a weapon? Maybe it was something to call their fleet.

Hanali had to act now. The light was dim, the street was crowded, and the music had grown deafeningly loud. "Take my next customer. I'll be right back," Hanali said to Yuma. She took her jar of money and marched toward the familiar stall of cooked meats.

The man with the bushy beard stared her down and said, "You again? I told you—"

Hanali spilled a small mound of gold onto the counter and snatched a skewer of lamb from the display. Then, while the cook was distracted, Hanali pocketed a small knife from his cutting board. Without a word, she turned and walked away.

Of course, that was after catching the expression of pure disbelief on the chef's face.

Hanali slipped into the crowd seamlessly. The scarred man split off from his female companion and meandered down the street. Floating through the swarm of islanders, Hanali caught up to the spy as he neared a fisherman's wares. She passed the jar of gold into a child's arms and did not bother observing his total confusion. Her hands needed to be free.

The bombardment of trumpets, cymbals, and delighted screams threatened to dull Hanali's focus. Nonetheless, she walked steadily. She held the lamb skewer with her teeth. Then, without hesitation, she tapped on the scarred man's shoulder.

As he turned, Hanali unveiled her knife from a pocket and stabbed into the man's torso in three quick successions. She cut through his stomach, liver, and lung. Before the spy could scream, the damage took away his strength to stand. Hanali lowered him down to sit on a barrel in front of the fishing wares. Swiftly she threw an empty sack over his bloodied shirt like a blanket. "You're—" the spy croaked so weakly only Hanali could hear. The moonlight made the scar over his brow less pronounced. No one noticed the killing, the festival's commotion veiling the assassination.

After the man fell back against the wooden stall's post, Hanali swapped the object in the spy's hand for her knife. She observed the prize, a glass container of shimmering red fluid... with a fuse trailing off the lid. The Marauders planned to bomb Somerset. How many explosives were already on the island? And how many did the Marauder fleet carry on their ships?

Hanali lit the fuse on a sparkling stick someone held close by and threw the bomb high in the air. She used the wind to take it up and away from the island of Somerset. *Boom!* Celebrants of the Spirit Festival gasped and cheered at the red explosion of light in the sky. That was a signal to the other spies. Wherever they were, the Marauders would know that they had been exposed. Now it was time to find Commander Julian or Captain Katya to inform them of the enemy plan. It didn't matter if Hanali was punished.

Looking at the moon, Hanali realized midnight would come soon. The Marauder fleet could be only a few hours away. She dropped her food and began pushing through the crowd. Where was her Templar?

Then a curious sight took Hanali's attention. She watched a procession of masks drift down from the sky. Islanders ceased their cheering and gawked at the bizarre sight. A mask of a crying clown fell into the hands of a woman next to Hanali.

"Who's giving out the masks?" the lady asked a man who had his arm around her waist.

"The street peddlers keep stepping up their tricks," he responded while covering his face with a bear mask.

One by one, masks dropped into islanders' hands. They put them to their faces and laughed with each other. A mask landed on Hanali's foot. She glanced at it and saw a white-skinned, smiling face with rosy cheeks. These had to be from the mask salesman, Hanali determined. How could he pull off such an elaborate showing?

The mask at her feet spoke to her: *Rest in me. Rest in me.*

A strong desire to wear the clay mask overcame Hanali; however, she needed to reach her commander. Pulling her gaze away from it, Hanali stepped over the mask.

Suddenly, a dreadful sound pierced Hanali's ears. The woman near her shrieked and clawed at the clown mask on her face. Its clay material sizzled against her cheeks, appearing to sear itself to her skin. Her body began to change. Dead skin flaked off her arms, and black smoke spilled from the mask's eyeholes. The man she was speaking to doubled over in pain, the bear mask scorching his flesh.

Music faded out with the twang of a broken string as cries of agony echoed down the street. The transformation was occurring to islanders in all directions. Masks latched onto their faces and burned with black smoke. Their skin became rotten and gray while they cowered in agony. Hanali spotted the little boy with shaggy red hair and a face painted to resemble an eagle across the road. The child's mother gripped his hand as a laughing mask consumed her face. Dropping her food, Hanali pushed through screaming masked faces and black smoke. She had to reach the boy.

"Mom?" the red-haired boy said warily. Hanali got close enough to hear him. She knocked a yelping man over and darted toward the child.

It was too late. His mother tackled him, and as he squealed, Hanali became surrounded by rough, dead flesh. The boy was lost. Murky yellow eyes locked onto her from behind the many masks.

She didn't have time to think. Hanali swung her arms out and unleashed a shockwave of wind. The masked islanders were blown back, but she had only drawn more attention to herself. A man with the face of a bear scrambled over Hanali's victims and held out something toward her. She stared into a smiling, rosy-cheeked mask. Punching forward, Hanali sent a gust into the man's chest. He flew backward, and more masked islanders swarmed toward Hanali. There were too many; it was a sea of masked faces. Summoning all her ki, Hanali jumped from the ground with a booming explosion of air.

Hanali sailed over the two-story shops of the market street and landed on a roof with an awkward tumble. Down below, masked islanders scaled the side of the building Hanali stood upon. She'd have to keep moving. Taking a running start, Hanali leaped onto the next roof. Inhabitants of Somerset were being rooted out by the cursed populace. Hanali watched as terrified islanders were torn by black fingernails until they stopped squirming. Then, a mask would be placed over the face. A horde of masked children toppled Hanali's face painting stall. She saw Yuma's hand reach out for salvation as tiny hands ripped her skin and placed a mask over her gaping mouth.

Hanali couldn't save anyone, not by herself. She wasn't great at sensing the ki of others, but two streets over, she felt a familiar presence. It came from the direction of Somerset Inn. Perhaps Commander Julian still rested in the hotel.

A red mask and grimy fingers poked over the roof Hanali sprinted across. Without breaking her stride, she smashed her foot into the hidden face and kept running. The cursed islanders trailed her from the ground and climbed up the buildings ahead of Hanali. How much longer could she outmaneuver them?

❰ ☆ V ☆ ❱

Julian's fingers felt numb and unsteady as he reached into the leather pouch. His skin scraped against the rough interior, finding nothing of value. "Are — are we out?" he asked the redheaded woman shivering under his bedsheets.

"Dresser," Rosemary moaned.

He rolled off the bed, completely nude, and stumbled into the dresser. There was a line of black powder near the candlestick. Not hesitating for a moment, Julian snorted the drug and felt the remainder of his consciousness slip behind a thick haze. His reflection stared at him in judgment. Two bloodshot eyes with massive pupils looked him up and down. "Shut up," he groaned. Fighting now was pointless. If the Marauders came, he'd defend his life as long as he desired. Everyone on Somerset would die eventually. At least he could meet his end while riding a wave of ecstasy.

The floor swung upward suddenly, and Julian lay against it. Drool flowed from his tongue onto the hardwood.

"Look," Rosemary said to him.

Rolling onto his back, Julian followed her finger to the slightly ajar window. Something floated inside their room, a frowning mask with two comically large tears sprouting from the eyeholes.

Rosemary sat up and let the mask hover into her grip. The grime that once smeared the blacksmith's body had been replaced by a heavy sweat. She had scars on her wrists and burns on most fingers. As she held the mask over her face, the bedsheets came loose from around her chest.

"It's cute," the blacksmith said from behind the mask.

"Off," Julian grumbled. "Take...off." He could sense something horrible coursing through the clay material on Rosemary's face. It reminded him of the mask salesman's nauseating laughter.

She screamed a kind of vicious holler, something an animal might produce while being slaughtered. Rosemary keeled over on the bed and spasmed uncontrollably. Her skin burned away, revealing gray, dead flesh underneath.

Julian could not will his body to move. Every part of him felt weary and disconnected. He managed to slide his heels against the floor. The cart full of weapons sat near the door. There was no way he could reach it.

Black smoke spilling from her eyes, Rosemary stood up on the bed. The sheets hung around her naked body and concealed it from view. She dropped onto the floor and drifted toward him. Her foot kicked a small chest in his direction; one Julian had nearly forgotten about.

The chest tumbled onto its side, partly open. As Rosemary kneeled down, Julian concentrated on his right arm. He instructed it to move toward the chest lying by his thigh. His thumb twitched, but nothing else followed Julian's command.

A burst of black smoke tore away Rosemary's flesh. She became a being of pure shadow, the frowning mask cracking on her face.

Move, Julian told himself. Rosemary slashed jagged, shadowy fingers against his chest. Blood gushed from the wound, and the jarring pain was enough to stir Julian's limbs awake. He stuck his hand in the strongbox, yanked its contents free, and pulled a silver trigger.

Betrayer, the Crimson Pistol, fired a line of red-hot energy. The thin ray blasted through the frowning mask and out the wall of Somerset Inn. Rosemary fell back limply, black smoke rising from the hole in her head.

Still disoriented and trembling, Julian got to his feet. He stood over the creature that was once Rosemary. Just before the frowning mask completely crumbled, her corpse evaporated into a black mist. This was a powerful and horrific curse. Some time ago, he'd read about such a thing, but his mind felt too dull to recall anything soundly.

Groans and sickening squeals echoed from the window. Not having time to mourn his lover, Julian staggered toward the cries and peeked onto the street. Hordes of masked islanders roamed the town. Some sprinted erratically in all directions, searching for living flesh. Others stumbled about seemingly without purpose, their heads hung low.

Julian pushed the window open a crack wider. A barely audible squeak from the window's hinge caused every monster below to turn their masked faces in his direction. Stumbling back, Julian was startled by a thud against his suite's door. Another crash made him jump. Animalistic yelps from the hallway mixed with the loud bangs. They were trying to knock his door down.

His body acted on its own volition. A force deep within Julian's gut compelled him to survive. He felt the panic and frenzy that fueled his life in the capital's slums. No more self-pity; he could not afford it. It was time to kill.

After pulling on his new combat pants, boots, and thin chainmail shirt, Julian dragged the weapon cart close to his bed. The door barely clung to its frame as he strapped a short sword to his waist, two daggers at his lower back, and five knives across his chest. He adjusted the leather belts circling his body and then threw on his Templar jacket. Tugging on the jacket's ends, Julian started the fabric's enchantment.

The jacket began to stitch itself together, repairing the many holes. Bloodstains, sweat, and dirt faded from the fabric as it changed shape to fit Julian's needs. He now wore a black hooded vest.

Shrieks from outside had gotten closer. A masked face poked through the window and gawked at him. Moving swiftly, Julian tossed a knife from the weapon cart at the cursed islander's skull. His form felt awkward and sloppy, yet it was enough to drop the man from the inn right as Julian's door was busted open. Four shadowy creatures crawled over each other.

Instinct drove Julian to grab Betrayer from the dresser and fire. Four shots pierced through the masks and dropped each creature to the floor. His fingers shook against the trigger, unable to suppress the drug creeping through Julian's veins.

Hands piled onto the windowpane. At least three of the monsters were throwing themselves into Julian's room. He fired at one of them before jumping over the broken door and into the hallway.

Lines of blood were splattered across the walls and floor. Two masked islanders held down a woman with short, choppy hair and readied a mask to place on her face. Julian unsheathed a dagger and jammed it into a gray, rotten neck. The other monster made a jump for him, but Julian fired a red beam from Betrayer in his other hand.

Shadow creatures ran around the corner toward them. Before the woman underneath him could scream, Julian grabbed her hand and yanked her along. They only made it a few steps before a masked creature hurled itself out of a suite. It tackled the woman and slashed shadowy, sharp fingers across her neck. Julian fired Betrayer and watched the creature tumble over. The woman's dark eyes stared upward, dead.

Something shimmered in the dead woman's hand. Julian backtracked towards the body and saw a glass container filled with glowing red liquid. He turned his head and looked into the suite just next to the body. Dozens of the bombs were laid out on the floor. A fuse was already lit and burned quickly toward a single container.

Julian sprinted down the hall and jumped up the stairs just as the explosion rocked his senses. Red fire surged all around him. Flames crept up from the wood beneath Julian's feet. Struggling to focus, he barely saw the masked faces crawling up the stairs, beating against one another to reach him first. Their bodies carried the flames and spread them like a cancer.

He couldn't descend; flames rose from the old steps. Masked islanders jumped up at him from down below. The fire burned away the decaying flesh of their cursed bodies and left them with shadowy, ominous forms as they darted up the stairs.

Julian rushed up the staircase and fired three more shots from Betrayer at the monsters tailing him. They fell back and toppled the crowd of shadows at their heels. It only slowed them for a moment, though. The cursed islanders rushed through the fire, unfazed by its scorching heat.

He'd die here. This island would be the death of him.

((☆ *VI* ☆))

Ike tore through the forest, his feet pounding against the grass path. Trees withered and shed black leaves all around him. The foliage was dying.

A multitude of multicolored dots swarmed from the direction of the Great Spirit's dwelling place. They soared by him in a fierce gust of wind that made him stumble for a few steps. After they passed, a single green speck of light trailed his shoulder. Lotis appeared from it and flew next to Ike as he sprinted onward.

"Lotis, where is he?" Ike demanded.

"Who are you?" she asked him cautiously.

"It's me," he responded, "Ike."

They neared the massive hollow tree housing the Spirit. Its leaves were darkening and floating to the ground. Ike slowed to a steady march.

"If you are Ike," Lotis said, unsure, "then you've really changed. Did you deliver my mother's Power of the Storm?"

"Yeah," Ike confirmed. "It's in me."

"Oh!" Lotis exclaimed as she examined the tattoo on his wrist. "I see. You're *him*."

The mouth of the Spirit's dwelling place was only a few steps away.

Lotis withdrew slightly from Ike. Her expression seemed serious and slightly frightened. "My mother has entrusted everything to you," she said.

Ike sighed. "What was she thinking?" he murmured more to himself than Lotis.

The nymph shimmered back into a dot of light and hid among the decaying trees. Ike stepped into the Spirit's lair. Above him, the many branches and trunks forming the massive tree unwound themselves and fell backward with a mighty crash. Now the Great Spirit's statue was visible in the harsh moonlight. Before it, a huge orange gemstone and a thin, scarred man lurked.

"Mako!" Ike shouted without thinking.

A black mask turned to face him. Mako removed a hand from the Spirit's statue. Ike saw something in his grip. He was too late. Clutched between Mako's fingers was a wooden mask, the Great Spirit's heavenly features apparent on its surface. Behind him, the statue's head looked smooth and void of any detail. Her face had been stolen.

Ike had already failed to save the island. The grass at his feet shriveled and turned dark. He felt a tremble, like the island itself had shaken.

"Who are you?" Mako inquired curiously.

Lightning sparked on Ike's knuckles. After everything Mako did, he didn't recognize him?

Mako took a single step forward and tilted his mask in observation. "No...No, you should be dead!" Mako shouted and glided across the dead grass toward him with impossible speed. He pressed his mask against Ike's nose while taking his right wrist. The gaping, round eyes of his mask fell onto the tattoo. "This is—"

Ike sent a fist into Mako's chest, throwing his entire weight into the strike. Sparks burst from Ike's punch, and Mako slid backward, dirt piling behind his heels. The masked man came to a stop just before the statue. "Ike Ryder is dead!" he screamed once again. "I killed him!"

Feeling the veins in his neck tighten, Ike said firmly, "If he is dead, then his will is alive in me!"

Mako bent his fingers like claws and readied himself to leap forward. Ike spread his feet wider and took a breath. He had no idea what he was capable of now. Still, he had spent his entire life training to be a warrior. The forms, stances, techniques—everything was in his head. Now was the time to use it.

Suddenly, Mako let his arms drop. A giggle fluttered out from behind his mask. It grew into a chuckle and then a high-pitched, hysterical laugh. "I didn't think I'd meet you so soon," Mako said through the crazed laughter, "*Deathrid.*"

A shiver raced down Ike's spine. He knew that was what he had become. But to hear the word out loud terrified him.

"I hoped to steal the Great Spirit's face before you all returned," Mako explained, "and I did." He waved the wooden mask above his head. "But if I knew you were taking the body of such a…pathetic creature, I wouldn't have put so much pressure on myself."

"Hm?" Ike mumbled. He had been staring at Alina's gemstone and became distracted. How was he going to free her? That was his mission here. Together they could overpower Mako.

"Wha—I said you're—Did you not hear me?"

"You talk too much," Ike explained, "and I'm done listening."

Mako laughed a single, raspy cry. "I guess dying gave you a sense of humor. Fine, I'll kill you a second time if you're so anxious for it." A puff of black smoke summoned a familiar dark blade to Mako's hand.

Right, Ike needed a sword. He had one hope for obtaining such a weapon. His mother's words returned to him: *Only a warrior with Storm Paladin blood is able to call upon its strength.* Ike held out his right hand. He called out in his thoughts for a sword he had admired what seemed like a lifetime ago. Just as he thought how ridiculous this gambit was, something strange occurred.

The white stone and blue stained glass of the Temple to El unfolded in Ike's mind. He saw the gray sword named Dreamblade shimmering above the altar. It twitched and shuddered. *Come to me*, Ike commanded again.

Dreamblade spun off the temple wall and flew through stained glass. Ike felt it tear through trees and the night air. The sword raced across Somerset's dying forest and found its place in Ike's hand. He clutched the black fabric binding its hilt and marveled at the gorgeous metal blade.

"Huh," Mako giggled while darting toward Ike. "That looks like a toothpick in your hand." The Face Stealer swung his sword at him from the side. Ike blocked with a single hand on Dreamblade, feeling his ki pump through every muscle. He kicked Mako in the chest, making him flip backward and land with a flourish.

His enemy had been right. This sword was too small for Ike to use. He needed it to be bigger, much bigger. In response to this thought, Dreamblade sparked with lightning and blue energy. The sword began to change shape, becoming massive in size. Ike clutched the hilt with two hands and observed his weapon become as large as his own body. It had a single edge, like an enormous butcher's knife, and the black fabric covering its grip dangled from the long hilt.

Dreamblade was now exceedingly heavy, yet Ike held it with ease. He charged Mako and slashed down with the mighty sword. Giggling as he did it, Mako parried with his weapon. Their blades remained locked, blue sparks and black smoke bursting from the tension between the swords.

"The Great Spirit's face is mine," Mako stated gleefully. "Your mother and Alina are mine. This island will soon drop into the sea. And then I'll take the face of every spirit and ki-wielder. What do you hope to accomplish here?"

Ike's arms trembled as he attempted to keep his blade steady. Pulling away Dreamblade, Ike prepared himself to unleash a flurry of strikes. He moved faster than he ever had before. Three times he brought Dreamblade hurtling toward Mako. His enemy ducked, blocked, and leaped into the air.

Floating above him, Mako put one leg over the other. "I really don't see much of a difference from before," he mocked Ike. The taunt was empty. Three red lines were cut open across his body. Ike had made contact with each strike.

Gritting his teeth, Ike focused on the clouds above them. He held up a hand, remembering how ferociously his mother held this pose and called on the storm. "Fall!" His arm swung toward Mako.

A bolt of lightning slammed into the Face Stealer and sent him crashing into the dirt. Electricity jolted from his scarred skin as he pushed himself up. Ike had seriously injured him, beyond what any ordinary ki-wielder could tolerate. And that seemed to make the Face Stealer shutter with fury. "That—" Mako muttered gaily, "that's better."

In a flash, Mako appeared at the side of Ike. He didn't feel his enemy's blade touch him, but then a burst of blood erupted from between Ike's ribs. Before he could react, Mako slammed an elbow into his eye. The cursed blade then cut across Ike's chest and shoulder. Dazed, Ike staggered backward and lowered Dreamblade. Mako took advantage of his dropped guard. He grabbed Ike's face and slammed him to the ground. Ike felt the earth beneath him crack from the impact of his own body.

"Do you see the disparity between us?" Mako said slyly, his grip tight on Ike's cheeks. "Deathrid or not, the body you possess is human and weak. It's insulting to me that you thought yourself my equal."

Every part of himself aching, Ike clutched a fist and commanded lightning to fall. Electricity ripped through Mako and flooded into Ike's gut. Instead of feeling pain, the lightning joined the flow of ki racing through Ike. He felt strengthened, rejuvenated even.

Twitching from the electrical current in his body, Mako jumped backward about twenty feet. Ike managed to get to his knees. "I understand now," Mako told him. He poked sharp fingers into a large burn on his shoulders. "Your dormant ki-wielder genes have awoken… thanks to the Deathrid's power. Lightning strengthens your cells just as sunlight strengthens your father. It's the perfect blend of your two clans."

Ike sucked in air. He picked up Dreamblade and drove it into the earth to help him stand.

"But let me tell you something, Deathrid," Mako said with his sword outstretched toward Ike. "I feel like I need to put this situation in perspective for you. If this entire island was the full extent of my capabilities, I have only been using this much of my strength." Mako reached down and plucked a single blade of dead grass. He held it out and locked both enormous, sinister eyes on Ike. "You won't ever win against me."

The ground beneath them shook. To the left of Ike, a chunk of earth crumbled and sunk. Ike looked into it and saw rock dropping through Somerset to the ocean below. Breathing shakily, Ike spoke to Mako. "Thank you for that."

Mako twitched his head to the side.

"But I don't remember saying I came here to beat you," Ike said frankly.

Ike focused on the clouds and sent a bolt of lightning for the gem imprisoning Alina. The electricity spread a thin crack across the surface.

The Face Stealer looked back at the gem and then to Ike. "Oh, that's been your play from the start!" he laughed.

Ignoring him, Ike darted toward the orange gemstone. He'd never be able to reach it; Mako was beginning to move. Raising Dreamblade over his head, Ike threw the massive sword at the gem with all his strength.

While Mako kicked Ike hard in the stomach, he watched his weapon spin in the air and collide with its target. The sword sparked against the gem and ricocheted off. A deep scratch had formed over Alina's cheek. She still slumbered peacefully within it.

Ike had been knocked down by Mako's kick. He rolled over and spat up blood. "You'd risk another life just to free her, huh?" Mako said coldly.

"We'll—" Ike groaned. "We'll stop you together... and take that mask." He got up much slower than before. The Face Stealer guarded the gem with his black blade outstretched toward Ike.

"I'm bored," Mako stated. He rushed to Ike faster than he could react. The cursed sword cut through Ike's gut, and the familiar intolerable pain returned. "Everything's just as before. You've lost." Mako teased. "Don't get up this time." He thrust the metal deeper until the cross-guard slammed into Ike's torso.

No, it was impossible. He couldn't die, not again. Ike grabbed Mako's shoulder to steady himself. *No.* The word thundered in his skull. *I have to live.* A beastly power surged free from Ike's heart. His tattoo lit up with blue light, and his veins throbbed with the immense energy.

Ike shoved a single hand into Mako and felt a shock of lightning throw his enemy backward. Mako caught himself in the air and hovered there, a ghastly scorch spreading across his upper body. "What," Mako muttered. "What have you become?"

Snarling, Ike pulled the cursed sword from his flesh and tossed it aside. The deep wound sealed itself with fresh skin.

Freeing Alina could wait. First, Ike would tear Mako apart. "Fall," Ike commanded.

Heaps of lightning bolts descended from the clouds. Mako dropped to the ground and pranced between them, managing to dodge any fatal strike. He reached Ike and unleashed an assault of kicks and punches. Ike saw every movement clearly. He blocked each attack with little concern, then threw his fist forward. An incredible blast of lightning boomed from Ike and shredded a massive hole through Mako's chest, bigger than the mask hiding his face. For a single moment, Ike swore he saw the flash of lightning take the shape of a fearsome wolf.

The Face Stealer fell backward with an undramatic thud. Within Ike, the strange power retreated to his heart. He took a few steps back before collapsing from exhaustion. His tattoo's glow faded. It was all over.

"I'm dying," Mako's voice called out feebly. Ike looked at him in disbelief. How could he speak? His lungs were blown to ash. "So, this is what you felt like." The Face Stealer sat up, the hole still in his chest. Golden light spread to the wound from Mako's hand, which rested on the Great Spirit's face. "I'll admit it. You won, Ike."

Mako loomed there, the black mask fading away from his face in a cloud of smoke. Now the mask of the Great Spirit hovered just before his skin. "You are the first to ever best me," he said, commending Ike. "Too bad I'm as immortal as you now." None of his features were visible behind the wooden guise. The Face Stealer placed the mask against his face. Ike watched bark spread down Mako's neck all the way to his toes. Golden light spilled from the Face Stealer's mouth and eyes as his body changed. When the light faded, Mako's eyes were black and filled with stars. He still looked masculine; his body was slightly bulkier than before. Bark filled the gruesome hole in his chest.

Mako drew a single breath, and fire bloomed atop his wooden head. Unlike the Great Spirit's rolling locks of flaming hair, Mako's flame stuck straight up like a hot knife. He levitated up from the dirt, admiring himself.

"Wow," Mako giggled, "this is great. I mean, this face is weaker than it should be since you took the Power of Lightning—"

Ike's eyes went wide. He knew.

"Don't give me that look, Deathrid. How else could you learn to control lightning so quickly?" Mako teased. "There's four other Powers of the Storm to claim, however. I'm furious with you, but I'm going to try to be patient. They'll all be mine in the end. I'd just like you to be a little more worthwhile before I take your ugly face."

The Face Stealer flicked his wrist. Trunks of wood sprouted from the earth and bound Ike. He screamed as he felt the restraints crushing bone. "Then again," Mako said quietly, "it is annoying to think that I'm going to let a Deathrid roam around in this pitiful body I killed."

Thorns jetted from the wood around Ike and cut deep into his skin. Where was that tremendous power from moments ago?

A beam of green light shot into Mako's face. His body flew back across the dead forest. As he soared out of sight, the bindings around Ike fell apart. He looked to where the blast had come from and saw Lotis flying down to his side.

She tapped his shoulder, sending a wave of warm energy into Ike. He felt his injuries partially heal and his will to fight return. "Hey," Lotis said with a sly smile.

"Thank you," Ike told her as he stood up tall.

"Thank the forest," Lotis stated with an eye on where Mako sailed off to. "It gave me this power with its dying breath…to protect you."

"He'll kill you if you stay."

"My life is tied to this place," Lotis said. She knit her brow and became abnormally stern. "When the island falls, so will my sisters and I."

"There has to be something we can still do—"

"Survive this night," Lotis cut him off. "Do not let Mako leave Somerset with my mother's face. Whatever the cost. This is what my mother burdened me with telling you, Deathrid."

"Ike," he said to her.

Lotis hesitated before nodding. "Ike," she affirmed.

A screech bellowed from the darkness. "Go away!" Mako cried while he zipped across the sky at Ike and Lotis. The green nymph held out her hands, and a dozen green dots of light appeared, dancing up her body. She sent them all racing toward Mako. He flew erratically in all directions to dodge them. Each light seemed as if it would reach him but instead exploded with emerald energy just out of range.

The Face Stealer landed with a crash before them and raised a hand at Lotis. She rose up and gripped her neck, an invisible force strangling her. "Stop!" Ike screamed. He ran toward Mako and threw a punch. Using his free hand, Mako slapped the attack away.

Not willing to surrender, Ike jabbed twice more. Mako deflected each blow with a growing disinterest and then flicked a finger at Ike's forehead. The Great Spirit's power was so immense that a single finger blew Ike backward like a leaf caught in a hurricane. He smashed into a tree and felt his vision blur. Ahead of him, Lotis struggled in the air.

"The power of the Great Spirit made you," Mako spat at Lotis, "and now it will *unmake* you." The green nymph's skin turned gray and thin. She shrieked in agony, her body beginning to change shape. Ike witnessed Lotis burst away in a frenzy of black smoke. In her place loomed a monstrous creature. A beastly muzzle and jagged teeth growled into the night. Made of dark shadow, the monster's body seemed to be a blend of animal and man. Nearly nine feet in height, it dropped onto the ground and stretched its bulging muscles.

Somerset shook once more, this time enough to almost topple Ike.

"Time to go," Mako announced. He wafted his hand, and Alina's gem came to his side.

"I hate you," Ike said weakly from against a broken tree. The Face Stealer had to search for him in the dark forest. When his black eyes found him, they narrowed. "You'll pay…I'll make you suffer…Whatever it takes. I'll break every mask you hide behind and shatter that gem apart."

The monster that was once Lotis took thundering steps toward Ike. "This thing I made will tear you to bits," Mako said as he and the gem passed by in the air. "And then you'll be buried with this sad island. If you survive all that, maybe I'll think about taking your face." Mako and Alina flew through the forest in the direction of town. As they passed into darkness, the monster in front of Ike howled a cry of bloodlust. Drool trickled from its long tongue.

Ike held out his right hand. Dreamblade spun into the air from the ruins of the Great Spirit's dwelling place. The sword glided into his grip, and Ike walked ahead to meet the beastly creature between the many dead trees of Somerset's forest. He wouldn't lose, not again. Nothing would stand in his way until Mako laid dead. The monster growled while rushing toward him. Ike slashed Dreamblade straight for the creature's skull.

(☆ *VII* ☆)

Sweat seeped from Julian's skin as he burst through the door onto the roof of Somerset Inn. A pack of masked islanders bolted through the raging fire at his heels. He spun around and fired Betrayer into the flaming doorway. Four monsters dropped dead with burning holes between the eyes of their masks. One managed to reach Julian, yet the Templar unsheathed a dagger and sliced through its neck. A shadowy head with long black hair toppled onto the roof.

Screams bellowed from down the stairs. Fire seemed to harm the creatures, but it was not enough to stop their pursuit. Exhausted and slowed by his drug-filled veins, Julian squatted down. His gaze remained fixed on the doorway, flames clawing out of it. How much longer before the building crumbled and sent him to his death?

Another masked islander crawled over the pile of corpses. This one's flesh had been burned away, leaving only a black shadow in its place. A cracked, blushing mask obscured the face. Without bothering to stand, Julian fired a beam from Betrayer into its head. Before the creature hit the floor, Julian's hand burned horribly. He dropped Betrayer and saw that its handle had gotten red hot. Sighing, Julian realized that the weapon had overheated. Carefully, he went over the number of shots he fired from Betrayer that night. Julian counted sixteen shots before a cooldown was needed.

Two masked men hurled themselves through the collapsing doorway. Just as Julian readied a knife to throw, a gale of wind tossed the enemies off the roof. Hanali touched down next to Julian on the sizzling wood. She didn't appear badly hurt but had scratches running up her legs and arms. "Seems you found the bombs, my Templar," Hanali said through dense breaths. "What's happened to this island?"

"A powerful curse," he told her. "Seems like the mask salesman had some special inventory." Warily, Julian touched the golden handle of his pistol and felt no heat. That was about ten seconds before it was ready to use again. He tucked the firearm in his belt.

"Strange weapon," Hanali remarked. When Julian did not respond, she went on to say, "There is a word in my tribe for creatures such as these, but we dare not speak it."

"Jiangshi," Julian said with vacant eyes, "they're called jiangshis by the Templars. They're what happens when a body continues on without a soul." His mind had cleared enough to remember the creatures' nature.

"Then they are already dead," Hanali confirmed. "They do not have any ki that I can sense."

"I thought Marauders would be killing me tonight," Julian said bleakly. "This is much worse."

"I do not plan on letting us die here," Hanali declared. She uncorked a tiny bottle of lilac paint on her belt. Julian eyed her, mostly disinterested. "This is a technique known only to my people," she told him while making brush strokes on the hot wood below them. "When I left my tribe, I was told to never use this unless I meant to kill all observers." She painted two wings under herself. "So don't look, Commander."

Julian put a hand under his chin and stared at her.

"It was a joke," Hanali said, flustered. She slammed a hand down on the painted wings and yelled out, "Soar, *uwohali!*"

Hundreds of lilac feathers bloomed from the paint and circled Hanali's body. They fused to her back and stretched out into large, beautiful wings.

Underneath them, the wood cracked open. Fire lashed up from the decaying building. Julian began to fall, but two hands took hold of his arms. Hanali's wings beat down with enough force to scatter the raging flames. Somerset Inn collapsed as she took flight with Julian in tow. Looking down, Julian saw dozens of jiangshis yelping underneath the burning wood.

"You're too heavy!" Hanali cried, her grip on Julian's arms slipping. From the street below, jiangshis took notice of their presence. They followed their path in frenzied, disjointed dashes.

"Just don't land anywhere too open!" Julian instructed. "We need a tight place to defend!"

"I can't—falling," Hanali grunted. Her wings went limp, and they descended to Somerset in an unsteady glide. Julian couldn't see where they were headed; a rushing wind blinded his eyes. They met stone pavement in a hard tumble. Quickly, Julian bounced to his feet and pulled Hanali up. Her wings dispersed to familiar lilac feathers and faded away.

"Where are we?" Hanali asked, visibly fatigued.

Julian turned in a circle. They stood in a large paved area with shops and other buildings in the distance. A fountain was just behind them, and in front stood a massive temple made of white stone. They had landed in the very center of the town square. What seemed like hundreds of jiangshis wandered the open space, masks clutching their decaying faces.

"This is the worst place we could have landed. Am I correct?" Hanali said.

Jiangshis darted in their direction from the street they had flown over. Julian pushed Hanali behind him. Other masked islanders responded to the cries of bloodlust and joined the growing flock of jiangshis in their pursuit. Within moments, every cursed creature in the town square swarmed toward Julian and Hanali's position. "I've got the right. You guard left," Julian said to Hanali. She nodded while painting what looked like tiny eagles all over the stone tiles and her arms. Her fingers moved with tremendous speed.

A jiangshi sprinted for her as she said, "Hunt, *uwohali.*" From the tile she just finished painting, an eagle made of lilac energy burst free and slammed through the chest of the shadowy creature by Hanali. He fell forward, and the glowing eagle pierced the hearts of three more jiangshis before bursting away.

Julian gawked at the spectacle for just a moment. He knew of Totem Animals and their power, but Hanali's eagle was the first he'd seen in action. A savage screech from a jiangshi diving for him forced Julian to refocus. In one movement, he freed his short sword and sliced clear through the crooked mask on the undead creature's face. With so many enemies advancing, Julian would need to conserve Betrayer's sixteen shots.

Unveiling his pistol, Julian fired five red beams into the sea of approaching jiangshis. Shadowy claws cut his left bicep. Acting on instinct, he slashed through the attacker's neck with the blade in his opposite hand.

Behind him, Hanali sent out three lilac eagles that tore through the rotten body of any jiangshi that got within five feet. She used gusts of wind from her fists to keep back the masked faces that broke through the defense. Julian almost smirked. His lieutenant was highly skilled.

In the heat of combat, a cursed woman made a jump for Hanali's throat. Julian caught the attempt in his peripheral vision and fired Betrayer behind his head. The jiangshi fell lifelessly, and Hanali unleashed two more eagles to replace the ones that just dissipated.

They couldn't keep this up much longer. There was no end to the enemies' forces. "Help!" Hanali screamed. Julian threw two knives at advancing jiangshis and shot a glance back. The jaws of a cursed man clenched the base of Hanali's neck. His snake mask was broken halfway down, revealing sharp, black teeth that dug into Hanali's skin.

Betrayer blew the head off Hanali's attacker, and Julian caught her falling body. Clutching Hanali to his chest with one hand, Julian fired Betrayer rapidly at the onslaught of jiangshis swarming from all sides. Each shot impaled a masked face, never missing and never proving less than absolutely fatal. Shadowy bodies dropped all around them. Julian moved his arm in a circle and bestowed death to any jiangshi that lashed out for his flesh. His shots cut through three, sometimes four cursed beings. He couldn't miss; he would never miss. That was his burden, his curse. He was a master of death.

Julian's hand sizzled against Betrayer's burning grip. A horde of jiangshis dove for him and his lieutenant. He pulled the pistol's trigger and felt nothing release.

Suddenly, a wave of fire blew apart the masked creatures in front of Julian. The flames encircled him and created a spiraling barrier. Jiangshis threw themselves into it and burned away to black smoke. Out of the flames came a feminine figure clad in navy captain's armor with metal shoulder pads. Her hips swayed to each side while she walked, like a ballerina Julian once saw in the capital. Captain Katya's expression was stern and unwavering as she marched to Julian's side. "Can she go on?" the captain inquired with a finger pointed at Hanali. "Or will she transform into one of those things?"

"No!" Julian said much harsher than he meant to. "The curse happens through the masks."

"I can stand," Hanali announced suddenly and pushed off Julian. The wound wasn't very deep, but the veins surrounding it were turning black.

"This is a wound to her ki," Katya said, sounding somewhat surprised. She poked the darkening veins, and Julian saw her send ki racing into Hanali. The silver-haired girl shrieked in surprise as black smoke fled from the bite mark into open air.

"Their scratches don't poison," Julian confirmed, examining his own wounds. "Just the bites."

"Then we won't get bitten," Katya said coldly. The spiraling flames dispelled, leaving them vulnerable once again. Jiangshis surrounded them and stood motionless. Julian felt the heat leave Betrayer's grip. "Was this the Marauders' doing?" Katya asked Julian.

"It wasn't them," he said. "I've seen these masks on someone, a salesman. I don't know who sent him, but this was his work. I'm sure of it."

Katya produced a flame in her hand. As it grew slightly in size, the coloring became the shade of a rose. "Then it'll be his head I take," she stated.

The three of them prepared for the jiangshis to advance. Instead, the many cursed islanders remained completely still. Broken masks stared onto them from all directions. What were they waiting for? Under their feet, the island trembled heavily.

"Templar Julian," Hanali uttered quietly and pointed up in the sky. Floating above them was a thin man swathed by a ragged, black robe. A dark mask with bulging eyes veiled his face from view.

"You..." Julian whispered. The man above looked quite different from the one he knew to be responsible for all this, yet Julian was positive that he was the same person. He was the mask salesman in his true form, all tricks withdrawn.

A large orange gem floated next to the man. Julian saw something encased within it, a copper-skinned girl with flowing cords of gold, auburn, and ginger hair. He clutched Betrayer so tightly his knuckles went numb.

The masked man spoke in a familiar, giddy tone. "Hello—"

Julian shot Betrayer without thinking. The red beam slammed between the mask's hideous eyes. His head fell back, and Julian felt time slow for just a moment. Had he killed him? Laughing as he did it, the floating man swung himself forward. There wasn't even a dent on his ridiculous mask.

"I thought you never miss, Templar," he teased Julian. "That was your one shot."

"Who are you?" Katya yelled up at him.

"Quiet," the masked man groaned. "Your voice is annoying. My friends call me Mako, but I'd prefer if you just said nothing at all."

Julian fired Betrayer at the orange gem holding Alina. The beam bounced off, but it produced a visible crack across the glassy surface. Despite his face being hidden, Julian was sure the masked man named Mako felt fear.

Smirking, Julian discharged four more shots. Before they reached his target, the masked man appeared in front of the gem with outstretched arms. Each beam ripped into his torso, and he moaned a cry of agony. "I knew you'd be trouble for me, Markus Julian," the masked man mumbled. "But even you were arrogant enough to allow me on this island. You had your suspicions but thought you could kill me if I revealed myself as a threat. In my opinion, you're to blame for this night."

Julian let no expression overcome his face.

"Am I wrong?"

"You fiend!" Katya screamed. The rose-colored fire in her palm burned hotter. "Why did you do this? If it was Alina you were after, why unleash this hell upon us?"

"For fun," the masked man said with a shrug. Julian felt the island shake once more, this time more intensely. Every jiangshi surrounding them, at least a hundred, began to bubble and melt into a black liquid. Their masks crumbled to dust as the revolting fluid flowed to a single point underneath the masked man. The thick liquid melded together into a massive blob and then began to change shape.

Not wanting the bizarre ritual to complete itself, Julian fired madly at the floating man. He was too blinded by rage to count the shots, but he aimed every one at a vital organ. Thin rays pierced the enemy's flesh in rapid succession. Betrayer turned hot in Julian's hand. Still, he pressed the unresponsive trigger several more times in desperate defiance.

The masked man wiped blood from his stomach and giggled. "If you had done that this morning," he said, "I would be very dead right now." There was another mask in his left hand, one made of wood. A golden light flowed from the simply carved mask into his veins. Julian observed the many wounds close themselves. That mask could heal him.

His attention could not linger on the floating man. Hanali grabbed Julian's arm, and he looked toward the mixing, shadowy fluids underneath Mako. There, out of the bubbling black liquid, a horrifying creature rose. It had four arms, two reptilian heads, and the torso of a muscular man. Looming at least twenty feet above them, it had no legs. Instead, its waist protruded from the mass of dark fluid conglomerating on the ground.

"Back to business," the masked man declared. "I've made this stop to test my little friend here. I call him *Jiangshi Hydra*. Who will win? Let's see! Fight, fight!"

Katya and Hanali kept their gazes on the masked man, who was clearly readying an attack. "Look at me," Julian instructed them. They gave him their attention. "Our only chance is to get that other mask in his hand. I saw it heal him. Then I'll shoot him in the heart." Julian stiffened his hold on Betrayer, feeling blisters across his palm.

"Understood," Hanali said hurriedly.

"What if you're wrong?" Katya interjected. "You can't possibly be sure that mask healed him."

"This is an order," Julian barked.

Jiangshi Hydra swiped one of its enormous palms at the three of them. Katya unleashed a torrent of rose-colored fire to block the attack. Julian rolled to the side and fired Betrayer into the monster's two heads. It recoiled, then two lilac eagles drove themselves into its chest. The mask man's creation bellowed and released dark yellow fire from its mouths. Diving away from the flames, Julian lost sight of Hanali and Katya under a cloud of smoke and debris.

As he got himself up, the gargantuan enemy punched down toward him. The giant fist impacted Julian's entire body. He crashed into the ground, Betrayer still clutched firmly in his grip. Jiangshi Hydra raised its hand once again.

Screaming with the effort, Julian fired Betrayer into the monster's incoming fist. He would have his revenge. The masked man would not leave here alive.

《 ☆ *VIII* ☆ 》

Ike darted through the decaying trees of Somerset's forest. The shadowy beast that was once Lotis followed close behind on all fours. He'd led the creature on a chase to find a tighter area for battle. Despite the ridiculous length of Ike's sword, the monster's size gave it the advantage in a wide clearing.

Shriveled vegetation surrounded Ike on all sides. This was the location he needed. Feeling ki bolster his strength, Ike slashed Dreamblade through a rotten trunk of wood. As the tree fell onto his opponent, Ike slid in the dirt and turned to face his pursuer.

The monster caught the trunk with a single claw and tossed it at Ike. Reacting quickly, Ike slashed down his blade to break the incoming tree in two. Broken wood flew to each side of Ike, and the beastly creature closed the distance between them.

Ducking under a deadly swipe of the beast's claw, Ike slashed upward with Dreamblade. His sword sliced across the creature's shadowy skin, forcing black smoke to explode from the wound. The monster hollered in pain and staggered back.

"Come on!" Ike hollered madly.

Seeming to recognize the taunt, the monster stood upright and held a claw over the forest floor. A weapon sprouted from the dirt, a humungous black cleaver with a wooden hilt. The blade was larger than Dreamblade and twice as thick.

Ike held Dreamblade toward the sky and called down lightning. Electricity raced down the gray metal to reach his veins. He felt himself grow stronger, as if he'd just awoken from a restful slumber.

The beast took up its weapon with a single hand and swung at Ike. He countered with Dreamblade but stumbled back a step from the tremendous force behind the cleaver. Gritting his teeth, Ike dug both feet into the dirt. *You won't move me again*, he resolved.

Two beastly cries of rage echoed throughout the collapsing island of Somerset. Dreamblade bashed against the monster's cleaver. Ike shook under the monster's strength, yet his stance remained firm. They pulled their blades apart and clashed once more. Moving faster now, Ike yanked his sword away just to send it hurtling back at the shadowy creature with more intensity.

Sparks and dark smoke leaped from their blades as the two of them collided again and again. Ike parried strike after strike, his feet sinking in the dirt yet never moving backward. He swung Dreamblade with more speed than he ever thought possible. Rapid strikes of their swords bounced off one another, completely equal in power.

Ike searched for an opening, a moment where his blade could strike true. With every swing of his sword, Ike waited for the chance to kill.

Shrieking in frustration, the monster raised its cleaver for a mere second longer than his previous strikes. *Now,* Ike thought. He drove Dreamblade upward from his hip to over his opposite shoulder. The enormous sword cut through dense, shadowy flesh. His opponent yelped as dark smoke fled from the wound in a fierce burst.

Giving Dreamblade a final flourish, Ike watched the abomination fall back with a mighty thud. It was over. Ragged coughs wheezed out from the dying beast. Ike went to its side and knelt down. One murky yellow eye settled on him. He recognized something within it and felt his eyes swell with tears.

"I'm so sorry, Lotis," Ike said miserably. "If I was stronger—I could have just—" He clutched a handful of dirt and choked back one heavy sob. The earth beneath him shook violently. He heard the creature's breaths grow softer and more docile. Ike searched for Lotis in the depraved eyes of the beast and placed his palm on the shadowy muzzle. "I've never killed anything," he admitted, "not even a sick sheep. But I know if I leave you like this, I'll only be sparing myself."

He raised a trembling hand toward the clouds. "I'll make it quick," Ike uttered. No tears rolled down his cheeks. The beast's eyes appeared to be pleading with him. *Do it*, they said. His hand came down, and a bolt of lightning followed it. Sparks reduced the monstrous body to a plume of black smoke. Ike followed the rising vapor with a wide, empty gaze. Something felt lost inside him. A hole had opened somewhere in his heart.

Footsteps and what sounded like the scraping of wheels grabbed Ike's attention. He stood with Dreamblade in hand. Through the dark forest, Ike saw a hunched man lugging a cart behind him. "Hey!" Ike called out.

The man turned his head to the noise and sprinted for him, yapping like a crazed animal. The cart fastened to his waist by rope slowed him down immensely, giving Ike time to think of a strategy.

As the man neared, he could see a white rabbit mask on his face. Ike threw down Dreamblade to catch the strange man's flailing arms. Tossing one wrist to the side, Ike tried to yank the mask from his face. It resisted him at first, but Ike's strength proved enough to pull away the clay face.

Dark smoke puffed from the man's eyes and mouth. Around his decaying head was a ring of burned flesh from where the mask once rested. As he fell dead, Ike recognized the man's thick mustache. He had been the baker from the Spirit Festival that Peeko pestered. Baked goods, as well as jars of different colored drinks, filled his cart.

What had Mako done? Ike stood frozen above the baker's corpse. He knew this couldn't be the only victim. The Face Stealer sent hundreds of masks flying in the direction of town. Who would be left to evacuate from the falling island?

A quick flash of yellow light passed by Ike's peripheral. It came from behind a tree on his left. Suspecting its source, Ike sidestepped slowly toward the tree. When he got close enough, Ike dove and grabbed Mako's nymph companion from her hiding place. Oddly, there was some weight to the glowing ball, perhaps a few ounces. She vibrated in his hand, attempting to escape Ike's strong hold.

"Got you," Ike said to the yellow ball.

The nymph shook herself violently.

"Mako called you Echo, right?" he asked. "How long have you been watching?"

There was only a more adamant rattling in his palm.

"What happened to that man over there?"

Light pulsated off the nymph.

"Can you not speak?"

"Of course I talk!" Echo shouted. Her voice sounded girlish, high-pitched, and oddly alluring. Still, Ike's eardrums rattled from the obnoxious shouting. "I just don't speak to pimple-faced wankers like you!"

"I don't know what wanker means," Ike said truthfully.

"It's, uh—" Echo stammered, then spoke with much more volume than necessary. "Well, I heard dwarves use the word, and its context was highly offensive!"

"No one says it here."

"Then you should travel more!" she spat while shaking herself furiously. "This floating turd is revolting to look at anyway."

"Somerset is all I know," Ike admitted, "and your friend Mako has destroyed it. He's destroyed everything." Lotis's blushing green cheeks passed by his mind.

Echo calmed her quivering somewhat. The island dropped about a foot. Ike felt the sudden acceleration underneath him.

"You tried to help me before," Ike told her. "I can tell you're not like him."

The nymph's light dimmed slightly. "You don't know anything about me," she said calmly. "...or Mako."

"Help me understand then," he said. "What has he done to my people?"

"He's killed them and used their bodies for a powerful curse," Echo divulged.

"Is there a way to undo it? Or to stop Somerset from falling?"

"No," she said bluntly. "You'd need the Great Spirit's face, and getting it from Mako would be impossible, you whiny jackoff."

"All right, I know what that one means," Ike stated while getting irritated. "Is he still on the island? Do you know?"

"Duh, is he still on the island? Duuh?" Echo yammered in a mockery of Ike's voice.

Holding the nymph firmly, Ike went over to the baker's cart and emptied a jar of punch. He stuck Echo in the container, managing to close the lid before she could fly out.

"This is cruelty!" she yelled from inside. "You're inhumane! Let me out!"

"The nymph Mako just mutilated could've broken out of this in a second."

"Well, we can't all be so lucky!"

There was a string handle on the jar that Ike fastened to his belt. "Help me, and maybe I might let you go when this is all over," Ike said. "Where's Mako?"

Echo slammed against the sides of the jar and shouted, "Fine, he's in town! I feel his presence there. He took the Great Spirit's mask off. That much power must have taken a tremendous toll on his body. It seems like he's just having some fun before this booger in the sky falls apart."

Dreamblade flew into Ike's hand. He sprinted toward town with the huge blade on his shoulder.

"What do you plan on doing?" Echo yelled. "He'll just kill you again!"

By now, the trees of Somerset forest had shriveled up completely. Dead leaves and blackened branches covered the soil as Ike ran. "I can't beat him how I am now. I know that," Ike said. "But I won't give up on my home and its people. If there's a chance I can get that mask and free Alina, I'll take it."

"You're an idiot," Echo muttered, "but taking me back to Mako is exactly what I want. So, you better hurry. If everyone here dies, he's just going to get bored and leave."

A low rumbling reverberated through Somerset. Chunks of earth sunk into the soil around Ike. He jumped over the hazards and let his ki power both legs. Exhaustion threatened to cripple his body, yet he pressed on. The dead forest passed by in a blur. Soon he'd see the stone path leading to town, or whatever was left of it.

"The one thing you can count on is that mask will be right with him," Echo stated. "Mako keeps his new toys very close."

(☆ IX ☆)

Julian rolled forward to avoid a blast of yellow fire. Feeling Betrayer's cooldown end, he shot three times into one head of Jiangshi Hydra. The monster spasmed, but its second serpent-like face unleashed more fire at him.

Katya appeared at his side, sending a wave of her own rose-colored flames to counter the attack. Smoke and heat bellowed out before them. In that second of rest, Julian continued his strategizing. Killing this creature seemed nearly impossible. Every time substantial gaps formed in its dark flesh, a jiangshi would hurl itself into the monster and melt to a grotesque, black liquid. The fluid would then be absorbed in order to heal Jiangshi Hydra's fatal wounds. This creation was truly a killing machine. What could Mako be planning to use it for? In his words, the battle was a mere "test" for him.

One of Jiangshi Hydra's colossal hands swept Katya into its grip. She squirmed and shouted for help. Julian cut through the creature's wrist with an onslaught of red beams. As Katya fell, Hanali used a gust of wind to slow her descent. The three of them regrouped about thirty feet away from the creature. Demolished stone and watchful jiangshis framed the battle. Above, Mako rocked back and forth in the air as if he were reclining on a lounge chair. In one hand was the strange wooden mask that healed him before. Alina's gem rested directly behind him. That was it. Mako protected that gemstone with his own body. If Julian seriously threatened its integrity, the masked man would have to descend and deal with him. That would be their chance to get the wooden mask.

"Katya, cover me," Julian commanded quietly. "Hanali, ready an eagle and watch close." They both nodded. Bruises, blood, and dust coated their bodies, yet the Knights' eyes remained determined. A masked woman threw herself into the ginormous monster, and its missing hand began to reform.

Markus Julian, the Fourth Templar of Tenshi, darted toward the left side of Jiangshi Hydra. That put Mako directly overhead as well as the orange gem. Katya produced a brilliant ball of fire that bashed into the creature's left shoulder so Julian could slide under its two arms unnoticed. Aiming Betrayer for the side of Alina's gem, he fired twice.

Two cracks sprouted over the Starchild's cheek. Mako flinched his veiled face toward Julian. *Got you now, asshole*, Julian thought. Jiangshi Hydra appeared to respond to Mako's panic. By now, there were too many wounds for the creature to mend. Webs of shadowy flesh sought to pull together huge gashes in its body to no avail. This wounded state triggered a chaotic, frightening focus in the monster's yellow eyes. It turned while raising a fist to smash Julian's head in. The Templar dove backward, and if it wasn't for Hanali disrupting the monster's aim with a huge blast of wind, he would have been crushed.

As Julian got up, he fired Betrayer without looking at his target. Knowing he cracked the gem further with the shot, Julian rolled to the side, expecting Jiangshi Hydra's wrath. It came in an explosion of dark yellow fire that singed his vest. Kneeling on the ground after his maneuver, Julian saw grimy, dirt-filled toenails before him. He glanced up at a frightening black mask.

Mako tried to kick Julian in the jaw. He dodged it easily, but before Julian could do much else, he was thrown by an invisible force. Skidding on broken stone, Katya stopped Julian's floundering body and helped him up. Hanali breathed sluggishly fifteen feet away on his left. Now Julian was back where he started, standing directly before Jiangshi Hydra. However, Mako walked on the ground with them. The ghastly eyes of his black mask were fixed solely on Julian. This was it.

"No one has dodged me in a long, long time," Mako stated, sounding very pleased. "There was quite the commotion when you won the Templar Trials, Markus Julian. You're certainly not the typical Templar raining down hellfire, smashing mountains, and whatever else. But I think your abilities are much more fun than all that."

Jiangshi Hydra slithered two tongues out from its mouths in waiting. Julian dared not look at where Hanali stood for fear of giving away their plan. The wooden mask was held loosely in Mako's left hand.

"The meditation you perfected is called *Yoken Sa Reta*, right?" Mako asked while he meandered toward Julian and Katya. "It allows the user to foresee an event a split second before it happens. But you took it to a new level, my friend. From what I know, you see an enemy's weakness with a single glance, you feel every trace of ki move in the air, and you never, ever miss an attack."

"That's not quite how it works," Julian uttered, "but you're close enough. I do see your weakness quite clearly."

Mako came to a stop ten feet from them. His monster smashed down two of its arms out of boredom. Dust spun into the night air. "And what's my weakness?" the masked man asked with a giggle.

Julian caught Hanali in his peripheral and said, "You're watching me."

A glowing, lilac-colored eagle flew toward Mako from behind. Its beak opened for the wooden mask. Katya created a flaming dragon from her fist that rushed straight for Mako to keep him focused on them. He held up his free hand to block the intense ki attack, and Julian readied Betrayer to pierce Mako's heart. Everything would happen at once. The eagle's beak closed on the target. Julian held his finger against the Crimson Pistol's trigger. Why did he feel like Mako was smirking behind his mask?

Just before the dragon of fire touched Mako's palm, he closed his right fist. Julian, Katya, and Hanali froze in place. Katya's flames instantly dissipated in the air. Struggling to even flinch his finger, Julian grunted through unmoving teeth. An unseen force emanating from Mako had overcome their bodies. It held them tightly, restricting every possible movement. Julian felt haunting, gaping eyes glaring into his soul. Hanali's lilac eagle clutched the wooden mask. The bird fluttered its wings vehemently; however, Mako held onto the mask with only two fingers. Managing to twitch his eyes, Julian noticed that black smoke spun up and down his own body.

"You think I need this mask to win here?" Mako spat. He jerked the wooden face from Hanali's bird and used it to smash the eagle into specks of glowing ki. "You're wrong, wrong, wrong, Templar. The only reason I'd let myself remain on this floating rock is that no one could ever hope to harm me. I've studied ki-wielding arts that even the Templars are ignorant of. I've grown stronger than a god, with or without the Great Spirit's power." Jiangshi Hydra's twin jaws fumed with yellow flames. "Let's end this. The whole thing has become annoying. You should be thankful that it's my power that will kill you instead of Somerset crashing into the sea."

The monster made from black shadow prepared to rain down death. Hanali's eyes darted toward Julian. Tears streaked down her blood-caked cheeks. Katya's body shook from head to toe as she continued fighting to break free. Julian relaxed and prepared for Mako's creation to slaughter them. Murky, yellow flames began to surge forth.

Suddenly, Jiangshi Hydra shuddered in pain. Its two heads unleashed blasts of fire in random directions, tearing through distant buildings and the white temple. Julian, Katya, and Hanali remained untouched. They all looked to the cause of their salvation.

Standing just underneath the colossal monster, with a giant gray sword thrust forward in his hands, was a tall young man. He wore a tattered silvery gi, which barely held onto his blood-soaked body. Chestnut hair with flashes of blond fluttered in the cool breeze. Behind him, a massive tear in Jiangshi Hydra's flesh sparked with electricity.

The mysterious ki-wielder walked forward. Julian saw two gray eyes booming with the intensity of thunder clouds. Jiangshi Hydra fell onto its two faces with a deafening crash. Watching the creature struggle on the ground, Julian realized it was readying a final attack. One scaly jaw opened and filled with fire.

Before it could complete the assault, the young man spun back while pointing his massive blade at the monster with a single hand. Lightning surged from the clouds and shredded Jiangshi Hydra apart into a pervasive cloud of dark smoke. The surrounding masked islanders scattered in what must have been fear.

Somerset shook fervently as the stranger looked at Julian, Hanali, and Katya, who gawked back with complete confusion. His gaze then went to Alina's gem before finally settling on Mako. They stood only a few feet apart. The masked man had turned around to face him. Veins bulged on Julian's forehead. He wouldn't surrender like this. Using every ounce of his strength, Julian fired Betrayer into Mako's left wrist.

A thin beam blew a hole above the hand clutching Mako's wooden mask. Julian and his comrades felt Mako's control over them disappear. While the masked man turned to his attacker, Julian foresaw the movements of his left hand quite clearly. He unleashed three more shots, which cut through Mako's flailing wrist. The wooden mask and Mako's hand fell from his body in a downpour of blood and dark smoke.

Julian's pistol scorched his palm with heat as he saw a lilac eagle sweep toward the ground. It caught the mask and flew toward Hanali, who stood in deep concentration. Mako reached out for the bird, yet he changed his remaining hand's course when the gray-eyed warrior brought down his sword. He caught the huge blade between his thumb and forefinger. *Eight more seconds*, Julian thought.

Katya ran to confront Mako from the side and released a barrage of three fiery, rose-colored dragons that engulfed his entire body one after another. He remained planted on the ground, mere singes covering his skin. Sighing, Mako kicked the young man in his gut and sent him tumbling over. At the same time, he wafted his finger at Katya, making her flip backward in a heap of limbs.

Four more seconds.

Hanali waved her hands forward. Five glowing eagles raced from the paint covering her arms. Every bird collided with Mako's body in puffs of lilac light. Their enemy stood unaffected. Her eagle holding the wooden mask soared about overhead. She was making it a difficult target, but that wouldn't be enough. Mako snapped his fingers at the bird. Its coloring faded to black, and its light was corrupted with dark smoke. Taking control of Hanali's Totem Animal, Mako willed the eagle to fly toward him with the mask.

One more second.

Julian aimed for the masked man's heart. He pressed his finger against the trigger and prepared to fire.

CRASH! An explosion of deep red energy blew apart the ground between Mako and Julian. The Templar was thrown back by the incredible force without a single shot leaving the Crimson Pistol.

《☆ ✗ ☆》

Ike held his aching gut and looked onto the red explosion in awe and confusion. The Templar lay on his back against the ruins of the town square's fountain. Running toward the unconscious man was the silver-haired ki-wielder. She must have been his Knight.

Straining his eyes in the darkness, Ike searched for the enemy. Mako remained veiled from view by ash and dust. That blast seemed to have come from the sky. He spun around. Above the eastern shore of Somerset, Ike's eyes met a fleet of six ships that sailed through the air. They loomed over the island, casting a deep shadow. "What—" Ike muttered.

"Marauders," Katya said as she limped to his side. "They've come."

At least twenty streaks of red light soared upward from the Marauder battleships. When they began to descend toward Somerset, Ike saw that they were huge glass spheres containing gallons of glowing, scarlet liquid.

"Ki-bombs!" Katya screamed while tackling Ike onto crushed stone.

Explosions pounded against Ike's eardrums. He held onto Echo's jar tightly as if that might protect her. Katya groaned from the immense heat burning her back. The bombs had landed all throughout the town. From where he lay beneath his captain, all Ike could see was a single red flash.

Katya fell to the side. Ike's vision felt mottled and unsteady. He got up and tried to help the captain stand, but then his eyes fell on a dark figure moving through the shroud of dust. Mako the Face Stealer floated out of red ash toward Alina's cracked gem. Flames burned away the ragged robe clothing him. Blood still dripped from where his left hand once was. The bulging eyes of his mask stared at Ike, taunting him. Laying on the ground between them, surrounded by falling ash, was the Great Spirit's face.

They both darted for the mask in the midst of growing fire and booming explosions. Mako came down from the air, and Ike dove forward on the pavement. Their hands grasped the wooden face almost at the same moment. Ike and Mako rose together, and each pulled with all their might on the mask. Despite using both hands, Ike could barely rival Mako's one-armed strength.

The Face Stealer kicked Ike in the ribs, and he almost lost his grip on the wooden chin. Mako could still overpower him. Ike had no hope of tearing the Great Spirit's power away from him. Desperate and losing hope, Ike remembered the message Lotis delivered, *Do not let Mako leave Somerset with my mother's face. Whatever the cost.*

Ike gave a single look into the haunting eyes of Mako's black mask. He felt no fear, no doubt of his purpose. This was *his* war to win. Somerset may be lost, but all of Dawn could be saved.

Releasing his right hand from the Spirit's face, Ike called Dreamblade to his hand. The remaining lightning in Ike's veins surged into the mighty sword. Electricity rippled across the gray metal. He raised the blade and readied to strike down. Just before Ike's sword met the wooden mask, Mako shrieked, "No! You can't!"

Dreamblade shattered the Great Spirit's face in two. Golden light and bright smoke burst free from the pieces and trailed into the rising dust of Somerset's ruins. The breaking of the mask produced a shockwave that pushed Mako and Ike apart. Two explosions of Marauder bombs illuminated them in harsh, red light.

"You ruined everything! EVERYTHING!" Mako screamed madly, hurling his piece of the broken mask into the distance.

Clutching the Great Spirit's jaw and part of her cheek, Ike realized he was not done fighting. Raising Dreamblade once more, Ike stared at the Face Stealer. Mako appeared desperate, defeated, and… terrified. Ike threw his sword with every ounce of strength he had left. The blade spun in the air toward his target. It reached out for the orange gem imprisoning Alina. Before, he could barely nick the surface; however, the gemstone was badly damaged now. Also, Ike had never wielded Dreamblade with so much desperate force. This would be enough; it had to be. *Please, God*, Ike pleaded.

Mako appeared before Alina's gem in an instant. He kicked the sparking sword at Ike with his bare foot. Throwing his shoulder back to dodge, Ike observed his blade pierce the ground behind him in a rush of electricity. A line of blood dripped across Ike's chest. Seething with rage, he looked back to the Face Stealer and Alina.

Nothing. There was only smoke and cinders. Mako had vanished with Alina, Somerset's Starchild. Fatigue dropped Ike to his knees. Plumes of red energy burst throughout the town around him. The island dropped five feet, making Ike almost topple over. Somerset could not be saved without the mask Ike just tore through. Dawn was spared, but Alina and his home were lost. Had Ike just returned from the dead to fail? Everything he had done was not enough… None of it was close to enough. Perhaps he was still the beaten-down Squire Asim tortured. The power of the Deathrid could not overshadow Ike's weakness.

"Get up, Ryder," Captain Katya demanded. Her forehead bled heavily, and burns dotted her skin in wide blotches. The armor that once shined so pristinely had been nearly ripped apart. She grabbed Ike's arm and pulled him to his feet. "Listen to me," she said intensely. More bombs tore into Somerset in torrents of vivid light. "I don't know how the Spirit has changed you," Katya said. Her hand came around

the back of Ike's neck to hold him close. "But I always knew–
– I knew who you could be."

Ike's eyes were wide and unwavering. He took in his
captain's words as the Marauders rained down destruction.
From somewhere far away, the screams of cursed islanders
rose into the night.

"Go on from this place," Katya told him. "Survive this
night and go on! Avenge our home. Avenge our people. *Kill
Mako*. I am putting my faith in you, Last Son of Somerset."

The Temple to El exploded near them, red heat shredding
the ancient stone. Katya pressed her head against Ike's and
shut her eyes. Ike stared at the blood on her cheeks.

"Now run," the captain commanded after pulling away.
"Take the others and go. I'll cover you for as long as I can."

Shaking his head, Ike said, "Captain—"

"This is my last order! Run!" she cried while producing
two flaming dragons. They rocketed overhead and pierced
two bombs in the air above them. Red sparks poured down
on the ruined street.

Ike's head felt light and unsteady as he ran from his
captain to the Templar and his companion near the fountain.
The silver-haired girl was just getting the man to his feet
when Ike reached them. They both seemed dizzy and badly
wounded. "Follow me!" Ike yelled over the booming
explosions.

He sprinted ahead of them; however, Ike kept glancing
over his shoulder. Katya had risen in a torrent of rose-colored
flames. Her dragons tore through ki-bombs in the sky to
protect Ike and the others. One bomb slipped through her

defense and detonated just underneath the captain. Deep red energy swelled all around Katya. Ike kept running ahead.

Sinkholes opened everywhere he could see. Pits of crumbling earth threatened to kill the three survivors if they managed to avoid the relentless barrage of bombs. Ike witnessed the blacksmith shop collapse into the depths of Somerset. As they turned the corner on a street leading out of town, Ike saw a pack of masked islanders scrambling in all directions. The buildings that remained standing under the Marauders' assault burned with scarlet fire. Many cursed inhabitants crawled about clothed in deep red flame.

These were the people Ike had known his entire life. They waved hello in the morning and bought his wool on quiet evenings. They mourned the victims of war together and celebrated whoever returned home safely. Names passed through his mind, too many to count or make sense of. Ike recognized no one behind the hideous masks and burning flesh. They were already lost.

Four cursed creatures spotted Ike and his followers on the long stone road between houses. Realizing Dreamblade was still in the town square, Ike called the weapon to his hand. Before it could reach him, the Templar threw two knives into a rotting neck. The girl with silver hair created a gust of wind that flung another masked islander into red flames. As one of the remaining two creatures reached them, the Templar stepped in front of Ike to slash through his mask with a dagger.

Dashing for Ike was the last cursed islander. He wore a mask of a pouting little girl. Shaggy brown hair poked out around his large ears. Dreamblade found Ike's hand. As the masked creature lunged for Ike's neck, he swung down the sword. But then something halted his blade just before it crashed into the man's shoulder. Who was it that he was about to cut down?

The Templar stabbed his sword through the man's mask and left it there, protruding from the creature's skull. Black smoke fled from the cracking porcelain face. "Faster!" the blond man yelled while tugging on Ike's gi.

Ahead was the edge of town on the western side. The Marauders had appeared over the docks in the east, a smart move on their part. Ike didn't know how they'd get off the falling island before it hit the ocean. All that mattered right now was getting distance between them and the Marauder ships.

A shadow blocked the moonlight above Ike. He looked up and saw a ki-bomb descending toward them. Sooner than Ike could panic, the bomb was split open by a dragon of fire. The explosion reverberated through the air as Ike caught one last glimpse of Katya. She stood hunched over at the other end of the street. Burns, blood, and a maimed arm distracted Ike from her expression. Masked faces threw themselves over her weakened body. Katya disappeared under the rotten, shadowy figures.

Ike ran forward. They passed into the grass clearings of Somerset, yet all life was now deceased. Only dirt and blackened vegetation surrounded the road. The echoes of Marauder ki-bombs barely registered against Ike's pounding eardrums. Underneath them, the island dropped what must have been fifteen feet. They all fell forward from the island's sudden descent. Picking up Dreamblade, Ike led the Knight and Templar behind him onward.

"Where are we going?" the girl at his heels asked after what felt like endless running.

"There," Ike huffed. They came to a fenced pasture housing the corpses of his sheep. Behind it, Ike could see the edge of Somerset in clear view. He pointed to the cliff.

"What the hell happened here?" the Templar said in disgust.

"The edge is…only a little way down there," Ike panted. "The Marauders came over the docks. The elevator above it—"

"Is the only way down," the Templar completed his thought. "So, how do we get off this deathtrap?"

"I can carry you down with my wings," the silver-haired Knight told the Templar.

"That didn't exactly work last time!" he shouted back.

Somerset quaked violently. "We don't have a choice, my Templar!" she asserted and then looked at Ike with sorrow. "But I could only carry one person."

"It's fine," Ike responded quickly. "Take him and go. When you hit the water, swim straight that way." He pointed ahead to where the Cove, his old hangout spot, rested out at sea.

"What will you do?" she said warily.

"I'll be right behind you two," Ike stated.

They took a few quick steps, and then the Templar turned back to Ike. "Who are you?" he asked with what seemed like genuine intrigue. His eyes went down to Echo's jar.

"Ike," he replied simply.

The Templar turned away without another word. Ike watched them sprint to the island's edge. Glowing lilac wings illuminated the female Knight and her Templar. She fluttered above the cliffside, and the Templar took hold of her legs. They then descended out of sight. And Ike remained alone in his pasture.

Dreamblade felt exceedingly heavy in his weakened grip. Just as he thought this, the sword changed shape in a flash of sparks. Glancing at his right arm, Ike saw that the blade had become a thick metal band around his wrist. While inspecting Dreamblade's new form, Ike wandered through the broken fence and climbed the ladder into his treehouse.

When he swung open the trap door, Echo spoke for the first time in quite a while. "Hey, bonehead, you just killed us by letting that Dajo girl fly off."

Ike said nothing. He pulled an old knapsack from under his bed and mindlessly stuffed things inside while the island trembled. First, he packed a tin box housing the marble game he spent years playing with Nathan. Then he threw in a waterskin, a wool shirt, and bread. The bag had been waterproofed with a layer of wax. Every time he visited the Cove, the knapsack followed. This time was no different.

Moving past his bed again, Ike found himself picking up a framed picture on his nightstand. Staring back at him was his family. Mom and Dad engulfed Ike, Bridget, and Alina from above. Everyone seemed so young. They smiled as if the moment would never end.

He stuffed the picture in his bag, feeling nothing as he did it. Next, Ike undid his belt to put Echo's jar in the knapsack. "What do you think you're doing?" she shouted.

"Safer this way," he mumbled.

"I took you to Mako," Echo said heatedly, "so let me go! That was the deal! Hey! Listen to me!"

Ike placed the jar gently on the shirt. Then he realized the Great Spirit's jaw had been tucked in the waistline of his pants. Not remembering when he'd stuck it there, Ike tossed the broken piece of mask into his bag. With his possessions packed, Ike fastened the bag shut and drifted to the door. He gave the room one last glance. This morning Ike knew that he would be leaving this place, whether it was with the Knights or to abandon his duties. Despite all that, part of him thought that he would die here as a worthless shepherd. For a long time, he felt that was the absolute truth. Somerset was to be his grave. And it had been.

Chunks of dirt spiraled downward as the island continued to tremor. Ike walked methodically to the cliffside. Sulfur and smoke filled his nostrils from the fire miles away. He remembered when the scent of sea salt and fresh grass prevailed here. He recalled gripping his mother's hand and strolling down Somerset's green hills.

His feet came to the very edge. Rocks were slipping off the cliff and tumbling into the distant ocean. How many feet was this jump? The island had dropped significantly in the air; much more than he realized. Anger knit his brow. He wanted to test his resurrected body, see how much it could take. If this stopped him, he deserved to die again.

Ike took ten steps back. The island swayed and descended rapidly. This drop felt different than the other times. Before, it was like the ground dropped to a new resting place. Now the island simply fell without end, and Ike still stood on its surface. He ran shakily to the edge.

"Stop, stop! I feel like you're gonna jump!" Echo screamed herself hoarse from his bag. "We're dead! You're gonna kill us!"

Ike Ryder pressed his foot against the cliff of Somerset and jumped. His body twisted in the air. He could see the jagged chunk of earth that was his island drop beside him. Wind piled against his body and slowed his descent.

The floating isle of Somerset crashed into the Aged Sea underneath Ike. Tremendous waves gushed forth from the impact. Ike kept his body tight and smashed into the rising tsunami. A chaotic, swirling force took hold of him. The pressure cracked his bones, rattled his senses, and threatened to drag him into unconsciousness. He felt a familiar presence lurk into his heart…death.

No. Ike would not be defeated. As air spilled from Ike's mouth, he felt an intense power radiate from his chest. It felt overwhelming and uncontrollable. Deep beneath the crashing waves of the Aged Sea, Ike's tattoo glowed blue. The light illuminated the ocean like a beacon.

☆ *XI* ☆

Julian hung onto Hanali's legs with a firm grip. She had turned slightly in the air so they could observe the massive waves roll out from where Somerset dropped into the ocean. A wall of water raced toward them with fearsome speed. "Fly higher!" he yelled to Hanali.

She screamed in pain yet flapped her shining wings mercilessly. As the tsunami came for them, Julian held his legs to his chest, so the water passed by just beneath him. After it passed, Hanali's wings immediately dissipated. They fell what felt like a hundred feet into the Aged Sea. Julian swam hard for the surface. He drew in air and searched for Hanali. She popped up at his side.

"I see the spot," Julian said. By chance, he was looking right at a tiny speck of land. It looked to be a small beach hidden by a sharp rock. They swam toward it, and Julian kept his gaze fixed on the single palm tree. He didn't let himself feel exhaustion until the sand came under his hands. The two of them crawled onto land. Julian reached the palm tree and propped himself against it. Hanali lay on her back in front of him. Their frantic breaths mixed with the crashing of waves. The tsunami had drenched everything around them. Even the palm tree above Julian dripped water onto his forehead.

"Did he…survive that?" Hanali muttered weakly.

"No," Julian wheezed, "no one could."

He was only strong enough to keep his eyes half-open. Far away, the Marauder ships flew over where Somerset once was. They'd be sailing home now. How the hell did they make their ships fly? And had their attack really been strong enough to drop the entire island? That didn't seem likely. The ground had been trembling before they even arrived. Perhaps it had been Mako. He was good, that enemy.

Julian realized he still held Betrayer. Even when he gripped Hanali's legs, Julian used his arms so the pistol could remain at the ready. He tried to open the fingers wrapped around the golden grip; however, that prompted frightening pain. The constant overheating had melded his burned flesh to the pistol. Accepting the consequences, Julian used his other hand to rip Betrayer off his skin in a single hard pull.

Blood splattered onto the wet sand. He spat drool but did not scream. His many meditations had taught him to greet pain as an old friend. Burned flesh stuck to the Crimson Pistol's handle. Julian's blurred vision stared at his right hand. The skin seemed almost completely removed. It felt raw and agonizing.

He failed them. The Starchild, his regiment, that entire island. His reasoning for donning the black vest on his back seemed distant and unreachable now. Everyone had been right. He was a sham Templar. The silver pendant against his chest caught a glimmer of moonlight. Julian recalled four years ago when he made the title of Templar his goal. What had he told the other sewer rats living in the capital slums? *They can do whatever they want.* That's what he said.

Pain and fatigue took Julian into an empty, aching slumber. He came to what must have been a matter of minutes later. Hanali seemed to be floating between unconsciousness and anxious vigilance. The fear written on her face would last for a while, maybe forever.

For some reason, Julian imagined himself speaking out loud. *Templars are supposed to be shields*, he would say to Hanali.

She couldn't move much, but perhaps her head would turn on the sand to look at him. He'd meet her sky-blue eyes with his own gaze.

Before today, I never lost a fight, he would tell her. *I never met an enemy I couldn't finish with a single move. I'm an assassin. I wield death as my weapon. I see every weakness, no matter someone's strength. Mako was right about that.* The ocean breeze felt bitterly cold on his wet skin. *But I lost today because I'm not what a Templar is meant to be. It doesn't matter who I kill…if I can't protect those entrusted to me.*

You protected me, Hanali would say softly.

Julian stared out at the black ocean. *That's not enough*, he'd whisper. The truth crept into his mind. If he hadn't been high for the last three days, Julian could have done more.

A figure crawled onto the beach. He observed the gray-eyed ki-wielder cough up water on the shore. Something perplexed Julian. There was a cut on the young man's chest before. In fact, there had been several bruises and deep wounds on his body. Now he seemed completely healed. Regeneration would explain how he survived the island's descent into the sea, but that was an extremely rare ability. No way this boy could pull off something like that. His form with that huge sword had been sloppy, like it was the first time he ever used it.

Julian locked eyes with him. Then Ike stood up to face the ocean. As he turned, Julian noticed a strange tattoo on his right hand.

⟨☆ *XII* ☆⟩

Gone. It was gone. Everything Ike knew lay buried beneath the Aged Sea. He glared at the empty ocean seeing only dark waves and relentless night. His head spun enough to make him double over. No one was left. He lost everything to *him*, to Mako. Tears rose in his gaping eyes, yet they refused to fall. It felt as if fire pumped through his every vein. Clutching both knees, Ike bellowed a horrific scream. The flesh of his throat cracked and ached.

Dropping back into the sand, Ike let his mind fall numb with pain. For a while, he rested there, knowing what the road ahead would be. The ocean drowned his spiraling thoughts in an endless procession of crashing waves. No longer could he have dreams or hopes for the future like his mother so desperately wanted. There was only a single goal.

Hours passed before the strength to stand returned to Ike. He spent the time watching the moon sink further toward the horizon. When Ike stood, he noticed that the Knight and her Templar watched him closely. They'd both been passing in and out of restless sleep.

Ike reached into his pocket, hoping what he searched for had survived the perilous swim through the Aged Sea. It had. He displayed a silver chain before his two observers. At the end, a pendant of the numeral X swayed in the wind.

"Where'd you get that?" the Templar asked him.

"It was my mother's, sir," Ike stated furiously. "Mako killed her. They'll hold the Templar Trials now, right? To decide the next Templar?"

"Yeah," he said impatiently.

"I'm entering," Ike said.

The Templar scoffed.

"No one will wear my mother's pendant besides me," he said, clenching his jaw tightly.

"Look, kid," the Templar began, "they'll hold the Trials thirty-one days from now. That's if the League of Tenshi survives that long without Somerset. Your physical strength is okay, but your skills and ki control are abysmal. Maybe with some training, you could make lieutenant in the Knights. In ten years, maybe captain even. But Templars are the strongest ki-wielders in all of Dawn. You can't get that powerful in a month."

"I have to," Ike responded, swinging the pendant in the air. "Mako defeated my mother. She was one of the strongest Templars in generations. And now he's going after every spirit in Dawn."

The Templar sat up and said, "How do you know that?"

"I fought him," Ike stated. "That mask he held was the Great Spirit's face. That's what I broke."

"Congratulations," Julian said sarcastically.

"He means to destroy us," Ike said, unfazed. "Mako wants the face of every ki-wielder and spirit. He wants every shred of power there is. Somerset is just the beginning. So, I need to get stronger than any Templar alive. Winning the Trials is the first step."

"There are people that will fight on," the Templar said with growing frustration. "Don't you get it, kid? Be thankful you're still breathing. Others who are much more equipped to deal with Mako will kill him."

"With respect, sir, I don't believe they will," Ike said, stuffing the pendant back in his pocket.

The Templar looked at him with pure indignation. "Why do you care so much?" he said. "Your home's sunk. Nothing will bring it back."

"Mako has someone very important to me," Ike said through gritted teeth.

"Alina," the silver-haired Knight said. It seemed they knew her. The two of them must have belonged to her regiment, then. They were who she came here with.

"She is all I have left," Ike stated. "And Mako told me it'd take him a year to take her face. I can't rest while he has her. I just can't! Please. Help me. I'll do whatever it takes."

Groaning, the Templar stuck his chin toward the stars.

"I've heard stories," the Knight said dreamily, "of places within Dawn where time flows more quickly. Warriors have used these places to get months of training before a battle the next day."

"Time Slips," the Templar clarified for them.

"That's what I need," Ike said, taking an excited step forward.

"I'd go with you," the Knight said, getting onto her knees. "Alina is my friend. And your island was kind to me."

"You too?" the Templar said with a glare. "This isn't your responsibility, Hanali."

"But it is, sir," the girl said. She looked at her own hands. "Have you forgotten? We sailed to Somerset with Mako. I saved his life."

No one said a word for a moment. Ike obviously had questions to ask, though he bit his tongue. Now wasn't the time. The Templar appeared to be in deep thought. He watched the waves roll in with a sunken gaze. Finally, he said, "There's nothing left." Water leaked from his eyes in thin lines. "I lost five hundred Knights." He spoke with a trembling voice. "I lost an entire island, and you're both naïve enough to think you'd stand a chance? It's over. The Empire of the Great Sands rules the Aged Sea. Mako has the Starchild. Accept it. Walk away with your life. I am." His left hand yanked the necklace off his neck. With a dramatic swing of his arm, the pendant soared toward the ocean. Ike watched it pass out of sight. "I'm done," the Templar stated quietly.

Feeling desperate, Ike looked to Hanali for any sign of hope. The silver-haired Knight kept her eyes on the Templar. She sat up tall, spread her lips, and said, "Commander Julian—"

"Don't call me that," the Templar interrupted. "The Green Guard is dead. All of them. I command nothing."

"I'm not asking you to continue being a Templar," Ike said, unsure where his words were headed. "All I ask is that you guide me to where I need to go."

"No thanks," Julian said.

"It's all right," Hanali declared suddenly. "My new friend and I will find this place ourselves. You've done enough, my Templar."

Templar Julian settled his gaze on the girl. Ike tried to understand his expression. Did he feel insulted?

"I'm alive thanks to you," Hanali said with a smile. "Because of that, I can ask for nothing else. So, rest. We will find the Time Slip and train until our bodies nearly break. Then, Mako will answer to justice. If I die, that's okay. I'm not afraid."

Julian stared at his wounded palm. Gently, Hanali lay back on the cold sand. Her sky-blue eyes held a haunting awareness, as if an enemy might attack at any second. Swallowing hard, Ike turned to walk away from them.

"All right," the Templar said unexpectedly, "I'll take you to the Slip. But that's all."

Ike spun around and sighed with relief. He saw a weight leave Hanali's eyes.

Struggling to move his limbs, Julian reached into a pocket deep within his vest. From it, he retrieved a tiny vial of purple liquid. "This will make a portal," he explained, "but it takes three days to appear. I'll train you myself until then. After we sleep. For a while." Tucking the vial back in his vest, the Templar fell onto his side. His eyes remained partly open, but Ike suspected that his consciousness had withdrawn.

"I'm sorry," Hanali said to Ike, "for what you've lost." She shook slightly, perhaps from cold or lingering panic. Despite that, her words were warm and sincere.

Ike nodded, unsure what else to say. The Knight closed her eyes and held a wound on her neck. He drifted away from her to the rocks that hugged the beach.

☾☆ XIII ☼☼

Wanting to be alone, Ike had climbed onto the sharp boulders and sat down, so his back was to the others. Fatigue had dragged them into sleep, but not Ike. Hours had passed since he found his solitude, but now Ike finally allowed himself to cry.

Never again would his mother's smile fall on him. Never would he sit on Somerset's edge to watch the sunset. So many lives gone. And he was helpless to do anything but break their one chance at salvation. Lotis sacrificed herself just so he could have a chance at defeating Mako. This power inside him, the might of a Deathrid—he needed to make it his own. Exhaling deeply, Ike calmed his racing heart.

Sunlight peeked over the Aged Sea. The illumination was enough for Ike to spot a piece of peculiar wood wash up against a rock near him. Carefully lowering himself near the oncoming waves, Ike fished out the strange object. He raised the upper half of the Great Spirit's face to his eyes. Ike had broken the mask in a diagonal line right across the center. This piece of wood finding Ike through natural causes seemed impossible. Allowing himself to feel slightly hopeful, he yanked his piece of the Great Spirit's face out of his knapsack.

Unsure what may happen, Ike held the two pieces together. A second passed, then two, then a full minute. Cursing to himself, Ike put his hope to rest. He could not wish Somerset back to life. The past was finished, no matter how fresh the wounds were to his heart. There was still much to be fought for. Ike needed to focus on Alina.

Between the many rocks, he found a pocket of rough sand and gravel. Ike buried the two pieces of the wooden mask with a clear sense of finality. After turning away from the burial, Ike put his knapsack on the rock beside him and dug out Echo's jar. The tsunami had managed to wet some things and even spread a few cracks on the glass container. However, the nymph appeared to be all right.

"You've been quiet," Ike said to her.

"I have nothing to say to those two," Echo announced dramatically. "Besides that, Mako left me with *you*. He couldn't forgive me, and I don't deserve his forgiveness. It's time you let me out! I need to find him again. Maybe he didn't see me in town... Maybe..."

Ike felt his tone grow intensely serious as he spoke. "I told you. I'll let you go when this is all over."

"It is over! Your island is wiped out. You all lost. Are you listening to me? Hey!"

Growing tired of Echo's ranting, Ike set the jar aside back on the rock. Sorrow, regret, doubt, confusion — they all struggled for dominance within him. However, it was anger that prevailed over every emotion. An orange haze drew back the night sky. Somerset should have been basking in the morning sun. The Great Spirit knew Ike would have to destroy the mask of her face. She knew that the island was lost, that there was no way to stop Mako without sacrificing herself. It wasn't fair of her to make that decision for all of Somerset. She was supposed to protect Ike's people. How could she let them all die?

"Look at me — Wait. What is that?" Echo chirped and bounced toward where Ike buried the broken mask.

Ike whirled around. The pocket of sand housing the Spirit's face glowed with a faint gold shimmer. Two tiny, feeble saplings pushed through the thin gravel and stretched out fresh leaves. Shaking with anticipation, Ike looked to the Aged Sea. Specks of multicolored light rose from the ocean and danced into the sunrise. There were hundreds of them rising from Somerset's grave. All the nymphs of Somerset's forest came together in what resembled a rainbow overhead.

"It's beautiful," a familiar, airy voice said near Ike. She stood over the two saplings, a small child with green skin and glossy brunette hair. A single white flower was tucked behind her ear.

"Lotis?" Ike asked quietly.

The young girl smiled, and as she did, her body grew and matured in a matter of seconds. Grass and vines sprouted around Lotis's body to clothe her, much more modestly than when Ike had first met her. Now Lotis hovered a foot over the rocky island, a young woman in the prime of her beauty.

"I'm sorry," Ike said to her.

"For what?" Lotis responded and tilted her head. "You did what my mother asked of you. Mako did not obtain the Great Spirit's power. You won."

"No," Ike said sternly. "How can you say that? I lost everything I have ever cared about. Somerset is gone. Its people are dead."

"Tell me," Lotis said patiently and with a hint of playfulness, "is death the end?"

Ike knew the answer but chose to remain silent.

"Somerset lives," Lotis stated. "Not in the way you knew it, or perhaps in a way you can understand. But that is the nature of the forest, the nature of life. Death nurtures all beginnings."

Frustrated and confused, Ike followed the soaring nymphs with his gaze. "So, what is it I'm seeing?"

"Rebirth," Lotis said. "You've planted the seeds." She gestured to the glowing saplings. "And now the people you've lost live on." Lotis watched the dots of light mingle in the sky.

"What are you saying? Are my people the lights? They've become nymphs?" Ike asked, unsure.

"No," Lotis said gently. "Your people have become something else. They are the new children of Somerset's forest. Just like my mother, they are rising again. In time, the island will break free of its grave and rise higher than ever before, higher than the clouds."

Floating toward him, Lotis kissed Ike on the forehead and then passed over the open sea. "My sisters and the fledgling children could look to you as the Father of Somerset, its new guardian." She glanced over her shoulder bashfully. "I hope you will be here to witness our beginning…with me."

"I'm going to kill Mako," Ike said. Lotis halted in the air and stared at him calmly. "And I disagree with what you said…with what your mother wanted for us. Death isn't the end, but it's painful. It hurts. Rebirth like this isn't worth all that suffering."

"You're thinking like a human," Lotis said coldly. Her emerald eyes were unmoving and full of judgment.

"Your mother was supposed to be our protector," Ike said. "And she led us to ruin."

"Do not speak ill of her."

"I won't let this happen again," Ike spoke over Lotis. "I'll become the strongest Templar there has ever been. And I'll shield all of Dawn. No one else dies. Except the Face Stealer."

Lotis clenched her jaw and shot Ike a final glance. "We'll see how far that wisdom takes you, Deathrid." The green nymph retreated to a spec of light and glided away.

The days of the Great Spirit were over. Ike stood tall on the jagged rocks, the only relic of a sunken culture. Death dragged him to the deepest abyss, and yet he returned. This new life would not be wasted.

"The strongest Templar there has ever been, huh?" Echo recounted what Ike had said. "How do you plan to get that tough?"

"That's simple," Ike said. "You're going to help me track down the other four Powers of the Storm."

"Son of a bitch," Echo sighed.

"I'm assuming you and Mako have an idea of where they are."

"Yeah, and Mako is going for all of them now. Each Power of the Storm dwells within a powerful spirit. He'll take their faces to replace the mask you broke. Then, he'll wipe out the Templars, the League of Tenshi, the Great Sands, everything."

"Perfect," Ike said, "which Power of the Storm will he want first?"

"Well, lucky you…It's in a Time Slip, the thing blondie mentioned. If he's taking you where I think, you're headed right for it."

Staring off to somewhere far away, Ike said, "He'll have Alina with him. I know he will." Ike would free her, and they'd challenge Mako together. Letting Mako steal her face was not an option.

"You don't have what it takes to do this," Echo said gently. "That's the kindest advice I could offer."

With the morning sun bathing his face in soft light, Ike said, "Whoever you think I am died with Somerset."

Wind rippled through the Aged Sea. Somewhere in the war-torn realm of Dawn, an enemy prowled behind falsehood. He had no need to hide or lurk in the dark. Mako the Face Stealer roamed the world in bright, piercing daylight. His true face was forever hidden; his lies consumed all. One day soon, he would answer for what he'd done. Ike Ryder looked onto the tattoo etched in his pale skin, the mark of death.

Dawn Crusade

Epilogue

Destruction

❪ ☆ I ☆ ❫

The current rocked Flynn Quan back and forth. He sat against the ship's mast, blood spilling around the arrowhead lodged in his belly. It must have been close to midnight. Burning ships illuminated the night brilliantly. Their flames grew so fierce that the battleships almost appeared to be hot, floating suns kissing the water. Flynn's eyes no longer moved. Covering the deck within his vision laid rows of dead soldiers lit by the fiery parade of sinking timber. They were Knights and Squires, many of whom belonged to Somerset. Only a few Marauders lay dead, and one still drew breath.

Sitting across from Flynn was a bearded man with wild, matted hair. Scars crisscrossed his dark cheeks. He sat hunched over, four arrows lodged in his back. The man's dying eyes looked only at Flynn, who felt powerless to return the gesture. If he was able, it seemed the man would use his final moments of life to snap Flynn's neck.

Flynn himself didn't feel such motivation. Behind him, the Marauder ships sailed on to Somerset. Soon his island would be overrun and consumed. He thought of the girl he loved — Juniper. She'd die tonight too.

Footsteps creaked the wooden planks at Flynn's back. Black coattails passed into view. They belonged to Templar

Asim. Flynn was unable to look up at his face, but he seemed completely and utterly healthy. Not a scratch marked his pristine coat. The Templar did not notice him, or maybe assumed he was another corpse. Within a couple of minutes, Flynn would be.

Asim passed the living Marauder, who scowled and drooled on the bloodied deck. Without offering a glance, Asim kicked over a Knight's corpse on the left side of the deck. Slowly he knelt down and placed a palm on the wood. A purple glow rose from underneath his hand. Still pressing down on the deck, Asim snapped with his free hand to a spot just beside the snarling Marauder.

Near the dying man, a portal suddenly appeared. The passage looked oval in shape, just large enough for Asim to step through, and was framed by smoking purple light. Flynn could see only black sky within.

A strange wheeze crept out from the Marauder. Perhaps it was a laugh. "You've...had a portal waiting...coward...coward, Templar," the bearded man croaked.

Asim rose and marched briskly toward the Marauder. "You're their captain?" he inquired.

"Captain Farhad the Ruthless, bringer of torment," the man said with a blood-filled grin.

"Wonderful," Asim responded, stepping to the portal.

"That coat is wasted on you," Farhad spat.

Asim froze just before the doorway.

"How many could you have saved? How many could have fled through that passage?" Color faded from the captain's scarred cheeks. "So many lives lost in your defeat…and more lost to your pride."

"Tell me," Asim uttered, "how have I lost?"

Farhad grew furious and confused. "Your ships are burning," he moaned, "your Knights are butchered. I am dying, but my people carry on to Somerset."

"Yes," Asim confirmed. "You've won this battle. And that is a victory for me."

"Explain," Farhad demanded. His body became weaker, yet his voice only grew more intense. "Explain, you coward."

That word made Asim shudder. "I don't expect you to understand this," he said frankly, "but a battle means nothing to me. I am fighting a war for all of Dawn."

Farhad swayed forward, barely able to remain upright. "You've given us…this battle…and the isle of Somerset?"

"Smart boy," Asim chuckled. His foot passed into the portal.

"Your arrogance is pathetic," Farhad muttered. "We crushed you, and now you concoct fairytales. A true warrior would rather die than shame himself."

Asim clutched his fists and shook from anger. Taking a long breath, he knelt next to Farhad. For the first time, Flynn saw the Templar's gaunt face. He seemed focused and filled with hatred. "Die knowing this, savage," Asim spat on the captain's chin. "The destruction of Somerset will be the spark that lights a new era in this war. All five kingdoms under the League of Tenshi will unite without question to invade the capital of the Great Sands. The talks of a truce will dissipate. Civilian lives will be forgotten. No one will forgive the taking of such an ancient monument."

"You've sacrificed thousands," Farhad groaned.

"The invasion of Somerset began this war," Asim said ceremoniously, "and its complete destruction will end it."

Captain Farhad hung his head. The will to cling to his life withered away. Flynn wished he had the strength to cut through Asim's throat. Or perhaps he just wished he'd died before learning the truth. His eyes felt incredibly heavy now. Despite that, he kept them open to witness Asim passing through the portal.

Just after the glowing doorway snapped shut, Farhad's head rose. He stared madly at Flynn. Falling onto his belly, the Marauder Captain crawled toward him. Flynn's heart felt too weak to race, yet panic made his head swim. How could this man still be alive? Was this the strength of a true ki-wielder?

Farhad clawed up Flynn's legs with painstaking, agonizing grunts. He put a trembling hand on the arrow in his stomach then yanked it out. Flynn's eyes went wide, but he was numb to the pain. Dropping the arrow, Farhad placed his hand on the wound. Chaotic, cold energy passed into Flynn's body. He felt as if the ocean itself had poured into his flesh. Suddenly, the gaping wound began to close.

"Why are you doing this?" Flynn became strong enough to say.

"You know the truth," Farhad told him. His eyes were glassy and vacant. "We are enemies, but the truth...is an ally to all." The Marauder collapsed next to Flynn. Raised, white skin replaced the arrow hole in the Knight's gut.

Epilogue: Destruction

Alone on a battleship of Somerset, Flynn traced the fresh scar with steady fingers. Farhad's dead gaze gawked at him from the deck's floor.

(☆ *II* ☆)

Scraps of wood drifted on the Aged Sea's relentless tide. Flaming sails sunk beneath the waves behind the fleeing debris. There, on a lone chunk of lumber, Nathan Abara's corpse rested. Steel blades had ruptured his flesh in jagged, stark lines. His torso had been nearly split open by the many wounds. Veiling his dead eyes was a red strip of fabric.

A seagull landed on the wood sheltering Nathan's body. Its sharp beak poked at the decaying flesh. Soon a frenzy of scavengers would come to feast. Such is the order of all things. Death gives life, and so on. Destruction and creation are forever intertwined.

Two more birds joined the scout on the fresh corpse. They hopped near the deep wounds and eyed the body's insides. Their predecessor gnawed on the ear, testing its quality.

Just then, a hand snatched the pestering bird by its neck with enough force to snap it in two. The other seagulls retreated to the air in frenzied shrieks. Cold breath gushed into Nathan's throat. Red light gleamed within his veins and rushed to the gaping wounds. Immediately, his flesh began to mend itself. Soft, caramel-colored skin pulled itself together.

On his left hand, a glowing red mark had appeared. It resembled a very thick ring with only a dot of ordinary skin in the center. Nathan raised that hand to his face and removed the strip of fabric.

Cloudy, white eyes were overcome with a bright hazel coloring. Dark pupils dilated for the first time in low light. He stared at the black sky, thinking that perhaps nothing had changed. Then the thousands of shining stars came into focus. Nathan's lip quivered, and tears flowed down his face. Shaking slightly, he raised his left hand and examined its appearance. The glowing symbol faded to a strange black mark. Chuckling weakly, he felt the skin of his wrist and the tips of his fingernails.

He was alive.

CPSIA information can be obtained
at www.ICGtesting.com
Printed in the USA
LVHW041657120621
690064LV00003B/320

9 781737 185000